A WISH ON STAR CASTLE LANE

A MRS WISHMORE NOVEL

ALIX KELSO

LAKE FALLS PUBLISHING

Cover design by dmeacham design.

ISBN (paperback): 978-1-913098-09-4

Published by Lake Falls Publishing

For my husband, David.

PROLOGUE

Mrs Wishmore watched the world pass by outside the bus window as the early morning sunshine cast a thousand sparkling jewels across the waters of the bay. The coastal road twisted and turned as it meandered along the Argyll shoreline, revealing rugged islands rising from the grey-blue waters on one side and hills covered with heather and pine on the other. High on a rocky outcrop, Mrs Wishmore spied a red deer standing resplendent in the June sunlight, its magnificent antlers reaching impossibly high above its head as it surveyed its kingdom.

This tucked away peninsula on the Scottish west coast was a glorious part of the world, and Mrs Wishmore was thankful to find herself here. There could be no more wondrous sight than the view to which she was being treated this morning as the bus made its way along the winding route. She wondered, as she often did on these journeys, about the work that waited for her somewhere further on up the road, and about the new people she might soon meet.

Mrs Wishmore glanced around at her fellow passengers. There were around a dozen people on the bus, most of them glued to their phone screens and oblivious to the natural wonders that lay beyond the windows. No doubt they were all regular commuters on their way to work on the early morning bus service, and blind to the scenery they'd become used to seeing each day.

Such a pity, Mrs Wishmore thought, as she glanced out the window again just in time to see a pod of dolphins break the glistening surface of the waters in the distance as they breached and dived. Her heart lifted at the sight of the sleek creatures playing in the sunshine.

"Look, Mummy! Dolphins!"

In the bus seat in front of Mrs Wishmore, a little girl was bouncing and pointing out of the window, her eyes wide at the sight she'd just seen.

"So it is," the little girl's mother said, sparing a glance through the window before returning to her phone screen.

Mrs Wishmore smiled as the little girl continued peering across the bay, hoping for another glimpse of the dolphins. But their playtime must have been over, because there was no further sign of their fins slicing through the surface of the water, and after a moment, the little girl sighed and shifted around in her seat.

The child's gaze settled on the older lady, and she peered at her for a long moment before smiling.

Mrs Wishmore smiled back.

The little girl's eyes widened, and she waved to her over the back of the bus seat.

Grinning, Mrs Wishmore returned the wave.

For another long moment, the little girl studied her. Then her eyes grew wider still as she began bouncing again in her seat.

"Mummy!" she yelled, pointing to Mrs Wishmore. "There's an angel on the bus!"

Mrs Wishmore let out a warm chuckle as the other bus

passengers turned to see who the little girl was pointing at, their expressions amused. Perhaps they saw her cloud of silvery hair and her kind blue eyes and gentle smile and thought they understood how the little girl could have imagined that the elderly lady looked like an angel. Children's imaginations often ran wild, after all.

"Don't be silly!" the little girl's mother hissed at her daughter. "And stop pointing. It's rude!"

The little girl's smile dimmed. Feeling sorry for her, Mrs Wishmore winked.

The girl's smile reappeared. When her mother's phone rang, drawing her attention away, the child reached into the pocket of the blue nursery school sweatshirt she was wearing and pulled out a small bag.

"Do angels like chocolate buttons?" the little girl asked in hushed tones as she held out the bag of sweets.

Mrs Wishmore laughed. "I'm sure some of them do, yes."

The little girl considered this. "Do *you* like chocolate buttons?"

"Certainly."

The little girl reached further over the back of the seat until the bag of sweets was almost pressed into Mrs Wishmore's face. The older lady laughed again before reaching into the bag.

"Thank you, dear, that's very kind," she said and popped the chocolate treat into her mouth. It might be very early in the morning, but it was never too early to enjoy a chocolate button offered by a kind-hearted child.

The little girl chose a chocolate button for herself and watched Mrs Wishmore while they ate their treat together. A thoughtful look crossed the child's face.

"Where are your halo and angel wings?" the little girl asked.

Mrs Wishmore laughed softly. "You mean you can't see them?"

At this, the little girl's eyes flew wide as she scrutinised Mrs Wishmore's cloud of silvery hair and peeked at her shoulders, apparently searching for the accessories she'd asked about. After a few seconds of this, the child let out another shout.

"Wait, I see them!" she yelled. "I see your angel wings!"

"That's enough, Sophie!" the child's mother said in a fierce tone, the phone still at her ear as she pulled the child up from the seat and stepped out into the aisle of the bus. "Come on, it's almost our stop."

"Bye," the little girl said to Mrs Wishmore as she hurried with her mother to the front of the bus.

"Goodbye, Sophie."

At the next stop, the child and her mother disembarked from the bus. The other passengers once more favoured Mrs Wishmore with amused glances, as if they were all in on the joke about the little girl and her flights of fancy.

If only everyone could see what little Sophie had seen, perhaps the world would be a brighter place, Mrs Wishmore thought to herself.

But the world didn't work that way, as she knew only too well.

The bus trundled on, and a few minutes later a sign appeared up ahead, welcoming the passengers to the town of Balmarrie. Soon, little fishermen's cottages began appearing along the side of the road, their facades painted in pretty pastel shades of blue, pink, yellow, and lavender. Moments later, the bus swung onto the high street, which was lined with shops and cafes and ice cream parlours, and then on to a promenade that ran the length of the bay on the town's western shores. Residential streets spurred off from the main road, lined with a mix of terraced houses and grand villas and modest apartment buildings.

Balmarrie was a pretty little place, bustling with early morning activity as people made their way to work and school. But Mrs Wishmore sensed it was not yet time to get off the bus.

After pausing at several stops throughout the town, the bus left Balmarrie and continued north along the twisting coastal road. Mrs Wishmore gazed out at the sparkling waters of the bay and the dark islands in the water and the towering hills in the distance. A few minutes after leaving the little town behind, another sign appeared at the side of the road, this one announcing that the Star Castle Hotel could be found by taking the next turn on the right.

The Star Castle Hotel. It was a beautiful name, and Mrs Wishmore knew instantly that this was where she was headed.

Rising from her seat, she pressed the button to alert the driver that she wanted to get off at the next stop. The driver pulled the bus into a layby just beyond the sign for the Star Castle Hotel, and Mrs Wishmore thanked him. As the bus chugged off, she glanced around, taking in her surroundings.

On the other side of the main road, there was a T-junction with a red-topped road that disappeared into tall trees. On either side of the junction stood smart wooden signs that pointed the way to the Star Castle Hotel.

Hitching her blue handbag higher onto her shoulder, Mrs Wishmore crossed the road and followed the route into the trees. The air was fresh with the scent of pine and fir and warmed by the morning sunshine. After several turns, the trees thinned and the road opened up to reveal a sight so beautiful it made Mrs Wishmore pause in astonished admiration.

Beyond a wide expanse of dewy lawn, the Star Castle

Hotel stood in elevated and elegant magnificence. The four storey Scottish baronial building in pale grey stone boasted ornate conical turrets and an imposing keep and rows of tall windows, some with elaborate stone balconies, and with a grand canopied entrance that welcomed guests inside. The castle—now a hotel—was surrounded by gardens and edged with woodland that stretched off into the surrounding hills. As Mrs Wishmore drew nearer, she turned and saw the dazzling waters of the bay behind her in the distance.

The Star Castle Hotel was a priceless jewel on the coast, of that there was no doubt. Mrs Wishmore wondered what her work here might involve.

At the edge of the turning circle outside the canopied entrance, there were benches for guests to enjoy, and Mrs Wishmore made her way over to one of them and sat down. Although it was early in the morning, staff in smart hotel uniforms were coming and going as they went about their work, and there were also a few guests meandering out from the hotel to enjoy the fresh morning air.

Mrs Wishmore sensed that this was a special place. And she sensed, too, that because it was so special, her help here was needed urgently.

Closing her eyes, she let out a slow breath and settled her mind. If someone here in this beautiful place was about to send out a wish for a helping hand, she wanted to be ready to hear it.

Slowly, she began to sense what she might be here to do. Sometimes, Mrs Wishmore was called upon to help the broken-hearted, to help those who were lost, or to help those who'd become discouraged. When people needed a friend, or a shoulder to cry on, or some sage advice, Mrs Wishmore was there, so long as people wished for her to be there.

She sensed that the days ahead would bring tough challenges for someone inside the Star Castle Hotel. She sensed calamities waiting to upend the peace of this place, and make someone inside question themselves deeply. And she sensed that someone might soon need a word or two of comforting reassurance and a friendly nudge in the direction of their dreams.

If that was what had brought Mrs Wishmore here, then she would do whatever she could to help and be of service.

In the meantime, though, all she could do was wait for a wish to be made, a wish made in desperation and with little hope that it would come true. Only then could she get to work.

Mrs Wishmore sat in the sunshine as a new day began for the staff and guests inside the Star Castle Hotel, and waited for the wish that would set her to work.

CHAPTER ONE

Suzanne Kennedy paced the floor as she waited to be called into the managing director's office and fought the urge to chew on her fingernails. She'd painted her nails only last night, and didn't want to chip the bold red polish, but this imminent meeting was shredding her nerves. When she'd been summoned here five minutes earlier, Suzanne had been left in no doubt that she'd done something to upset the boss.

The boss also happened to be Suzanne's mother, Imogen Kennedy, a force of nature in the hospitality industry and a formidable business woman. After five years spent learning the ropes and working her way up the ladder at the family's luxurious Star Castle Hotel, Suzanne knew only too well that she'd barely scratched the surface of what she needed to understand in order to one day run the business. There was a lot of work ahead before she claimed the manager director's office as her own, which was just as well, because her mother had no intention of retiring from her job anytime soon. Until Suzanne's time came, she'd do whatever she had to do to prove to herself, and to her mother, that she was up to the challenge of taking the family business from strength to strength.

Proving herself wasn't easy, not where Imogen Kennedy was concerned. It often seemed to Suzanne that the mountain she was climbing only became steeper every day, and that the shoes she had to fill only got bigger and bigger.

The Star Castle Hotel was the jewel in the crown of the Kennedy family, and it held a special place in Suzanne's heart. Located on a breathtaking peninsula in Argyll on the west coast of Scotland, the eighty-room hotel enjoyed sweeping views of the rugged coastline on one side and glorious brooding hills on the other. When Suzanne's grandfather, Robert Kennedy, had bought the nineteenth-century castle forty years earlier, it had been little more than a dilapidated shell, abandoned by its previous owners because of high running costs and lack of vision. With twenty years of experience under his belt working in an international hotel chain, Robert had taken a gamble on the run-down old castle and transformed it into one of the premier destination hotels in Scotland. Encouraged by what he'd achieved through grit and hard work, Robert had added sympathetic extensions to the building that had expanded the guest capacity and grown the business further. When Suzanne's mother took over, she'd focused on the hotel's event business and on building its reputation as a wedding and leisure destination, increasing the hotel's profitability.

Suzanne was under no illusions that her grandfather and mother had worked hard to build the family business into what it now was. That this family business would one day become her responsibility filled her with both excitement and fear in equal measure.

"Suzanne, come on in."

Suzanne glanced up from her floor-pacing and saw her mother peering out from her office into the hallway. The look on her face was inscrutable, and Suzanne felt a pang of anxiety ripple through her.

"I've got a phone call scheduled in ten minutes, so we'll have to be quick," Imogen said, returning to the chair behind her desk.

Suzanne followed her mother inside. Beyond the windows of the office in the north wing of the Star Castle Hotel lay the breathtaking view of the deep blue waters of Balmarrie Bay and the Isle of Mull in the distance, the island shimmering beneath the early morning sunshine. It was a view that always lifted Suzanne's heart and her spirits. This was home and there was nowhere else she'd ever want to live. This landscape hadn't just given her family its livelihood. It had become part of her blood and her soul.

When Imogen's gaze levelled at Suzanne across the wide expanse of the walnut desk, Suzanne had to resist the urge to gulp.

"What did you want to see me about?" Suzanne asked.

"I spoke to Jeff first thing this morning," Imogen said, steepling her fingers as she leaned into her chair. "Why did you cancel the Silver Moon Jazz Quintet booking for the summer ball?"

Suzanne allowed herself a silent sigh. She should've known this was what her mother wanted to talk to her about. She should've known, too, that Jeff King, her deputy, would go over her head and attempt to get Imogen to overrule the decision she'd made.

"The band wanted to increase their fee at the last minute, with only days to go before the summer ball," Suzanne explained. "I think they assumed we'd have to agree in order to avoid losing our entertainment for the night. It was an underhand move and unprofessional. I called their bluff."

"The Quintet have been playing at the Star Castle Hotel summer ball for the last six years," Imogen frowned.

"Then maybe it's time for a change."

"The guests *like* the band, Suzanne. They're a big draw."

"The guests like the excellent meal and the wonderful service and the terrific atmosphere we create," Suzanne countered. "The music is an added bonus."

"But we need a band or it isn't much of a ball, is it? People expect to dance at a ball."

"Of course they do. Which is why I've already lined up a new band."

Imogen narrowed her gaze. "Who?"

"They're called The Soundscapes."

"I've never heard of them. What other places have they played? What's their background?"

"Actually, they've only just got together as a professional band and—"

"What?"

Her mother's tone made Suzanne shift uncomfortably in her chair. She reminded herself to keep calm and not let her mother's terrifying temper get the better of her. They'd forged a reasonable—if often prickly—working relationship during the years Suzanne had spent learning the business hands-on, but every employee here knew that Imogen Kennedy didn't suffer fools gladly. Which meant Suzanne had to convince her mother that the decision she'd made wasn't a foolish one.

"They're good, Mother," Suzanne said evenly. "Really good. They're young and energetic and they know how to get an audience into the mood. I believe they'll be a great fit for the summer ball and that the guests will love not only the change in musical style, but that they'll love this band in particular."

Imogen frowned and rose from her chair, and walked to the window where she stood looking out at the view. "How much are we paying them?"

When Suzanne told her mother the fee she'd agreed with the new band, she earned herself a hard stare.

"This new band is costing almost as much to hire for the night as the jazz quintet," Imogen said. "It sounds to me like we not only lost our reliable and popular musical act, but we're overpaying to replace them with an inexperienced group."

"You made me hotel deputy manager and put me in charge of event hospitality for a reason, Mother," Suzanne said. "And if I've learned anything since I came to work here, it's that neither you nor grandad made it in this business by letting people make fools of you."

At this, Imogen cut a glance in Suzanne's direction, her eyebrow arching. Suzanne knew that look only too well. It meant her mother was listening, but might not be for much longer.

"The jazz quintet tried to milk us for money they don't deserve," Suzanne said. "We agreed a fee with them, and they waited until the last minute to demand more, thinking we'd have no choice but to pay it. If the decision had been yours to make, would you have allowed yourself to be hustled out of extra money just for an easy life?"

Imogen's lips twitched. "Of course not." She gazed back at the view for a moment, slipping her hands into the pockets of her tailored trousers. "Every penny counts when it comes to running a profitable business. But I don't like losing the jazz band, Suzanne. The summer ball guests love them."

"They'll love this new band, too," Suzanne said, determined to hold her ground.

"Maybe." Imogen walked back to her desk and took her seat again, once more levelling her gaze at Suzanne. "What sort of music do they play?"

"They're a covers band," Suzanne said, and when she saw her mother's eyes widening she added, "They're not cheesy, in case that's what you're worried about. I've heard them play live and they're terrific. They'll bring something fresh to the summer ball, which is what I think it needs."

Imogen's eyes narrowed again. "Meaning?"

"The summer ball isn't as profitable as it used to be. I can show you figures, but the fact is that we're attracting the same crowd year after year and they're spending less while they stay with us—less money on their room bookings, less money in our restaurant and bar, less money on our leisure activities. I think it's time we targeted a younger demographic."

"This is a luxury high-end hotel, Suzanne. We didn't get that reputation by being filled with drunk twenty-somethings."

Suzanne smiled, sensing her moment. "Would it surprise you to know that the average age of the guests who come to the summer ball and book a two-night stay while they're here is sixty-eight?"

Imogen opened her mouth to respond, obviously surprised by this. "No, I didn't know that. But the older people we attract here have plenty of disposable income."

"Perhaps, but they aren't spending it while they're with us. That's the bottom line. The figures don't lie." Suzanne sat forward in her chair, keen to make her case. "I'm not talking about turning our summer ball into a rowdy booze-up. I'm talking about attracting people who are just a little younger and who want to have a great time with us, people who are in their forties and fifties." She watched her mother carefully, then risked landing a final blow. "You're almost fifty-three, mother. Do *you* want to spend an entire evening listening to easy listening classics from almost seventy years ago, played by a bunch of elderly men in sequined waistcoats?"

Imogen looked away and let out a short laugh. "Actually, no."

"There's nothing wrong with the music. But it isn't helping us stay profitable because it's not attracting guests who want to splash some cash."

"Even if you're right about this, people who have already booked tickets are expecting to see the jazz quintet."

"We'll inform them of the change to the entertainment. Anyone who doesn't want to come along anymore will get a refund. And anyway, the event has only sold about two-thirds of the tickets, and..."

"Really?" Imogen interrupted. "But it's less than two weeks away. Usually by now, we'd be sold out."

Suzanne waved a hand in the air. "Exactly. And when I looked at our figures for last year's ball, we didn't sell out then either, and we actually sustained a small loss on the night. Like I said, the summer ball isn't the terrific success as it once was. We need a change and we need to move with the times. I hope that once we announce the new band, we'll see a surge in ticket sales for the ball and for guest rooms, too."

Imogen tapped her fingers on her desk, thinking it over. "I'm worried about hiring such a young and inexperienced band."

"I understand. But I've checked them out, and they're committed and professional and keen to make a success of things. Playing at our summer ball is a big deal for them, and they know it's a wonderful opportunity to get their name out there and attract more bookings."

Suzanne could tell that her mother wasn't yet convinced. If Imogen refused to authorise the booking, she'd either have to go crawling back to the unscrupulous jazz quintet who'd tried to fleece her and accept their new terms, or find another band altogether. Although she wanted to appear confident and in control in order to convince her mother that she knew what she was doing, it hadn't been easy to find another band at such short notice. Worse, if her mother overruled her decision in this matter, it would send a terrible signal to the rest of the hotel staff and undermine her authority.

After spending so long working her way up in the business and learning what she had to learn, she'd been thrilled when her mother had appointed her as deputy hotel manager, with responsibility for special events. This matter concerning the summer ball was the first major decision Suzanne had taken in the role, and now that she'd taken it, she had to defend it. People like Jeff King, her deputy, already had doubts about a twenty-seven-year-old taking on so much managerial responsibility at the hotel. She didn't want him, or any other members of staff, to have their doubts confirmed.

"Trust me on this, Mother," Suzanne said. "You put me in charge, not because I'm your daughter, but because I proved I was up to the challenge. So, let me get on with the job."

Imogen held her gaze for a long beat before sighing. "All right. We'll go with your plan. It had better work."

"It will," Suzanne said, crossing her fingers out of sight beneath the edge of her mother's walnut desk.

"I remember locking horns with your grandfather on plenty of occasions when I was learning to manage this business," Imogen said, the ghost of a smile now at her lips. "He had his way of doing things and I had mine. We both had to practise some give and take. But both of us only ever had the hotel's best interests at heart."

Suzanne glanced at the framed photograph of her grandfather that sat on a bookcase across from her mother's desk. His fierce blue eyes shone out from the picture frame, his smile dancing as he grinned at the photographer behind the camera, Suzanne's grandmother, Margaret. Theirs had been a love story for the ages, and Suzanne knew there wasn't a day that went by when her mother didn't miss her parents, both of whom had passed away two years ago, within just a few months of each other. While Margaret Kennedy had been the warm matriarch of the family, Robert Kennedy had been their north star, the great man in their lives, the one person they'd all relied on to give them good advice that would keep them right.

"I'd never do anything to risk what you and grandad built here at the hotel," Suzanne said.

"I know that, Suzanne," Imogen said, her smile now wistful. "But your grandad helped me to avoid plenty of silly mistakes while I was learning this business, and now it's my job to help you avoid them, too."

Suzanne nodded, choosing her next words carefully. "I don't think it's a mistake to hire this band. I think it's a good move for us."

Imogen seemed to consider this before nodding. "I only hope you're right. The summer ball is important to this hotel. It's part of our identity. Your grandfather started the summer ball tradition not long after he refurbished the ballroom."

"Which is why I only want it to go from strength to strength."

"For the record, I'm not yet convinced. But I want you to run with it anyway and prove me wrong."

Suzanne decided to risk injecting some humour into the moment. "That's a tall order."

"I never said working here with me would be easy."

Imogen's expression gave nothing away. Suzanne rose from her chair to leave.

"I understand you didn't want to be hauled in here and asked to account for a decision you believe was yours to make as deputy manager," Imogen said. "But this is a tough business and the margins are razor thin. I want you to take over a thriving business one day, Suzanne, and that means we're going to have these kinds of conversations from time to time."

"You're the boss and I answer to you. Being your daughter shouldn't change that. But I don't want you to see me as a little girl who needs her mother looking out for her all the time. I want you to understand I've got what it takes to do this job and to do it well."

For the briefest of moments, Suzanne thought her mother would say that of course she knew her daughter had what it took to do the job, that she believed in her, that she trusted her judgement. But instead, she saw a flash of doubt in her mother's eyes, and it sent a stab of pain and regret straight through her.

She wished she could live up to her mother's high expectations. Imogen Kennedy was a survivor and a warrior. She'd had to be. She'd raised Suzanne as a single mother, after Suzanne's father had broken off their brief relationship and disappeared when Imogen told him she'd fallen pregnant with their child. While raising Suzanne by herself, Imogen had worked non-stop at the Star Castle Hotel, helping Suzanne's grandfather build it into a thriving success. The woman was made of steel and fire. Suzanne only wished she was made of the same tough stuff.

In her head, she told herself she *was* made of the same tough stuff. But in her heart, doubts lingered.

The phone on Imogen's desk rang just then. Her mother gave her a curt nod, her usual signal that she had to move on to other things. Suzanne took her cue and left the office as her mother answered the phone call. As she closed the door behind her, she could already hear her mother launching into a detailed discussion with whoever was on the other end about some aspect of the running of the hotel.

Imogen Kennedy was formidable, and her business acumen and judgement were beyond reproach. Because of that, Suzanne wished she could earn her mother's trust. But no matter what she did to prove herself, that trust was never fully there.

Wanting to clear her head after the meeting, Suzanne headed towards the exit behind the suite of staff offices at the back of the hotel. Outside, the June morning was already warm and freshened by the cool air blowing off Balmarrie Bay. An expanse of shrub-bordered lawn and garden lay to the rear of the hotel, which was always popular with guests spilling out from the bar terrace. Beyond this area, a narrow gravel lane led into a smaller garden and then to a patch of woodland on the northern edge of the hotel property. It was along this lane that Suzanne now walked, seeking the peace she always found there.

Her grandfather had put in the gravel lane over twenty years earlier, when Suzanne had been just six years old. Robert Kennedy had doted on his granddaughter, and when she'd told him she thought the patch of wild roses rambling through the hedge on the old dirt track reminded her of a pathway into an enchanted forest, he'd been charmed and had set about creating an actual enchanted forest for her to enjoy.

The gravel path led through the hedge, still covered in wild roses all these years later, and down into a clearing in the trees at the edge of the woodland, where Robert had placed a collection of carved wooden toadstools and cute fairy hut dwellings that he'd commissioned from a local carpenter. The enchanted forest illusion had been complete, and both the winding lane through the hedges and the sweet cluster of toadstools and fairy huts had become popular amongst the families who visited with small children. To this day, no visit to the Star Castle Hotel—either to stay overnight or to enjoy lunch in the restaurant—was complete unless any small children in the party had explored the winding path and run amongst the bright red toadstools and in and out of the little huts, searching for the elusive fairy folk who were rumoured to live there.

At the head of the lane there was an aged wooden sign that read 'Star Castle Lane', with a carved arrow pointing into the rose hedges and towards the enchanted forest beyond. Suzanne ran her hand across the silvered sign as she passed it, remembering the day her grandfather had installed it and the little unveiling ceremony he'd put on for her benefit. She could still remember his amused smile as she'd screeched in delight when she saw the sign for the first time. Even now, she loved to read the lettering there. There was something about those words—Star Castle Lane—that seemed so magical.

As she paused at the old sign, the scent of wild roses thick in the fresh summer air, Suzanne thought she could use a little magic in her life right now.

I wish I could make my mother believe I'm up to this job, Suzanne thought to herself as she strolled along the lane. *And I wish I believed I was up to it, too.*

This last thought stopped her in her tracks. She doubted herself too often these days. Despite the certainty she'd conveyed back in her mother's office about the Star Castle Hotel summer ball and the decision she'd made about the night's entertainment, Suzanne wasn't sure if she'd done the right thing or not. Lately, the self-confidence she'd once enjoyed seemed to have deserted her.

Had she made a mistake in cancelling the agreement with the jazz quintet? Had she been too rash in hiring an unknown band to fill their shoes? What if the guests didn't like the replacement band she'd chosen and the summer ball ended in failure? It would be her fault if that happened, and she'd be jeopardising the future of an event that her grandfather had started many years ago, and that meant a great deal to the hotel.

Had she made an error in her calculations when she'd examined the figures for previous summer balls and detected a decline in profit?

Did she have any idea what she was doing at all?

"I wish I could trust myself," Suzanne found herself muttering as she walked along the lane.

The sound of Suzanne's phone ringing pierced the soft stillness of the summer morning. When she answered the call, it was from Pauline, one of the staff members at the hotel front desk.

"There's a woman in reception who says she starts work here today," Pauline informed her. "But when I rang through to the back office, they said the HR manager was off on holiday and I should speak to you instead."

Suzanne didn't usually deal with hotel staffing matters, but knew that the human resources manager was taking annual leave with her young family. As next in line in the management chain of command, it stood to reason that the matter would fall to her, although she was surprised the HR manager hadn't mentioned a new staff member arriving today in her absence, so she could be prepared.

"I'll take care of it," Suzanne said. "Would you ask Jim to dig out the woman's files so I know what we've hired her to do?" she added, referring to one of the administrative staff in the back office.

"Will do."

"Thanks, I'll be there in a minute," Suzanne said, and hurried back into the hotel to deal with her unexpected task, grateful for the diversion from her gloomy thoughts.

CHAPTER TWO

The Star Castle Hotel lobby was an open and airy space, expanded from the reception hall of the castle into a glassed atrium and boasting polished wooden floors, tall windows, and the original grand staircase that led to the floors above. When Suzanne got there, Pauline glanced up from her computer at the reception desk and nodded across the lobby to the array of sofas on one side, where an older woman sat flicking through a magazine from the stack on the coffee table. Suzanne walked over to greet the woman, taking in her soft cloud of silvery hair and warm smile and bright blue eyes.

"Hello, I'm Suzanne Kennedy," she said, offering her hand. "I understand you're here today to start a new job?"

The older lady set aside the magazine and rose from the sofa, adjusting the red cardigan she wore over her cream blouse. "That's right, dear. I'm Mrs Wishmore, Doris Wishmore. It's very nice to meet you."

They shook hands. "I'm sorry to say I'm not up to speed on your new position here with us, Mrs Wishmore," Suzanne said. "Our HR manager is away on holiday, and I haven't yet laid my hands on your paperwork. Would you give me just a minute to look at our files and I'll be right back?"

"I'd be glad to, but perhaps I could save you the trouble and tell you what I'm here to do?"

Suzanne had been about to hurry off to the back office, but paused. Before she could say anything, Mrs Wishmore spoke again.

"I'm here to work as a front of house assistant," the older lady said proudly. "And very excited I am about it, too. As I understand it, I'll be helping to look after the guests and assisting other members of staff with whatever they need me to do."

Suzanne frowned at this. The job description seemed incredibly vague. Hotel staff were usually given specific roles and tasks.

"I'm only here on a temporary contract to help plug some staff holiday absences," Mrs Wishmore continued. "I got the impression that the hotel needed to hire someone who was happy to be flexible in their role and be a bit of a gopher and a dogs-body." The older lady chuckled. "I suppose in a fine place like this, there must always be some important task that needs to be dealt with, but not always someone around who can take care of it."

"Well, that's certainly true," Suzanne said, knowing only too well the endless work associated with running such a large hotel.

Still, she found it hard to believe that the HR manager would have hired someone without a defined set of responsibilities. Perhaps she planned to discuss specific tasks with the new hire once she was working here, although such matters should surely have come up during the interview process?

Suzanne reminded herself that this wasn't her problem to fix. The HR manager had hired a new member of staff and knew what she was doing. There was always some confusion and crossed wires when someone new joined the team until they found their feet and their place inside the hotel.

But Suzanne couldn't help but wonder at this new woman who'd come to work for them. She was easily well into her sixties, if Suzanne's guestimate was right, and the temporary job she was here to do wouldn't be for the faint-hearted. Hotel work was physically demanding, whether it involved standing behind the reception desk for long periods helping guests check in and out, or running around in the restaurant and bar serving guests, or helping in the leisure facilities which incorporated a gym, pool, sauna and spa. The temporary staff they hired in the busy seasons tended to be much younger than this woman.

Not that she was about to say anything like that. Suzanne wasn't about to land herself in hot water by questioning this woman's ability to do the job she'd been hired to do before she'd even got started.

"We're happy to have you join our team," Suzanne said. "Let's sort you out with a fresh uniform and get you started on the front desk."

"That sounds wonderful," the woman said, picking up her large blue handbag from the sofa, along with a cheerful red anorak that was draped over the seat cushion.

As they walked towards the reception counter, Suzanne pointed to Pauline behind the desk. "Pauline can show you the ropes with the check-in process and how the computer system works. It can take a little while to get the hang of it, so don't worry about learning it all right away."

"I'm sure I'll be fine," Mrs Wishmore replied. "I've worked in many hotels in my time and I'm familiar with the standard systems."

Suzanne was pleased to hear this. There was no point hiring someone temporarily to help with busy spells during the hotel's summer season if it took ages for them to learn how everything worked. Temporary staff had to hit the ground running, and she hoped Mrs Wishmore could do just that.

"Oh, doesn't this look like a splendid event?"

Pulled from her thoughts, Suzanne looked up to see Mrs Wishmore pointing at a poster hanging on the wall beside the reception desk advertising the hotel's upcoming summer ball. The poster depicted a montage of photographs from the hotel's grand ball room, showcasing beautifully laid tables and shimmering candlelight and fizzing champagne, along with the dancing that took place once the meal was over.

"Our summer ball is a highlight of our entertainment calendar here at the hotel," Suzanne told the woman. "We're looking forward to this year's event very much."

"I should think you are," Mrs Wishmore said, still admiring the poster. She pointed to the line of printed text along the bottom, which advertised the Silver Moon Jazz Quintet as the featured band for the evening. "Oh, I'd heard there was a different band playing at the summer ball this year."

Suzanne turned to the woman in surprise. No one knew about the change in the entertainment plans except for herself, her mother, her deputy, and the new band who were taking over. After all, they'd only just agreed to the change. "Where did you hear that?"

Mrs Wishmore shrugged. "I'm not sure. I think I might have heard something in passing while I was waiting in the lobby."

Suzanne frowned. Nothing had yet been announced about the change, and it seemed unlikely that anyone would be discussing the matter. Before she could ask Mrs Wishmore who she'd heard talking about it, the older lady spoke again.

"It will be very exciting to have a new band playing at the

summer ball," she said. "The Silver Moon men have done it for so long and I'm sure it will be lovely to offer your guests a change."

Suzanne's eyes widened. "That's exactly what I think, too."

The older lady chuckled. "It sounds to me like you have a good head on your shoulders, in that case."

"Thanks, Mrs Wishmore," Suzanne laughed, feeling oddly touched by the woman's kind words.

"Please, call me Doris."

"All right, then. Doris it is."

Suzanne glanced back at the poster for the summer ball, making a mental note to add an amendment to the advertisements with an update about the new band who would now be playing. A thought occurred to her as she filed the task away, and she turned back to Doris.

"It sounds like you must be local, or familiar with our hotel, if you know which band has played at our summer ball these past years?"

The older woman glanced back at the poster for the summer ball. "I'm not local," she said with a somewhat mysterious laugh. "But it seemed only right that I learn as much as I could about this wonderful place before I came to work here. Your grandfather started the summer ball many years ago, is that right?"

When Suzanne gave her a puzzled expression, Doris added, "I recognised your surname when you introduced yourself, dear, and saw the likeness to photographs I came across of your grandfather on your hotel website. I understand he was well-known and highly respected in the local area and in the business community."

Suzanne smiled. "He was a true legend."

"I was sorry to hear of his passing."

"That's very kind, thank you."

"I'm sure he'd be very proud of all your hard work at this fine hotel he built," Doris said. "And I'm sure he'd be very proud of what you're doing to keep the summer ball thriving, too."

"It's a big event at the hotel and we want our guests to enjoy it."

"I hope I'll have the chance to help you make it a success. Perhaps I'll be lucky enough to be working a shift here on the night of the ball."

"You might wish otherwise once it gets underway," Suzanne grinned. "It's one of the busiest nights of our summer season."

"Well, I'm up for the challenge," Doris said with a wink.

They'd reached the reception desk, where Pauline was assisting guests and pointing them towards the restaurant where breakfast was being served. "Let me introduce you to Pauline and once she's sorted out your new uniform and given you a quick tour of the computer system, I'll show you around the rest of the hotel."

"Oh, there's no need for you to do that," Doris said. "I'm sure I can find my way around just fine. You must have more important things to do than run after me."

"Well…" It was true that Suzanne had a to-do list longer than her arm, but she didn't want to abandon this new recruit only minutes after welcoming her to the hotel.

"Pauline and I will get acquainted," Doris said, smiling at the other woman on the reception desk, "and then I'll make myself useful with whatever she needs me to do."

"Are you sure?" Suzanne said, feeling torn about leaving the new staff member to her own devices.

"Quite sure," Doris said with a smile, then reached out and squeezed Suzanne's arm. "After all, I'm here to help."

The generous smile on the older lady's face, coupled with the warmth in her bright blue eyes, left Suzanne encouraged that this new employee would quickly find her feet after all.

Suzanne's phone chirped, reminding her of an errand she had to run in town to meet with one of the hotel's local suppliers.

"Well, if you're sure, I do need to hurry off to an early morning appointment," Suzanne said.

Doris gave an easy wave of her hand. "Off you go, dear."

Suzanne lingered for a moment and then nodded. "I'll be back in an hour or two and I'll check in to see how you're doing."

"I'll look forward to it," Doris said. "Now don't be late for your meeting!"

With a smile, Suzanne waved goodbye to the older lady and hurried to grab her bag and car keys from her office. Meeting with her mother, and then with the new recruit who'd come to work at the hotel, had left her running behind, even although it was only eight-thirty in the morning, and she was determined to catch up.

As she hurried to her car and began the drive into the nearby town of Balmarrie, two miles south on the shores of the bay, her mind turned once more to the hotel's summer ball and how much was at stake with the new musical act she'd hired, and whether a shake-up in the entertainment was really what the guests wanted.

Suzanne pushed the anxious thoughts away. She wasn't the only one who thought it was a good idea to freshen up the musical offering for the summer ball. The new staff member, Doris Wishmore, thought so too.

Perhaps the older lady's vote of confidence was an encouraging sign that she'd made the right decision, Suzanne thought with a wry smile as she sped towards town.

Probably not. But she was grateful for it, just the same.

CHAPTER THREE

Kyle Lawson was running late, which was par for the course these days. If he didn't leave the house in the next five minutes, his boss would never let him hear the end of it. He was already in Frank Hill's bad books, and couldn't risk displeasing the man any more than he already had these past few weeks.

"Jamie, are you ready yet, buddy?" Kyle called up the stairs.

"Almost, but I can't find my homework."

Kyle glanced into the small living room across the hall, where a pile of exercise books lay on the coffee table. "I think it's down here."

Thundering footsteps pounded across the upstairs landing and down the stairs. When Jamie appeared in the hallway and dashed into the living room, Kyle saw that the boy's school tie hung loosely around his neck and that his pullover was on inside out.

"Let's fix your wardrobe malfunction before dropping you off at school," Kyle grinned, gesturing to Jamie's tie.

As Jamie scooped his school books into his backpack, he

glanced down at his clothes. "I hate ties, Uncle Kyle. They're stupid."

"Come here and I'll help you tighten the knot."

With a sigh, Jamie traipsed over. As he straightened the tie, Kyle pretended to tighten it hard enough to choke the boy, which always got a laugh out of the seven-year-old. Seeing his nephew's expression lift and hearing him giggle made Kyle's heart clutch.

Five weeks ago, Kyle's sister Erin had moved into his house along with her son Jamie, and since then Kyle had felt like everything in his life had been turned upside down. Erin and her husband, Lee, had separated after nine years of marriage when she'd discovered he was having an affair with a work colleague. The shock of the betrayal had hit Erin hard, and so too had the realisation that, once she'd thrown him out of the house, she couldn't afford to keep their rented property on her own nursing salary alone. When Kyle learned of his sister's financial troubles, and saw how hard it was for her to find an affordable new place to live, he'd insisted that Erin and Jamie move in with him while Erin worked out her next steps. Kyle's terraced house wasn't enormous, but he had a guest room going spare and had turned the box room he used as a home office into an extra bedroom.

Kyle understood how hard all these upheavals were on Erin and on Jamie. His sister's stunned anger at what her husband had done was bad enough, but Jamie was suffering in a different way, struggling with the sudden absence of his father from his everyday life. Lee had already moved fifty miles away to live with the woman he'd been having an affair with and had only seen his son once since the separation. Kyle could understand a marriage failing, but couldn't understand a man turning his back on his own child the way Lee had done. Anytime Kyle could make the boy laugh—as he could now, by joking around while he fixed Jamie's school tie—he'd take it. Kyle couldn't replace the father that Jamie adored, but he could be a fun and loving uncle, and show his nephew that not all men were selfish, no-good cheats.

He might be able to make Jamie laugh from time to time, but there was plenty that Kyle knew he was getting wrong. Erin had been working a string of nursing dayshifts this past week, which required her to start at seven in the morning, leaving Kyle in charge of getting Jamie ready for school and dropped off at the gates. It stood to reason that Erin and Lee must have worked out a decent system between the two of them in order to manage their work patterns while also taking care of their son, but as a single man with no experience of dealing with kids, Kyle found the new responsibilities hard to juggle. Although Erin always made sure that Jamie's school uniform and lunch box were organised the night before, Kyle still ended up running late every morning as he hustled his nephew through washing and dressing and breakfast. Jamie liked to dilly-dally over his morning cereal while playing on his tablet, and Kyle was clueless about how to hurry him up. He couldn't force the cereal down Jamie's throat, after all. And no matter how much work Erin did to lay out Jamie's clean clothes for the next day and organise his school bag, Jamie still took a lifetime to change out of his pyjamas and into his uniform, and brush his teeth, and present himself in the hallway so that Kyle could run a comb through the boy's hair before bundling them both into the car and setting off for school and work.

With luck, he'd soon get the hang of wrangling a seven-year-old boy. In the meantime, he had to hope he wasn't missing anything important when it came to looking after him. And he had to hope that, in doing what he could to help his sister and nephew through this hard time in their lives, he didn't end up losing his job in the process.

His boss, Frank Hill, had been utterly uninterested in Kyle's excuses for coming in late to work twice this week already. The landscaping firm the man owned didn't foster a workplace culture that permitted much leeway on account of family issues.

For the past few months, Kyle had been working on a plan to leave Frank Hill's employment and set up his own business. Hill Landscaping was an all-service company that did everything from garden clearance to patio paving to routine maintenance and lawn-mowing, and although Kyle enjoyed all those aspects of the job, his true love was garden design. He loved taking overgrown or unloved patches of land and transforming them into something beautiful, using thoughtful planting, architectural know-how, and clever reimagining of the space. Lately, there hadn't been much of that type of work happening at Hill Landscaping, and Kyle missed the challenge and the opportunity to use the skills he'd learned at horticulture college. He'd always wanted to work for himself one day, seeking out jobs that pleased him and clients who wanted his skills and creativity. The start-up costs were high, and time and investment were needed to make sure there would be clients in place and cash coming in, but Kyle had worked hard on his business plan and was ready to take the leap. He'd squirrelled away enough money to tide himself over for at least a few months while the new business found its feet, and had spent time identifying the equipment he'd have to buy or lease, and exploring local suppliers and marketing options.

Despite being ready to start the business in every practical aspect, it now seemed like the wrong time to make such a huge change in his life.

With Erin and Jamie staying with him while his sister searched for a new place to live, and with his help required to look after Jamie while Erin held down a job, Kyle had put his business plans on the back-burner. Family came first, and his sister and nephew needed him right now. Starting a new business could wait for a few months, but helping Erin and Jamie couldn't, and he wasn't about to leave Erin to struggle with childcare on her own, while also reorganising her torpedoed finances and finding a new place to live.

Making a success of a new business would take every minute of his time. Now that he was cluelessly juggling Jamie's school drop-offs and pick-ups into his schedule, and dealing with breakfasts and dinners depending on Erin's shift patterns, and helping with any number of other tasks he'd been astonished to discover were part and parcel of looking after a seven-year-old boy, Kyle knew he had to bide his time and put his new business plans on hold.

If doing that meant he could help his sister and nephew as much as possible, then it wasn't even a close contest. Family was important to Kyle Lawson.

Unfortunately, putting the brakes on his new business plans meant having to tolerate Frank Hill for a little longer than he'd like, and do his best to keep the boss happy. After working hard to save every spare penny in order to one day get a new business off the ground, he couldn't risk losing his job because he kept turning up late each morning after Jamie's school drop-off. The last thing he wanted was to use his carefully saved cash to fund himself through a job lay-off, and he couldn't start a new business while giving as much time as he could to helping with Jamie's childcare.

Which meant he had to get his act together and arrive at work on time. As Kyle glanced at the clock on the wall, he knew he was about to anger his boss yet again.

"Ready to go now?" Kyle asked Jamie as he smoothed down his nephew's pullover after taking it off and putting it back on again, this time the right way round.

"Ready," Jamie said, grabbing his school backpack.

"Don't forget to put all your homework in your bag," Kyle said, nodding to a stray exercise book Jamie had set down on the hallway table and already forgotten about.

"Okay," Jamie said, stuffing the homework into his backpack and pulling his jacket from the peg beside the front door.

"Have you got your lunch?"

"Uh, I don't know."

Kyle hurried to the fridge and found Jamie's boxed lunch still inside. "We don't want you to starve, do we?" he asked as he handed over the lunch box.

"I suppose not."

Before Kyle could stop him, Jamie had opened the box and begun examining the contents. "Mum put an apple in here. Do I have to eat it?"

"Apples are good for you, buddy."

"Can I have a chocolate bar instead?"

"I don't think so."

"Can I have crisps?"

It was obvious that the boy was testing the limits of what his Uncle Kyle would and wouldn't allow. "No chocolate, no crisps," Kyle said, trying to sound authoritative and as if this was definitely the last word on the matter. "Now, let's get out of here."

He grabbed his phone, car keys, and the bag containing his working gloves and other things he used on the job, as well as his own packed lunch. At last, they were ready to leave.

"Uncle Kyle, can I get a hamster?"

Kyle laughed in surprise at the unexpected turn in the conversation. The kid had almost worn him out already and the day hadn't even started yet. "I think that's a question for your mum, buddy."

"But she'll just say no."

"Well, in that case, maybe it's something you two can chat about tonight, and in the meantime you can think of ways to convince her to say yes. But right now, we need to go."

He felt bad about encouraging Jamie to come up with arguments in favour of getting a hamster, just so he could spring them on his mother later tonight. But Erin was better at dealing with this stuff than he was, and he suspected that if he gave the kid any more leeway in this conversation, he'd find himself at the pet shop and purchasing a hamster before he knew it.

Finally, they made it to the car and got moving. Kyle dropped Jamie at school, which ran a morning club so that working parents could drop their children off early. But it was still eight-forty when Kyle arrived at the Hill Landscaping premises on the outskirts of town. As he was supposed to start at eight-thirty, Frank Hill made a point of staring at his watch as Kyle parked his car and jumped out.

"I'm sorry I'm late, it won't happen again," Kyle said.

"You said that last time," Frank scowled.

"I'll work late tonight at the yard to make up for it."

"You'd better. And if you can't get here on time in the future, I'll have to find someone who can." Frank thrust a job sheet at him. "Start at the Gallagher place. We need that patio paving job finished today."

Frank stalked off towards his office, housed in a small brick building to one side of the premises. The other employees were almost finished loading the trucks for the day, and Kyle pitched in. Checking the job sheet, he saw that most of the day's work would involve laying patio paving and dealing with the grunt-work of hard landscaping. It was set to be a tough, physical day.

Kyle hopped into the truck alongside the two other Hill Landscaping employees he was listed as working with today. As team foreman, Kyle took the wheel. One of the other guys announced he wanted coffee before they set off for the job, and Kyle was secretly glad to hear it. After the trials of getting Jamie off to school this morning, he needed another hit of caffeine to supplement the mug of instant he'd bolted down before leaving the house.

He drove to a café near Balmarrie town centre that they often used because of its easy parking. When they arrived, Kyle volunteered to go inside for their hot drinks, keen to make things up to his colleagues for not being there on time to help load the trucks for the day.

He was walking around the corner towards the café when someone hurrying from the opposite direction along the pavement ran head-first into him.

"Ooft!" Kyle grunted in surprise as the woman he'd collided with staggered backwards and dropped the stack of folders she was carrying.

"Ouch!" The woman's hands flew to her face which had connected squarely with Kyle's chest.

"Are you okay?" Kyle peered at her face for any signs of a bloodied nose or split lip, and was relieved to see none.

"I'm okay," the woman blinked. "Just a bit startled, that's all." When she saw Kyle staring at her, she dabbed at her nose as a worried look crossed her face. "I'm not bleeding, am I?"

"No, you're fine. But that must have hurt. Seems like you hit me at about fifty miles an hour."

When Kyle rubbed at the spot on his chest where the woman had smacked into him, she winced.

"I'm so sorry, I hope I didn't hurt you?" she said.

"Of course not, I'm fine."

As she smiled in obvious relief and blew out a breath, Kyle took in the woman properly for the first time. She looked like she was in her mid- to late-twenties and was tall and willowy in an elegant blue trouser suit and smart summer loafers. Her chestnut hair was tied into a sleek ponytail except for a few stray strands that had flown loose when they'd collided. Surprise had lit up her green eyes, and in the early morning sunshine Kyle saw amber flecks burning there.

He realised he was staring, and quickly glanced away towards the folders the woman had dropped when they'd smashed into each other. Stray papers were already tumbling from the open document wallets and threatening to blow away in the breeze.

"Let me help you with these," Kyle said, gathering up the papers and folders.

"Oh no, let me do that." She hurried to scoop up her paperwork from the street. "This was my fault, anyway."

He picked up some of the papers and handed them over. Smiling as she took them, she let out a quick laugh and thrust the paperwork inside the folders.

"I had all these papers in order, and now I won't have a chance of finding what I'm looking for when I get to my meeting," she said with a resigned shrug. "It's my fault for running late."

"I know all about running late," Kyle grinned. "I think they might make me the King Of Running Late, the way things are going for me this week."

She laughed and pointed along the street. "I ought to get going. Sorry again for crashing into you."

"Don't worry about it. Just so long as you aren't hurt."

The woman rubbed her forehead. "I might see stars for the next hour, but I'll live."

Kyle laughed as the woman threw him a quick wave and hurried off along the street. It took him a moment to remember he was supposed to be buying takeaway coffees at the café. The woman's startled expression after she'd run into him, followed by her smile, had left him with a warm glow.

As he walked inside the café, he groaned when he remembered calling himself the King Of Running Late. What did that even mean? The woman must have thought he was a proper twat, saying something as nonsensical as that.

While the staff behind the café counter brewed his takeaway coffees, Kyle decided he needed to brush up on his skills with the opposite sex. He hadn't been out on a date for almost two months and he'd clearly lost the knack of casual conversation with pretty women. Since Erin and Jamie had come to live with him, a social life had been a little hard to come by, and before that he'd been working so much on the plans for his landscaping business that he'd let fun stuff like dating fall to the wayside.

The last relationship he'd had was with Emily Jones, the cousin of an old school friend. For the first few weeks, things had gone well between them and they'd enjoyed each other's company. But one evening, during what was supposed to be a romantic dinner at a local restaurant, Emily had taken issue with a nasty graze on Kyle's hand, which had happened while he'd been digging out an old rotted fence at a job he'd been working on that day. Cuts and scrapes weren't anything unusual in his line of work, but Emily hadn't been impressed and had quizzed him about how much longer he was planning on working as a 'labourer', as she put it, and why he hadn't already found himself a better paid job that could be done indoors. When Kyle had been too stunned to respond, Emily had back-tracked and tried to pass her comments off as a joke. But Kyle understood that she'd meant what she'd said, and that while she might like him enough to date him, she was secretly embarrassed by the physical nature of what he did for a living. Some people were snobs that way, as Kyle knew only too well. After that awkward dinner, they hadn't seen each other again.

It had occurred to Kyle to tell Emily about his plans for

going into business for himself and build a reputation as a garden designer and skilled horticulturist. In the end, though, he hadn't bothered. He didn't want to be with someone who'd look down on him because of how he earned his living, and he wasn't interested in changing Emily's perceptions by sharing his dream about being his own boss. They'd had some fun together, but the chemistry hadn't sparked between them, and so when it ended, Kyle wasn't devastated about it.

Although he could have done without Emily's hurtful comments about his line of work.

As Kyle carried the cardboard tray of coffees back to the men in the truck, he wondered when he'd ever get back out there again and give dating another go. It was something he ought to make time for, because it wouldn't just magically happen otherwise. He was already thirty-two years old and, as Erin had reminded him repeatedly since moving in, the clock was ticking and all the good women his age would soon be gone if he didn't get a move on.

Maybe because of how things had ended with Emily, he'd been too hesitant to try again. He shouldn't let her stupid, hurtful comment about how he made his living put him off. It was her issue, not his. He loved his work, and he'd love it even more once he had his own little company up and running, and no longer had to put up with his unpleasant boss and his constant scowling. Frank Hill ought to try smiling once in a while, Kyle thought with a grin as he got behind the wheel of the truck and handed the coffees to his men.

The thought made him think of the smile the pretty woman had given him outside the café, right before she'd hurried off. That had been quite a smile.

I wish I could see that smile again, Kyle thought as he pulled the truck back out into the road and drove towards their job site for the day. *And I wish I'd asked her name, too.*

Whoever the pretty woman was, she was probably already in a relationship or married. She had to be. With looks like that, it stood to reason that some smart guy would've snapped her up.

Still, that smile…

Kyle turned his attention to the road, where it belonged. He had a full day of patio laying ahead of him, and the hard, back-breaking work would leave no room for daydreaming.

CHAPTER FOUR

By the time Suzanne got back to the Star Castle Hotel following her meeting with the wholesale supplier, followed by a bunch of other business errands she'd taken care of afterwards, it was almost noon. The lobby was buzzing with people arriving for lunch in the restaurant overlooking the waters of the bay, and the reception desk was busy with guests who had late check-outs. As it was Thursday, the hotel staff were gearing up for another busy summer weekend, which always began early in the hospitality business. Suzanne knew the cleaners would be racing to turn around the guest rooms for new check-ins, while the staff in the leisure facilities would be preparing to greet new arrivals who'd come for relaxing spa breaks with plenty of pampering thrown in.

Suzanne was happy to see the new recruit, Doris Wishmore, looking comfortable and confident behind the reception desk, now wearing her hotel uniform and working at the computer while assisting a guest. The older lady glanced up from the keyboard just as Suzanne crossed the lobby and gave her a warm smile. Once Mrs Wishmore had finished helping the customer, Suzanne walked over to the reception counter.

"I hope you're settling in all right?" Suzanne asked.

"I'm doing just fine, or at least that's what Pauline tells me," Mrs Wishmore said with a chuckle, gesturing to the other staff member working with her on the reception desk.

"She's a miracle," Pauline told Suzanne as she pulled a sheet of paper from the printer and passed it over the counter so the guest she was serving could sign it. "She seems to know how everything works around here better than I do."

"Hardly," Mrs Wishmore said. "Pauline is an excellent teacher, and I simply listened to what she said and then did what she told me."

Pauline waved off this modest comment and returned to the guest she was helping.

"I meant what I said earlier about giving you a quick tour of the hotel," Suzanne told Doris. "New guests often have questions about our facilities when they arrive, and being familiar with the hotel layout and our services will help you answer them. Check-in starts at three, so we have time to fit in a quick walk around beforehand."

"In that case, I'm at your disposal," Doris replied. "I certainly want to make sure I'm able to give your guests a proper Star Castle Hotel welcome."

Suzanne smiled, pleased with Mrs Wishmore's enthusiasm for customer service. "Give me two minutes and I'll be right back."

After running through to her office at the back of the hotel and dumping her handbag and stacks of paperwork and folders on her desk, she pulled a compact mirror from a drawer and checked her face. The collision she'd had with the man on the street in Balmarrie had left her nose feeling tender, and she was more than a little worried that she'd end up with a nasty bruise or, worse, a couple of black eyes. When her morning meeting with the wholesaler had finished, she'd checked her face for signs of swelling and saw none, which was a relief because the last thing she wanted was to wander around town looking like she'd been the unlucky loser in a bad fist-fight. Now, as she checked her face again, she saw no signs of damage, which meant the nasty bash she'd taken had done nothing more than leave her feeling sore.

As well as a bit stupid. She'd been so consumed with the scribbled notes she was reviewing in her paperwork as she'd hurried around the corner, she hadn't even seen the man coming. The poor guy could probably have done without her thick forehead crashing into his ribs and leaving him winded. Although she'd be lying if she pretended she hadn't been more than a little breathless herself at the broad expanse of chest with which she'd collided. The guy had been both fit and gorgeous.

It was a pity she wasn't on the lookout for a handsome man, Suzanne thought with a sad smile as she freshened her lipstick while she still had the compact mirror to hand. Given the long hours she worked at the hotel, there simply wasn't time for romance. And even if there was time, romance just wasn't on her radar right now. She had enough on her plate proving herself to her mother, and proving she was up to the job of hotel deputy manager, without adding the complication of a romantic relationship into the mix.

Life was all about priorities, and Suzanne's priority was the Star Castle Hotel and the career she was forging there. Not even the gorgeous man she'd literally run into this morning could make her change her mind about that.

And anyway, even if she had been interested—which she wasn't—the man probably thought she was an idiot anyway, tearing around the streets of Balmarrie and barrelling into people and tossing her paperwork around the place like a crazy person. It hadn't been her finest moment.

Suzanne finished organising the stacks of paperwork on her desk, then opened the carrier bag she'd collected from the local printer in town and pulled out the contents. Stopping off at the printer's after her meeting with the wholesaler hadn't been on her agenda, but the detour had paid off because she was now in possession of a stack of new, glossy posters for the summer ball, updated with the name of the new band, The Soundscapes, who were now booked to appear. The Star Castle Hotel was a good customer at the printing office and she'd been able to negotiate a deal for the additional marketing materials, which meant the added cost of the new posters wouldn't eat into their profits too much.

Once the new posters were combined with a fresh online marketing and advertising push, Suzanne hoped that the remaining tickets for the summer ball would quickly sell out.

Suzanne carried the package of posters back into the lobby. While showing Mrs Wishmore around the hotel, she'd replace the summer ball posters at the same time. Pleased with the idea of dealing with two tasks at once, Suzanne got to work.

"Ready for the tour?" Suzanne asked the older lady when she reached her at the reception desk.

"Lead the way," Mrs Wishmore replied with a smile.

"First, I want to replace this old poster for the summer ball with this new one I had printed this morning," Suzanne said, gesturing to the poster on the wall beside the reception desk as she pulled a fresh one from the box she'd brought along.

"Let me help, dear."

Mrs Wishmore opened the silver-coloured plastic frame on the display case and pulled out the old poster, allowing Suzanne to slip the new one into place.

"Done in a matter of seconds," Mrs Wishmore beamed as she closed the poster frame. "We make quite a team, Suzanne."

"I appreciate your help, Doris. This would be a bit fiddly without an extra pair of hands chipping in."

"Teamwork will always get us where we need to go."

Suzanne smiled at the older lady, amused by her easy wisdom. Pointing to another bank of marketing posters on the other side of the lobby, Suzanne continued her work.

"So, tell me Doris, what made you want to come and work here at the Star Castle Hotel?" she asked as they dealt with the next poster.

"Well, this seems like such a lovely place, and it has such a rich family heritage. When I heard you were in need of help, I knew I had to come and do what I could."

Suzanne paused in her work, taking in the woman's reply. It struck her as a little odd, although not in any specific way she could explain. Most temporary staff would have said that the short-term contract suited them, or that they already had another position lined up for later in the summer, or something along those lines. And the hotel didn't need 'help', so much as it needed to plug a routine employment gap, which wasn't unusual. The hotel regularly hired people on temporary contracts during the busier moments of the year.

"Oh, I think that poster is a little squinty, dear," Mrs Wishmore said.

Pulled from her thoughts, Suzanne glanced at the poster she'd inserted into the frame and realised it was off-centre.

"Thanks, Doris."

"As I said, dear, I'm here to help."

Mrs Wishmore gave her a mysterious wink and looked rather pleased with herself. Suzanne decided that the hotel's new temporary member of staff was a bit of a strange bird.

Still, she couldn't help but like the older lady and her warm personality.

With the posters replaced in the reception lobby, Suzanne began the tour of the hotel for Mrs Wishmore's benefit. It was a pleasure to walk around the building, pointing out its various features and the services on offer to the guests. Suzanne's familiarity with the place meant it was too easy to overlook its many attractions as she went about her daily work. She enjoyed telling Mrs Wishmore a few facts about the history of the old castle, which were always useful when answering guests' questions about the building.

The castle had been built in the mid-nineteenth century as a country residence for a wealthy Glasgow merchant, who'd liked the idea of boasting about having a castle of his own with views of the sea and the hills. Subsequent owners had changed and adapted the building over the years, but many of the original features—fireplaces and intricate mosaic tile work and the grand staircase—remained, and the hotel guests often liked to know more about them.

With the history lecture over, Suzanne showed Mrs Wishmore around the beautiful restaurant with its bank of windows overlooking the bay, and the oak-lined bar and lounge beside it, before introducing her to the hotel's café and then the grand ballroom, followed by a trip to the modern annex where the leisure club and pool were located. After that, they toured the guest floors in both the main castle and in the extended building on the west side of the property. Suzanne showed her around an unoccupied luxury room in one of the curved turrets of the old castle, which were popular with guests on account of their quirky features and open views of the Scottish countryside. The turret rooms were also particular favourites of Suzanne's, who'd been charmed as a little girl by their curved walls and windows and compact tiled fireplaces.

"Gosh, this is a large hotel!" Mrs Wishmore exclaimed once they'd completed the tour and were descending the grand staircase that overlooked the gardens and terrace at the rear. "It was obvious when I arrived that this was a substantial building, but I must say the front façade is rather deceptive. I had no idea there were so many bedrooms."

"There have been plenty of additions to the property over the years which have expanded the original footprint," Suzanne said.

"And all those additions have been done with great taste and respect, if I may say so."

"That was something my grandfather insisted on when he developed the castle. He wanted to preserve the old and make sure anything new honoured it, while still making sure the needs of the business were met and the hotel could grow."

"Well, he certainly succeeded." On the staircase landing between the first and second floors, Mrs Wishmore pointed to a poster frame on the wall. "Oh, it looks like we missed changing this one."

"Nice catch, Doris."

They switched the old poster for a new one. Before they continued down the staircase, Mrs Wishmore paused at the tall picture window on the landing.

"Those are beautiful gardens, dear," she said, pointing to the expanse of lawn running down towards the gazebo and shrubs, and the patch of woodland beyond, above which the hills rose in the distance. "Are there any particular aspects of the gardens that you'd like me to point out to the guests?"

"Actually, yes, now that you mention it. We have a lovely trail that leads down into a small patch of woodland, and families with children often like to wander there, but they sometimes can't find the entrance to the lane. Come on and I'll show you."

Once Suzanne had stowed her remaining stack of posters behind the reception desk, she led the older lady along the wide corridor flanked by the restaurant and bar on either side, and then out through the glass doors to the terrace. She took the opportunity to point out the lawn bowls and skittles that were available for guests to enjoy before turning towards the lane that meandered through the rose hedges and off into the woodland.

"This really is a secret entrance!" Mrs Wishmore said as they turned off the paved pathway and onto the gravel lane. She smiled when she saw the fanciful old wooden sign that pointed the way into the rose hedges. "Isn't that lovely! The children who come here must enjoy seeing this sweet sign. It's like something from a fairy tale."

Suzanne returned the older lady's smile. "My grandfather put this sign up a long time ago when I was just a little girl. I always loved running around in this part of the garden. This is still one of my favourite places at the hotel. On busy days, or when things feel a little out of control and I worry I might be in over my head, I like to come here to gather my thoughts."

She wondered why she'd said this last part to Mrs Wishmore. It was personal information and not something she'd ever share with a member of staff. To cover her embarrassment, she began walking along the gravel lane through the rambling rose hedges.

"I can see why walking along this pretty lane would help to still your mind," Mrs Wishmore said, her gaze slanting towards Suzanne as they strolled along together. "And although it stands to reason that helping to run a fine establishment like this one must involve many difficulties and challenges, I'm sure you are never in over your head, dear."

Suzanne couldn't help but give a wry smile. "But it often feels that way just the same."

"You're doing yourself a disservice, I'm sure," Mrs Wishmore said. "After all, you just walked around the entire hotel replacing those posters for the summer ball, making sure that the best marketing materials are out there for the guests to see, so that the ball will be a tremendous success. That's not the sign of someone who is in over their head."

"I'm not so sure about that. If I hadn't cancelled the band who were supposed to be playing the ball and replaced them with someone else, I wouldn't have had to get new posters printed and hung up in the first place."

"But you did it for the good of the summer ball and for the hotel, didn't you?" Mrs Wishmore asked.

"Of course. But whether I made the right call is another matter entirely."

Once more, Suzanne wondered what on earth she was doing discussing this matter with Mrs Wishmore. Never in a million years would she explain her deep doubts about a key decision she'd made to a member of staff at the hotel.

Yet, as she talked to Mrs Wishmore, Suzanne didn't feel like she was talking to an employee, so much as she was talking to someone she'd known for a long time, even although this made no sense whatsoever.

"Why aren't you sure about the choice you've made regarding the entertainment for the summer ball?" Mrs Wishmore asked.

"The ball is a big part of our hotel's summer events calendar," Suzanne replied. "It used to bring in a lot of money, but we need to make a few changes to the event, like shaking up our entertainment, to keep it profitable. Plus, the summer ball meant a lot to my grandfather, and now that I'm in charge of running it, I want to honour his memory by making it as successful as I can. I can't help but worry I made a mistake when I got rid of the jazz quintet and chose something new and fresh."

"Change always comes with risks. Every time we're faced with a decision, we risk choosing poorly. That's simply the way of things."

Suzanne continued walking along the lane. Mrs Wishmore's words made good sense, but the kindly older lady wasn't telling her anything she didn't already know.

"I just don't want to make a mistake with the summer ball, the sort of mistake that we can't recover from."

"No mistake is ever that bad, dear."

"Some mistakes are exactly that bad," Suzanne replied, and then just as quickly regretted it.

Mrs Wishmore turned her gaze on her once more. "It sounds like there's something you'd like to talk about."

"No, I shouldn't have said anything. It's not appropriate."

The older lady only laughed at this. "We should always talk about things that trouble us. That's the only way to deal with them."

"Maybe. But you're a stranger, and…"

"I'm not a stranger, dear," she interrupted, and laughed again. "I'm Doris Wishmore, the newest employee at the Star Castle Hotel and only too happy to help in any way I can, even if only as a friendly sounding board for your concerns."

The warmth in the woman's expression seemed to wrap around Suzanne like a welcome hug. There was something so deeply comforting about Mrs Wishmore that she couldn't help but nod in agreement with what the older lady had said.

"I suppose it can't hurt to talk through some of this stuff," Suzanne smiled.

"Quite right," Mrs Wishmore replied with a nod.

They walked a few more steps through the winding hedges, the summer roses perfuming the air with the scent of pink lemonade. Suzanne felt no pressure from her companion to talk further, but she did it just the same. It almost felt as if this meandering stroll amongst the long hedges and wild flowers had put her under some kind of spell.

"I'm nervous about the new band I've hired for the summer ball, not so much because it was a sudden decision on my part, although it was, but because my mother doubts my judgement, and I doubt it, too," Suzanne murmured.

Mrs Wishmore considered this for a moment. "Your mother, Imogen, is the managing director of the hotel, isn't she?"

"Yes, that's right," Suzanne said. "You really did your homework before you came to work here," she added with a laugh.

"It's important that I know what, and who, I'll be dealing with," Mrs Wishmore replied.

Before Suzanne could ask what she meant by this downright mysterious statement, Mrs Wishmore smiled and laid a hand on Suzanne's arm. Immediately, Suzanne felt a warm wave of reassurance roll through her, and the older lady's strange comment suddenly didn't seem so strange after all.

"I'm sure your mother has every confidence in you and in your judgement," Mrs Wishmore said.

Suzanne shook her head. "She doesn't. And she's right to doubt me."

"Why on earth would you say that?"

Mrs Wishmore gave her a thoughtful look, her blue eyes kind and warm. The older lady's comforting presence by her side made her want to explain what she meant.

"I've never had to face the kinds of challenges in life that my mother faced, or my grandfather," Suzanne said. "I've had an easy life, thanks to their hard work."

"Isn't that what every family wants for its next generation? For children to thrive instead of struggle?"

"Of course. But a person learns something by coming through hard times. And because my mother knows I've been spared the sorts of troubles that she went through, and that my grandfather went through, too, I know she doubts that I've got what it takes to do the job and make the big decisions, because I've never really been tested."

Mrs Wishmore seemed to think about this for a moment. "What sort of troubles are you talking about?"

"Well, for one thing, my grandfather gambled his entire financial future on this place," Suzanne said, gesturing to the hotel and the grounds. "He had no guarantees it would turn out to be a success, and he had to work hard to build it into what it became. And as for my mother, well, as if taking on the responsibility of growing the business alongside my grandfather wasn't enough to be going on with, she found herself pregnant and raising me alone. She had to become this smart, savvy business woman and hospitality genius, while also bringing me up after my father left her for dust before I was even born."

"Both your mother and grandfather sound like remarkable people."

"My grandfather was a force of nature and my mother is just like him."

"And when compared to them, you feel unworthy."

Tears pricked at Suzanne's eyes at the sharp truth of the matter. "Yes." Embarrassed by her emotions, she gave an easy shrug and laughed. "Believe me, I know how ridiculous that sounds."

"It's not ridiculous in the slightest."

"Because of my family's hard work, I was able to study business and management at university, and then I walked into a job here at the hotel. I've had things easy."

"But you didn't exactly waltz into your current role as deputy manager the moment you graduated from university," Mrs Wishmore said. "Your mother insisted you start on the bottom rung of the ladder at the hotel so you would learn as much as possible."

Suzanne frowned. "How do you know that?"

Mrs Wishmore shrugged. "It's common knowledge amongst the other members of staff that you were no shoe-in to your current role and that you've worked hard to earn it. No one here thinks you were handed anything on a plate."

"But I've still got such big shoes to fill. I want to believe I can do it. But sometimes I worry I can't, and that I won't, and that this place..." Turning once more, Suzanne gestured to the hotel, still visible behind them beyond the wild rose hedges. "I worry that I'll lose this place because I don't know what I'm doing."

They walked a few steps in silence.

"Have you talked with your mother about any of this?" Mrs Wishmore asked.

Suzanne let out a sharp laugh. "The last thing I want to do is tell her any of this. It'll only confirm what I know she already thinks about me." She frowned at Mrs Wishmore, feeling suddenly awkward about having shared these personal doubts and fears. "You won't tell anyone I said any of this, will you? I can't have people knowing I feel this way and that I have these worries and..."

"I won't say a word, I promise," Mrs Wishmore interrupted. "You can trust me, Suzanne."

Reaching out, the older lady squeezed Suzanne's arm, and a warm feeling of comfort seeped through her. Instantly, she knew Mrs Wishmore would never gossip about what she'd just been told. There was something inherently good and pure about the woman—Suzanne felt it inside her heart.

"Anyway, it looks like we've arrived at our destination," Mrs Wishmore said with a smile as she glanced along the gravel lane to where the hedges opened up to reveal the clearing in the woodland. "And doesn't this look like a charming little place?"

As Mrs Wishmore bustled into the clearing, exclaiming at the sweet wooden sign that announced their arrival in the 'Enchanted Forest', Suzanne was relieved their conversational detour had ended. She wasn't entirely sure how the woman had steered her onto the matter in the first place, nor why she'd talked so much about her anxieties when it came to her ability to do her job. It was the first time she'd ever mentioned these feelings to anyone. That she'd shared them with a complete stranger was utterly baffling.

Except Mrs Wishmore didn't feel like a stranger—not anymore.

She joined Mrs Wishmore in the clearing as the older lady admired the wooden red-and-white toadstools scattered around the ground, and the adorable fairy huts dotted here and there. Scots pine and birch trees rose around them, filling the summer air with their sweet sap and leafy scents.

"I can certainly understand why children love coming here," Mrs Wishmore beamed as she inspected the wooden toadstools and the cute fairy huts. "This place is truly magical."

"I think so, too," Suzanne said. "I used to love coming here with my grandfather and running around in the trees. He put these wooden toadstools and fairy houses here to make it even more fun."

"He was a good man, your grandfather. Everyone thought so, and not just those folks who knew him through the hotel."

Again, Suzanne was struck by Mrs Wishmore's odd choice of words, but before she could ask the older lady just what she meant, the air was split by a loud cracking sound beyond the clearing, followed by a terrible crash that caused the ground to rumble beneath their feet.

"What on earth was that?" Suzanne said, hurrying across the clearing in the direction of the noise, with Mrs Wishmore at her heels.

"Oh my goodness!" Doris cried as they reached the edge of the woodland clearing. "One of the branches has fallen from that tree over there!"

As they hurried closer, Suzanne saw a scene of devastation at the edge of the little enchanted forest. A large, gnarly branch had fallen from one of the tall trees and landed on top of two little fairy huts that sat at the bottom of the trunk, smashing the cute wooden structures to pieces. Twigs and smaller branches had snapped off the fallen bough on impact, scattering across the ground and damaging the pathway underfoot.

"I can't believe this!" Suzanne said. "Look at those poor little fairy huts. They're completely destroyed."

"What a pity!" Mrs Wishmore said, her brow furrowing at the sight. She pointed a little further around the pathway and sighed. "And I think there might be more damage over there."

Suzanne followed the older lady's gaze and realised she was right. Beyond the clearing, there was a dip in the land where a narrow stream ran, and which was crossed by a small wooden bridge that allowed guests to continue further into the woodland. Suzanne's grandfather had commissioned the little bridge from the same local carpenter who'd constructed the fairy huts and carved the wooden toadstools, and the bridge adopted the same enchanted woodland style of the other decorative additions in the clearing, with pretty carvings along the handrail and colourful wooden fairy folk standing sentry at either end. Suzanne knew children loved running back and forth across the bridge, but as the edge of the fallen branch had damaged part of the handrail, it would now be out of bounds to the guests for safety reasons. The paved pathway that led to the footbridge was also damaged, and the paving stones beneath the fallen branch were badly cracked.

"What a mess!" Suzanne said, still surveying the damage. "I'm only glad the branch didn't come down when someone was walking here. If it had landed on someone's head, I can't bear to think how badly they might have been injured, or about how much trouble the hotel would have been in because of it."

"The angels were looking out for you," Mrs Wishmore said mildly. "The only damage is to those things that can be repaired or replaced."

Suzanne gave the older lady a curious glance. "You believe in angels, Mrs Wishmore?"

A surprised expression crossed her face. "Of course. Don't you?"

She wasn't sure how to respond to this. "I never really thought about it."

"Well, here's the evidence right in front of us of angels working on your behalf."

"Couldn't the angels have helped by not letting the branch fall off the tree in the first place?" Suzanne said with a laugh.

"I'm afraid it doesn't work that way, dear," Mrs Wishmore said earnestly. "And we can't always understand the whys and wherefores of how angels go about their business."

Suzanne gave Mrs Wishmore a long look, wondering if she was possibly a little loopy.

"Well, unless these angels you know so much about are going to fly down and help clear up this mess, I've got work to do," Suzanne said, pulling out her phone. "I'll have to contact our ground maintenance crew and have them clear away this fallen branch and cordon off the bridge. We can't risk any hotel guests getting injured."

"I'm sure they'll take care of this mess in a matter of moments."

Suzanne spoke to the ground crew supervisor on the phone for a minute, explaining what had happened in the woodland play area and the emergency plan they'd have to put in place to make the space safe. They agreed Suzanne would wait there until the crew arrived, in order to divert any guests who wandered by in the meantime. Once the plans were set in motion, Suzanne hung up.

"Our staff can clear away the fallen branch and put up a cordon," she said as she tucked her phone in her pocket, "but they don't have the skills to repair the wooden bridge or replace these cracked paving stones, never mind rebuild the damaged fairy huts. We'll have to look at hiring a contractor for the repairs. I think we should also get a specialist out here to look at this tree. Given that this huge branch just fell off it, I'm wondering if the tree might not be so healthy."

"What a pity if it has to come down."

"I hope it doesn't, but we'll have to find out either way. It's been a while since we've needed any special work done out here in the woodland, and I can't remember who we used in the past."

Mrs Wishmore nodded and waved a finger in the air. "In that case, allow me to deal with it. I'll speak to the staff in the office and find out who we should contact."

"That's not really your job, Doris. You're here to help our hotel guests, not me."

"The way I see it, if I can help you, then I'm also helping your hotel guests," Mrs Wishmore said. "Leave the matter with me. If I can't handle it, I'll let you know right away."

"Well..." Suzanne wasn't sure about the wisdom of leaving the new recruit to liaise with the back office staff in order to deal with this issue. Still, it was only a matter of asking them to dig out the contact details for the landscaping contractor they'd used in the past. "Okay, I'd appreciate that.

Once you've found the details for the contractor we use, let me know and I'll contact them myself."

"Of course," Doris replied. A warm smile came to her face as she added, "I'm impressed with how quickly you worked out just what has to be done here to deal with this emergency. Despite what we talked about earlier, you are a lot more capable than you give yourself credit for."

Suzanne couldn't help but laugh. "I appreciate the vote of confidence, Doris. But dealing with a practical problem like this isn't exactly in the same league as making major strategic decisions about the future of the hotel."

"Well, if you insist on arguing on behalf of your imagined limitations, Suzanne, then soon enough you'll make them real."

The sharp wisdom of these words caught Suzanne by surprise. She turned to see Mrs Wishmore watching her with a speculative look on her face. She was about to insist that the limitations she saw inside herself were far from imagined, but something in Doris's kind blue eyes stopped her.

It was almost as if the older lady already knew the thoughts inside her head before she'd uttered them.

Which was just about the silliest thing Suzanne could imagine.

The ground crew turned up just then, ready to shift the broken tree branch and set up a safety cordon. Once she'd chatted with the supervisor and was satisfied that everything was in hand for the time being, Suzanne and Mrs Wishmore returned to the hotel. When they reached the offices behind the reception desk where most of the administrative staff worked, Mrs Wishmore turned to Suzanne and smiled.

"Thank you for the tour of your wonderful hotel," she said. "I'll speak to you again just as soon as I have the information you need about the landscaping contractor."

With a cheery wave, Mrs Wishmore disappeared into the

small suite of offices behind the reception desk, and Suzanne headed to her own office further along the corridor to get on with the rest of her work day.

As she sat down behind her desk and opened her laptop, she thought about the new employee they'd hired, and how strangely easy it had been to chat to her during their tour of the hotel and their walk out to the enchanted woodland. Doris Wishmore really was a personable lady and just the type of employee they wanted helping their guests and making them feel welcome.

Suzanne thought, too, about the private information she'd shared with the older lady as they'd walked in the summer sunshine. She was so easy to talk to and Suzanne felt as if she'd confided in an old friend, not someone she'd only just met as a new employee a matter of hours earlier.

She wondered what it was about Mrs Wishmore that was so comforting and reassuring. But no matter how much she mulled it over, she couldn't quite put her finger on it.

The woman just had something about her, Suzanne decided. Something just a little bit *mysterious.*

CHAPTER FIVE

Kyle and his work crew had just stopped for lunch after a morning spent laying patio slabs in the back garden of the Gallagher house when his phone rang. Setting aside his sandwich, Kyle saw Frank Hill's name flash up on the phone screen. Tempting though it was to ignore the call while he finished eating, he knew he had to do whatever he could to stay in the boss's good books right now. That meant answering the man's grumpy calls, even during his lunch break.

"How's it going at the Gallagher place?" Frank barked down the line when Kyle answered the call, not even bothering with a 'hello' first.

"It's fine," Kyle replied. "We should be finished by three."

"Good. I need you to go to another job. Leave the men at the Gallagher place to get on with the work while you're gone."

"What's the job?"

"It's up at the Star Castle Hotel. This might be a big chance for us."

Kyle heard the excitement in Frank Hill's voice. It was the

first time in a long time that the man had sounded anything other than grumpy.

"They've got tree damage up on the hotel property and need someone to look at it," Frank continued. "A large branch came down and damaged a pathway and a footbridge, and they need it repaired. There might be other damage too that they need looked at. I'd be over there myself like a shot, but I'm down at the Dunmore job today."

The Dunmore job was thirty miles away. It was also a full day's schedule of work, involving extensive lawn-mowing and hedge trimming for a wealthy widow who lived in a big house with rambling grounds. Frank wouldn't want to leave the distant job, or the lucrative client, now that he was already there with a team of men in tow.

"You're only a ten minute drive from the hotel," Frank continued. "Go over there and inspect the damage and make the right noises about the work involved and our ability to handle it."

"Okay, no problem."

"They have their own grounds crew at the hotel, but it's a big place, and if we land this job, we might get more work from them in the future. I need you to handle this right and make sure they choose us for this job. Don't mess it up."

Before Kyle could respond, the line went dead. Frank had hung up on him. The man really needed to work on his telephone skills.

"Frank wants me to go and inspect a job," Kyle told his work colleagues, rising from the Gallagher's garden table where he'd been about to eat his lunch. "He wants you two to stay here and keep working. I'll be back as soon as I can to help you finish."

The two men grunted, more interested in eating their lunches than in hearing anything more about Kyle's errand. Picking up his lunch box, he walked around to the work van parked out on the street, stuffing half his sandwich into his mouth before he pulled out onto the road.

The Star Castle Hotel was a spectacular place, and Frank was right to get excited about the prospect of landing some work there. While the damaged footbridge and pathway and tree inspection he was going to look at didn't sound like big jobs, that didn't mean they were insignificant; once a client knew you could do decent work, they'd ask you back when they needed something else done. It was how Kyle would go about building his own business one day—one small job at a time.

If he handled the Star Castle Hotel client right, and got the work for Hill Landscaping, maybe it would keep Frank Hill off his back for a while. That prospect alone was motivation enough to secure the job for his cranky boss.

Kyle turned off the road and onto the country lane that led to the Star Castle Hotel, his fingers crossed as he steered the wheel that he'd play this right.

SUZANNE FINISHED DEALING with a batch of emails and was about to start work on spreadsheet files when there was a knock at her office door and Mrs Wishmore appeared.

"I have both good news and bad news," the older lady announced. "The bad news is that the landscaping company the hotel has used in the past is fully booked and wouldn't be able to send someone out until the end of next week."

"Oh, that's a shame," Suzanne said.

"The good news is that I've found another local landscaping company and they're sending someone over here as we speak."

Suzanne looked at Mrs Wishmore in astonishment. "Gosh, that was quick work."

"I saw no point in delaying."

"We'd usually perform some routine checks on a new company or contractor before we use them, Doris. It's hotel procedure."

Mrs Wishmore waved a hand at this. "Of course you would, dear, and there will be plenty of time for that, I'm sure. Their name is Hill Landscaping, and I put in a quick call to your grounds crew supervisor, who confirmed he's familiar with them and their work. As the footbridge in the woodland is now out of bounds, I thought it made sense to get the ball rolling on the repairs. I know how disappointed the hotel guests will be if their children can't enjoy the lovely woodland adventure when they visit."

Suzanne couldn't deny that Mrs Wishmore's logic made a great deal of sense. Still, she would've liked to look into this new company herself before inviting them to inspect a job.

"When will they get here?" Suzanne asked, hoping she might still have time to check out their website.

"I think the young man might be pulling up in front of the hotel right now," Mrs Wishmore said.

Suzanne frowned. "How do you know that?"

The older lady chuckled and pointed to the small window behind Suzanne's desk. "I just saw a van drive past outside with 'Hill Landscaping' printed on the side."

Suzanne laughed. "For a minute there, I thought you had some sort of sixth sense."

"No, I'm afraid not," Mrs Wishmore said, her tone serious. "I am lucky to have seventh and eighth senses, however."

Suzanne paused, staring at the older lady and seeing something distinctly mischievous in her bright blue eyes.

"Ha-ha," Suzanne said, picking up her phone and grabbing a notebook as she walked around her desk. "You're quite the joker, Doris."

Mrs Wishmore didn't respond. Instead, she just smiled mildly as Suzanne passed by her and out into the corridor.

When they reached the reception lobby, Suzanne scanned the people milling around the check-in desks, looking for the person who'd arrived from Hill Landscaping. A moment later, she saw a man walking through the hotel doors, wearing work jeans and a blue T-shirt with a 'Hill Landscaping' logo stamped on it. He was younger than she'd expected, and was tall and broad-shouldered, with a gunslinger's walk as he crossed the lobby floor. His face and arms were bronzed from working outdoors, and his dark blonde hair was streaked from the sun.

It took Suzanne a second to realise she recognised the man. Her eyes widened when it dawned on her that this was the guy she'd run into that morning on her way to the meeting with the wholesaler. She remembered the firm expanse of his chest as it had connected with her face, and the funny *ooft!* noise he'd made at the surprise collision. He'd been wearing a plain black sweatshirt over his T-shirt earlier, but had discarded that at some point, no doubt on account of the warmth of the summer's day. But there was no mistaking it was the same man.

"Oh, it's you!" Suzanne said as the man drew closer.

He'd been heading towards the reception desk, but his gaze now swung in her direction. When he saw her, he stopped walking and his eyes narrowed as he tried to place her. It didn't take long.

"Hello, again," he said, a smile now replacing his confused expression of a moment earlier. "Hey, how's your head?"

Suzanne's hand moved to her head, which was still tender from its previous impact with the man's chest. "It's fine. Well, I did black out earlier at my desk, but that was just for a minute or two."

The man laughed at this, which was kind of him because

Suzanne knew that what she'd said wasn't especially funny. Memories of the man's solid chest against her face, and the rippling muscles she'd felt beneath his clothes, had made her feel suddenly and stupidly girlish.

"So, you two already know one another?" Mrs Wishmore said, smiling as she glanced between them both.

"Not exactly," Suzanne replied. "We bumped into each other this morning while I was hurrying to my meeting."

"Well, isn't that nice?" Mrs Wishmore said. "It really is a small world, isn't it?"

Suzanne saw the light once more dancing in Mrs Wishmore's eyes, and saw her coy smile too, and couldn't escape the impression that the older lady wasn't remotely surprised to discover that Suzanne had already run into this man earlier in the day, although she wasn't at all sure why she thought this.

"You're from Hill Landscaping," Suzanne said, nodding to the logo on the man's shirt. "Thanks for coming so quickly. We appreciate it."

"Glad to find out if we can help," he said, and offered his hand. "I'm Kyle Lawson. I'm a foreman at Hill Landscaping. Nice to meet you."

"I'm Suzanne Kennedy, deputy manager here at the hotel."

They shook hands. Suzanne's hand seemed tiny inside Kyle Lawson's enormous palm. His were a working man's hands, strong and tough from digging in the dirt all day long, and feeling his fingers around hers gave her a little thrill.

Okay, get a grip, Suzanne told herself. This guy might be easy on the eye, but he was here for business reasons. If she was panting over him like this, then it was only because it had been a while since she'd enjoyed the company of a good-looking man—but that had been her deliberate choice. It stood to reason that she'd feel a little zing of electricity at this man's touch. Any woman would.

"Let's walk out to the grounds at the back of the hotel and I'll show you the work we need done," Suzanne said, all business now.

Kyle nodded. "Sounds good to me."

Suzanne nodded goodbye to Mrs Wishmore and then led the way outside. As they crossed towards the lane that wound into the woodland, she watched Kyle Lawson look around at the lawns and shrub borders.

"Your grounds crew does a terrific job," he said, gesturing to the expanse of gardens stretching down from the bar terrace. "I like what they've done with those rose arbours on the other side of the lawn. That involves skill and dedication."

"We're lucky to have wonderful staff on our garden team," Suzanne agreed. "All this takes a lot of maintaining. Because of that, we don't include non-routine tasks in their work schedules, and prefer to hire outside contractors when something big needs done around the place. Which is why we called your firm." She paused, thinking something over. "I'm happy you could come out so quickly, considering we only phoned a little while ago."

"We like to provide the best service we can," Kyle replied. "I was working on a nearby job, so it was easy enough to get here. The boss mentioned the work might be urgent?"

"The damaged footbridge and pathway are in a part of the grounds that our guests enjoy very much. We've cordoned it all off in the interests of safety, but we don't want the area to be out of bounds for any longer than necessary."

They'd reached the gap in the hedge where Star Castle Lane forked off from the main pathway around the lawns.

"This is special," Kyle said as they turned onto the lane, smiling at the old wooden sign as they passed by. "I've eaten lunch in the hotel restaurant a couple of times, but I never knew this hidden pathway was here."

As they were walking quickly, they soon reached the enchanted forest in the clearing amongst the trees. Kyle let out a warm, low laugh when it opened up before them.

"Now, this really is special," he said, glancing at the wooden toadstools and fairy houses. "If I'd known this was here, I would've brought my nephew along to see it."

Suzanne smiled. "He'd like this?"

"He'd love it. He's seven, so it might not be much longer before he feels too grown up for stuff like this."

There was a soft look on Kyle's face as he looked around at the enchanted woodland, and although Suzanne didn't know this man, let alone his nephew, she knew he was imagining his nephew running around the toadstools and checking out the fairy houses.

"You should bring him sometime," Suzanne said. "Once we get the place knocked back into shape, that is."

Kyle nodded and his gaze travelled to the northern corner of the enchanted woodland where plastic cones and barriers now cordoned off the damaged footbridge and pathway and the broken wooden huts. The shattered tree branch had been hauled to one side and now awaited inspection.

"When the branch hit the ground, it damaged the footbridge and cracked several pathway pavers," Suzanne explained as they walked over. "The noise it made when it hit the ground almost had me jumping out of my skin with fright."

Kyle's gaze swung in her direction. "You were here when it happened? Were you hurt?"

"No, I'm fine. I was standing over there in the clearing when it came down."

The obvious concern in Kyle's expression lingered for a moment before he looked away. Suzanne couldn't help but feel touched by his interest in her wellbeing, and the way his eyes had scanned her as if checking she was indeed unscathed.

She cleared her throat and pointed beyond the safety cordon. "As you can see, the branch smashed these little fairy houses, too."

"That's a real shame." Kyle lifted the plastic barrier and stepped closer to inspect the damage. "These are sweet fairy huts."

Suzanne grinned. "My grandfather commissioned them from a local carpenter when I was a little girl. They've stood the test of time, at least until now."

Kyle nodded, his expression focused as he continued his inspection of the damage. "So, you want this footbridge and paving repaired? And do you want us to rebuild these wooden huts, too?"

"That's right. Our ground staff are gardeners, not carpenters. Although, I now realise that a woodworking project like this might not be something your company does, either."

"Don't worry, we can handle this work," Kyle said quickly. "These wooden huts aren't too complicated to build and we can make sure the decorative finishes are in the same style as the existing huts."

Suzanne's eyes widened at this. "That's wonderful."

"As for the pathway, we'll lift the cracked paving slabs, level off the ground underneath, and lay new pavers in place. We might not get an exact match to what you already have here, but it'll be pretty close."

He gestured to the damaged handrail on the footbridge, then climbed down for a closer look, ducking beneath the struts and testing them with several firm shakes and slaps.

"From what I can see, this looks like cosmetic damage only, even although it does look bad," he said, still squinting at the little bridge. "The underlying structure is unaffected, which is good news. We can take care of these repairs to the handrail."

Suzanne blew out a breath. "That's a relief. What's the time scale for the pathway and footbridge work?"

Kyle gave a thoughtful shrug. "Probably a couple of days, maybe a little more if we hit any unexpected problems once we start."

"And the cost?"

"I'll take measurements and do some sums back at the office," he said, pulling out a tape measure. "The boss, Frank Hill, is in charge of signing off on quotes."

"How soon can you fit us in to complete the work? We can't let kids run around here until it's safe."

"Frank Hill will prioritise this job if you send the work his way," Kyle replied. "I wouldn't be surprised if we can fix your pathway and footbridge in the next couple of days. We might even be able to start as soon as tomorrow if Frank gets the quote to you later today and you're happy with it. The little wooden huts will take longer to finish, but you could still reopen this part of the garden while you wait for the replacement huts to arrive."

This was great news. The sooner the ugly plastic barriers were removed from the woodland, the better. Of course, before the hotel authorised any of this work, they'd have to be sure about the health of the tree that had caused these problems in the first place.

Suzanne pointed to the fallen tree branch on the ground. "We also need an expert opinion on this damaged tree. We can't have members of the public accessing this part of the hotel estate if there's any risk they might be injured by a huge tree branch crashing down on top of them."

"No argument there," Kyle said, his gaze lifting to the canopy overhead and to the tree now sporting a gash where its branch had once grown.

"I don't like the idea of chopping the tree down, because it's been there for decades and it's part of the woodland landscape, but on the other hand the hotel can't risk being sued."

"It's a fine looking tree and I agree it would be a shame to lose it. But I can't tell from down here whether there's significant damage or disease in the tree that means we'd have to chop it down. We need to get up there and inspect it properly."

Suzanne winced. "When can you do that? Will it mean delaying the rest of the repair work?"

"I hope not," Kyle said. "I'll ask the boss to send us out first thing tomorrow to complete the inspection, and that way we'll know what we're dealing with. If we confirm the tree is dying and has to be felled, we'd complete that work before starting the repairs on the footbridge and pathway. Tree felling is a messy business, and it makes sense to get it out of the way first."

"Of course." She glanced up at the tree, not wanting to imagine its sweeping canopy disappearing from the woodland. "Safety comes first, but I really hope we can save the tree."

Kyle smiled. "Me too. Cutting it down is the worst-case scenario. With this damaged branch already gone, the tree might now thrive. My honest opinion from what I can see from the ground is that the tree is probably fine. But we need to be sure."

"Absolutely."

He gave her a thoughtful look. "I'm sorry I can't give you a firm answer one way or the other and I hope that doesn't put you off hiring us."

"Why would it?"

"Because I'm sure any other landscaping companies you've arranged to come out here will just tell you to chop down the tree and be done with it. They make more money that way and you don't have to worry about your hotel's liability insurance. I don't think we should take drastic action unless it's the only choice, but I'd also hate to miss out on this job because I was honest about being uncertain."

His gaze stayed fixed on her as he talked. Suzanne liked his honesty almost as much as she liked the way his eyes held hers as he talked.

"I appreciate your honesty, Kyle," she said. "We want this work done as quickly as possible so we can put this woodland area back into use. We haven't called anyone else yet about this work, and if I like what I see once you send through your formal quotation, we may not bother calling anyone else, either."

Kyle nodded, and Suzanne saw a look of relief pass over his face. "In that case, I'll take some measurements so we can work on your quotation this afternoon."

Suzanne's phone rang just then. When she checked the screen, it was her mother calling.

"Hi, Mother," she said when she answered. "Can you hang on a second while I finish dealing with something?"

"Actually, no, I can't hang on," her mother replied. "You were supposed to be here five minutes ago for our meeting with the bar manager."

Suzanne checked her watch and saw it was almost one-thirty already. Where had the day gone? She'd forgotten all about the meeting her mother had scheduled with their bar manager to discuss new product ranges they were considering adding to their bar stock.

"I'll be right there," she told her mother and hung up, before turning to Kyle. "I'm sorry, I need to get to another meeting. Can I leave you here to deal with these measurements on your own?"

"Absolutely."

Suzanne pulled a business card from her organiser and

handed it to Kyle. "Use this email address when you're ready to send through the quotation."

"Will do," Kyle said, sliding the card into his pocket.

"And my mobile number is on there, too, in case there's anything specific you need to chat with me about once you've worked up the figures."

"We'll be back in touch before the end of the day."

He smiled as he said this, and the honest warmth in his expression was reassuring. At least things were moving in the right direction as far as the repairs were concerned.

She'd almost reached the hotel's back offices when Mrs Wishmore appeared in the corridor.

"Oh, hello, dear," Doris said. "I was just on my way to the reception desk. How did it go with that nice young man, Kyle, from the landscaping company?"

"He's taking measurements and we should have a quote soon."

Mrs Wishmore clapped her hands together. "I'm so pleased he's able to help take care of the problem."

"Thanks for finding someone to come here so quickly and look at the job. I appreciate it, especially considering this is only your first day here."

"I'm here to help in any way I can," Mrs Wishmore said with a smile. "Whenever you need a hand with something, just shout."

The older lady patted Suzanne's arm and added, "You'd better hurry along for your meeting. You don't want to keep your mother waiting any longer, do you?"

Suzanne was knocking on the door of her mother's office when it occurred to her that Mrs Wishmore couldn't possibly have known about the meeting she was going to, or that she was running late for it. So on how earth…

"Suzanne, you're here at last," her mother said as Suzanne opened the office door. "What kept you?"

"Uh, well…"

"Never mind, let's just get down to business," her mother said before she could answer, and gestured to the bar manager sitting beside her at the meeting table. "I have another appointment after this, and Carl has to get back to the bar after we're done here, so let's crack on."

Suzanne set aside thoughts about how Mrs Wishmore had known about her meeting schedule for the afternoon. It didn't really matter, one way or the other, and there were other things to worry about anyway—like the displeased expression on her mother's face as she eyed Suzanne across the table. Imogen Kennedy disapproved of people who arrived late for things. Tardiness was a sign of a disorganised mind and a lack of seriousness, in her view, two faults Suzanne did not want to be accused of.

Sitting down at the table, Suzanne pulled out her meeting notes and got to work.

CHAPTER SIX

By three-thirty that afternoon, Kyle and his team of workmen had finished laying the patio at the Gallagher job and were packing up the van. Kyle was hauling equipment when his phone rang in his pocket. When he fished it out, he saw it was Frank Hill calling.

"I've looked over the measurements you sent from the Star Castle Hotel," Frank said when Kyle answered. "It's a bigger job than I expected."

"They want the kid's play huts and the little wooden bridge put back as good as new, which will keep us busy," Kyle said. "I can handle the carpentry work, and replacing the smashed pathway slabs will be straightforward. They're keen to get everything fixed as quickly as possible."

"Any idea who else is quoting for the work?"

"I got the impression that if they liked our price, they might not bother with other quotes. They don't want the woodland play area cordoned off for too long."

"Good. But what's this you've put in your notes about us having to inspect a tree first thing tomorrow morning? Why aren't we just cutting the damaged tree down? We make more money that way."

Kyle should have known Frank Hill would latch onto this detail. "The tree might be sound and the client doesn't want to lose it. You said you wanted to secure this job and keep the client happy. If we can save that tree, and save the client some money, that will keep them happy, just like you asked. We're still charging a fee for the tree inspection, so it's not like we're making a loss."

There was a brief silence before Frank grunted down the line. "Hmmf. Anyway, I've finished the quotation, so when you get back to the yard this afternoon, I want you to print out a copy and drop it off at the hotel."

"The deputy manager gave me an email address to send it to."

"Fine, but I want a paper copy delivered, too. It looks good and shows we mean business."

Kyle smiled. Maybe old Frank Hill knew a thing or two about customer care, after all.

"We're just packing up at the Gallagher job," Kyle said. "Once we've unloaded the van back at the yard, I'll take care of the quotation."

"Since you were late to work again this morning, you can make up for it by starting on those woodland play huts for the hotel this evening."

"You want me to start the work before the hotel agrees to the quote?"

"It's a competitive quote and I think they'll go for it, especially if they're in a hurry. If they don't give us the go-ahead, we'll find another customer for the wooden huts. People with families like that kind of thing. It's not a risk for us to start the carpentry work."

"Fine by me."

Kyle would enjoy getting stuck into building the little

wooden play huts. They'd be easy to put together and fun to build. Knowing they were destined for that cute patch of woodland, where children would romp around and have fun, gave him a sense of pride about the new work he was about to undertake.

The call ended and Kyle returned to helping his men load the van. The sooner they were back at the yard, the sooner he could get that quotation printed and delivered to the Star Castle Hotel and—hopefully—secure the job. Landing this client would keep Frank Hill happy, and maybe put Kyle back in his good books, especially considering he was the only employee with the skills to build those play huts quickly and to a high standard.

Plus, Kyle wouldn't mind seeing the hotel's deputy manager again, Suzanne Kennedy. He'd been pleasantly surprised to see her at the hotel after their collision on the street outside the café earlier that morning. Getting the chance to see more of the woman who'd almost literally knocked his socks off the first time they'd met would be a big perk of the job.

"WHY DIDN'T you tell me about the damage out in the woodland play area?"

Suzanne looked up from her laptop to see her mother standing in the open doorway of her office. Suzanne hadn't heard her come in. She'd been absorbed in financial analysis, her mind whirring with numbers and revenue calculations.

"I meant to tell you about it earlier," Suzanne said, pushing back from the desk. "But we had so many things to talk about during the meeting with the bar manager, and the rest of the day has been non-stop. I was planning on coming by your office just as soon as I finished this work."

"But I heard that a tree has fallen down and damaged the play area," Imogen frowned as she closed the office door and stepped closer to Suzanne's desk.

"There's damage to the play area, yes, but it was only one branch that fell down, not the entire tree."

"Fine, I stand corrected. But the play area is important to the guests who bring children here and we need to prioritise getting everything repaired."

"Exactly, which is why I've already taken care of it."

Imogen's gaze narrowed. "By doing what?"

"I got a local landscaping company to come out earlier and quote for the repair work. They're also sending someone out tomorrow to do a specialist inspection of the tree."

"Oh, I see." Imogen looked surprised, as if she hadn't thought Suzanne capable of taking the initiative to deal with an unexpected problem like this one. "Well, that's fast work."

"Actually, I had help from one of our new employees," Suzanne said, uncomfortable with taking too much credit considering how it had all come about. "The landscape contractors we use weren't available, but the new staff member, Doris Wishmore, found another company who could come out right away."

"I didn't know we'd hired any new office staff," Imogen said.

"She's here on a short-term contract to deal with the front-of-house, but offered to lend a hand when we found the damage to the play area while I was giving her a tour of the hotel. She was a big help."

"And what about the damaged tree?"

"Hopefully it's fine and won't have to be felled, but if it does, we'll get the messy work finished before starting the repairs to the bridge and footpath. The landscaping company will send through their quotation as soon as possible, so we don't have to keep the area closed for long."

"Good." Imogen still looked surprised at the news that Suzanne had dealt with the problem without first consulting her, but her expression was quickly replaced by another frown. "I'm glad you've already got things moving on this, but we wouldn't usually authorise an external contractor before comparing at least three work quotations."

"I know, but time's a factor here," Suzanne replied. "I double-checked our booking diary and realised that the summer party we throw for the hospital Kids' Club is happening next Wednesday afternoon. If we can't get the woodland play area knocked back into shape, we'll have to hold the party in one of the function rooms, and I want to avoid that. Some of those sick kids are stuck indoors enough as it is, and I hate the idea of disappointing them. I don't want to cancel a party they're already excited about, or move it indoors, just so we can organise more quotations from contractors in order to save a bit of money for the business."

Imogen's expression softened. For the last ten years, the Star Castle Hotel had hosted a summer party for the Kids' Club run by the local hospital. Children who were receiving treatment for long-term health conditions, and who were well enough to attend the party, were invited to enjoy an afternoon of fun and games and party food laid on by the hotel.

Most years, they'd been lucky with the weather and been able to hold the event in the woodland play area, much to the delight of the children. Children who belonged to the hospital Kids' Club, but who weren't well enough to come to the party, received a special goody bag at home or on the hospital ward where they were being treated, delivered by the kids' entertainers the hotel hired for the afternoon, who stayed to chat with the children and do a few party tricks so they didn't feel left out.

Suzanne knew how much fun the children had at the

summer party, and how much they loved having the woodland play area all to themselves while enjoying the entertainment and games. While there wasn't much she could do if poor weather forced the summer party indoors, she wasn't about to let it happen just because they didn't get the play area repaired quickly enough. The last time she'd checked, the weather forecast for next week looked bright and sunny. It would be a shame to waste the promise of a wonderful summer's afternoon for the hospital Kids' Club party just to stick to hotel procurement rules.

The expression on Imogen's face suggested that her mother felt the same way.

"That seems fair," Imogen said. "We can set aside our usual contracting procedures if it means getting the woodland play area back into action. I don't want to mess around with the Kids' Club summer party any more than you do. The children enjoy it and it's an important part of the hotel's commitment to the local community. It also buys us a lot of goodwill with people who spend money in our restaurant and bar, and use us for their special occasions, as a direct consequence of it. We don't want to jeopardise that."

It was a typically hard-nosed business analysis from her mother. Perhaps Imogen saw the look on Suzanne's face, because she added, "We're running a business, Suzanne. Every decision we make has to be in the best interests of the hotel and its profitability. Pressing ahead with these repairs is good business sense."

"I get that."

"We can't do any of the philanthropic work we do—like the Kids' Club summer party—if we don't look after our bottom line."

"I get that, too."

Imogen peered at her for a long moment. "Are you sure about that?"

Suzanne felt a bubble of indignation rise. "I'm the one who fast-tracked the woodland repairs to avoid disappointing our guests." Frowning, she thought of something else her mother ought to be reminded of. "I'm also the one who fired the band we'd hired for the summer ball because they tried to fleece us out of more money. I understand what it means to take decisions that keep us in business and making a profit."

Suzanne watched her mother's expression as she debated how to respond.

"We still don't know if firing the band is the right decision or not, Suzanne."

"It *is* the right decision."

She said it with more force than she'd intended, and her mother's eyes widened at her tone.

"You think I'm foolish for cancelling the band who were trying to get one over on us, but you also think I'm soft for not wanting to let the kids down by making last-minute changes to their summer party," Suzanne continued. "But both these things are about doing what's right for the hotel."

"I never said you were foolish, and I certainly didn't say you were soft. I just sometimes wonder..."

Imogen stopped talking and waved a hand in the air at nothing in particular.

"You just sometimes wonder if I'm up to this," Suzanne said quietly. "Why don't you just say it?"

Imogen opened her mouth then plopped it closed again and let out a sigh. "No, it's not that at all." She gave an angry shrug, her brow furrowing. "Look, I didn't come in here to argue about silly things. I just came to find out what's going on in the woodland play area."

"Well, now you know."

Suzanne didn't mean to sound like a sulky child and wished she could suck the words back into her mouth. She also wished she could have these discussions with her mother without always feeling like Imogen was judging her abilities and finding her not up to par. Would things always be this way between them? Would Imogen always doubt the choices Suzanne made and question whether she could do this job?

But Suzanne knew Imogen could hardly be expected to have faith in her when she had so little faith herself these days.

"Look, Mother..."

Suzanne wasn't sure what she wanted to say. She was relieved when a knock at the office door stopped her having to scratch around for words she couldn't find.

"Come in," Suzanne called out.

The door opened and Doris Wishmore stepped into the office. She glanced at Imogen, who was still standing on the other side of Suzanne's desk, and then at Suzanne. "Sorry to interrupt, I didn't realise you were in a meeting."

"It's fine, I was just leaving," Imogen said and glanced at the name badge pinned to Mrs Wishmore's work shirt. "You must be the new member of staff Suzanne mentioned. Welcome to the Star Castle Hotel. I hope you enjoy working here with us."

"Thank you very much." Doris smiled and shook Imogen's hand. "And you must be Imogen Kennedy. It's a pleasure to meet you. You have an excellent reputation as managing director here."

"Well, thank you," Imogen said, the compliment softening her expression.

"It must be wonderful for you to work here alongside your daughter," Doris added.

"Yes, quite wonderful." Imogen glanced at Suzanne and then gave the older lady a brief nod. "Excuse me, I have to get back to my office."

Once Imogen left, Mrs Wishmore turned to Suzanne. "I hope I didn't come at a bad time."

"Not at all. How can I help?"

"The young man from the landscaping company is back. Kyle Lawson. He's prepared a quotation for the work in the woodland and wants to hand over the paperwork to you personally."

"I see." Suzanne closed her laptop and rose from her chair. "His company must really want our business."

"Of course they do. This is a fine establishment. Any local company would be honoured to do business with you."

Suzanne smiled at the older lady's words. "Is he out in the reception lobby?"

"He is." Mrs Wishmore's gaze raked over Suzanne's face, and her expression turned into one of concern. "I do hope you're all right, dear? I can't help but feel that when I came into your office just now, I might have interrupted a disagreement you were having with your mother. Neither of you looked particularly happy."

"I'm sorry, you shouldn't have to worry yourself about anything like that, Doris." Suzanne locked her office door and they headed along the corridor towards the lobby. "We were just having a difference of opinion about something, that's all. It's just part and parcel of running a business this size."

"I understand," Doris replied, and gave her a kind smile. "Perhaps you'd like a nice cup of tea while you meet young Kyle."

"Oh, no, I don't have time for that. I'll just grab the paperwork he wants to drop off, and then I have to speak to the head chef about something I discussed with our wholesaler this morning, and after that I need to finish running some numbers on my laptop."

"You have plenty of time for tea," Mrs Wishmore insisted.

They'd reached the reception lobby and Doris headed to where Kyle Lawson was lingering at the seating area. "And I'm sure Kyle would like some tea, too, wouldn't you young man?"

Kyle looked up from his phone, which he'd been tapping at while he waited. "Uh, well..."

"Perhaps you're more of a coffee person?" Doris said, then wagged her finger. "Of course you are. In that case, two coffees coming right up."

"Doris, wait," Suzanne said, but Mrs Wishmore cut her off.

"I know how keen you are to get the woodland play area back into good working order," Doris said. "Perhaps if you take a glance over the paperwork that Kyle has brought along, you'll be able to ask questions while he's here to answer them."

Suzanne was at a loss for words yet again. She'd only come out here to collect the quotation paperwork before getting on with the rest of her work. Now, Mrs Wishmore was setting up a friendly chat with the man over coffee.

She glanced at Kyle Lawson, who offered her a smile. "There are a few things in the quotation I'd be happy to go over and explain in more detail if you had a spare few minutes."

Suzanne realised it would seem rude not to agree to chat for a minute, especially as Doris had already offered the man coffee. "Yes, that's a good idea. Shall we grab a seat in the bar?"

"Splendid!" Mrs Wishmore beamed. "You two get settled at a table and I'll bring your coffee straight over."

They crossed the lobby and headed towards the bar. Suzanne pointed to a table near the bank of windows overlooking the gardens and terrace, and Mrs Wishmore hurried off behind the counter, where she chatted comfortably with the young woman who was working there while the two of them prepared the coffee order. Considering how the older lady handled the complicated coffee machine, and her easy camaraderie with the young bar staffer, anyone would think Doris was a long-standing employee of the Star Castle Hotel, rather than someone who'd only started work there that very morning.

Once more, Suzanne found herself surprised and baffled by the older lady and her remarkable competence.

"Here's the quotation my boss put together, if you'd like to look it over."

Suzanne was pulled from her thoughts about Mrs Wishmore as Kyle pushed an envelope across the table towards her. When she took out the paperwork, she glanced at the figure typed in bold at the bottom of the top sheet and let out a gasp of surprise.

"That's the price you're quoting?" she said, already flicking to the second sheet which contained the itemised plan of works. "It's less than I expected."

"That's good to hear," Kyle said. "The boss is keen to get your business and wanted to provide a competitive quote."

Suzanne looked back at the quote on the paperwork. "We don't want to pay over the odds but we don't want a sloppy job, either. The woodland play area is important to our guests and, by extension, to the hotel business, and we aren't interested in cutting corners to save money."

Kyle was already holding up his hands in a placating gesture. "We won't cut corners if we get this job. You'll get the best work we can provide, I promise you that."

Mrs Wishmore arrived at their table with at tray bearing coffees and a plate of small cakes and cookies. After serving their drinks and snacks, she smiled at Kyle, then gave Suzanne a wink and shuffled off with the empty tray.

Suzanne wasn't sure what the wink might have been

about. She felt a flush of heat at her neck as Kyle leaned over the table towards the paperwork, his hand brushing against hers as he pointed to the itemised work list.

"We already have the paving supplies you need in our stock yard," Kyle said, his finger tapping at the list printed on the paperwork. "They're not an exact match, but they're close enough that no one will notice the difference and that means we won't have to special order anything or purchase a minimum number of paving units from our supplier."

"Hmm, I see."

Suzanne sipped her coffee and concentrated on the business discussion she was supposed to having, instead of on Kyle Lawson's strong workman's hands as he continued pointing at the quotation. He was a good-looking man, but she was bemused at being unable to focus on what he was saying because of it.

She imagined how her mother would react if Imogen knew Suzanne was having hot flushes on account of the attractive landscaping contractor with whom she was meant to be negotiating a business contract. The mental trick conjured her mother's angry expression and disappointed tone, which had the effect of cooling Suzanne's temperature.

"What about replacing the fairy huts?" Suzanne said, shifting in her seat to avoid Kyle Lawson's hand brushing against hers again. "We don't want anything that looks poor quality or is made from cheap materials."

"That won't happen," Kyle said. "We only use high quality materials. And I can personally guarantee that the new fairy huts won't be poor quality, because I'm the one who'll be building them."

This news took Suzanne by surprise. "You're a carpenter as well as a landscaper?"

Kyle gave an easy shrug and swallowed some coffee. "I like to tinker in my spare time. I made a garden den for my nephew when he was younger, and it's not a million miles away from the fairy huts you need replaced. When Hill Landscaping needs some carpentry work done for a client, Frank usually asks me to take care of it because I know what I'm doing."

"Hmm, okay." Suzanne wasn't convinced, not because she thought the man wasn't telling the truth, but because her grandfather had commissioned those fairy huts and supervised their design and she wanted to be sure that the replacements would have the same attention to detail.

"I might have some photos on my phone of the hut I made for my nephew," Kyle said, pulling out his phone and tapping at the screen for a minute. He turned the phone around for her to look at.

Suzanne looked at the photograph on his phone, which showed a grinning little boy of maybe five years old peering through the open side of a wooden hut while brandishing a plastic sword. The little hut was incredibly cute, with an oversized apex roof made of blue-painted slats and a window on the side opposite the open end. It was obvious that a great deal of work and care had gone into building the play structure.

"It's lovely," Suzanne said. "And it looks like your nephew loves it to pieces."

"This photo is from a few years ago. Jamie's older now and doesn't play in it as much as he used to." Kyle flicked through the photos again. "Here's another shot with me in the frame to give it more perspective."

Suzanne looked again at the phone. In this next photo, Kyle Lawson was standing beside the play hut while pretending to wrestle with his nephew. Judging by the ecstatic look on the boy's face, the kid was loving every minute. Kyle looked like he was having a lot of fun, too, horsing around with the child. She glanced across the table at him, wondering about the soft side that lay beneath his rugged workman exterior.

"This hut I built for Jamie isn't as detailed or intricate as those fairy huts you have in your woodland play area," Kyle said. "But I can match the design and deal with the carved details around the little doors and so on. That won't be a problem."

Suzanne nodded and pushed the phone back across the table. "Each of the fairy huts has different designs carved into the wood, but they aren't easy to make out on the damaged huts because of how the wood shattered. I may have old photographs in our family albums from when the huts were first installed that show the original design. I could look them out."

"That would be a big help if you want the carvings to be as close as possible to what was there originally."

"And you're certain you can start work right away?"

"The boss already signed off on it. If you're happy with this quotation, we'll be back tomorrow morning to take care of the tree inspection. If that goes to plan and we confirm the tree doesn't have to come down, we should be finished with the pathway and bridge repairs by early next week. If we do have to cut down the tree, that will mean an extra half-day's work."

"We're holding a summer party for the hospital Kids' Club next Wednesday. We'd like to hold it in the woodland play area as planned."

"I see no reason why you won't be able to do that."

Suzanne couldn't have hoped for better news. After one last glance at the quotation paperwork, she turned to Kyle with a smile and offered her hand.

"In that case, I'm happy to agree to this quotation, Mr Lawson."

He grinned and shook her hand. “Call me Kyle, Ms Kennedy.”

“In that case, call me Suzanne.”

“We appreciate you giving us this job, Suzanne. I’ll let the boss know he can send us out here tomorrow for the tree inspection.”

“Wonderful.”

They were still shaking hands across the table and smiling at one another. It should have felt odd, but it didn’t. Suzanne was enjoying the feel of his big hand gripping hers. When he released her hand to pick up his phone, she was almost sorry.

“We’ll see you tomorrow, Suzanne,” Kyle said, draining his coffee cup and rising from the table.

“I’ll look forward to it.”

His gaze travelled to the plate of cakes and cookies that Mrs Wishmore had left on the table, a look of obvious longing in his eyes.

“Please, help yourself,” Suzanne laughed.

“Thanks.” Kyle grabbed a cookie and took a bite. “Wow, this is good.”

“Our pastry chefs here at the hotel know what they’re doing. These chocolate chip cookies are one of our specialities and always popular with our guests.”

“I can see why.” He wiped crumbs from his mouth and gave the plate of treats another glance. “I think I’ll buy a few of these to take home for my nephew. He’ll love them.”

“Don’t be silly, you don’t have to buy anything,” Suzanne said, stacking the remaining cookies into a napkin and folding the edges around them, before handing them over to Kyle. “As a small thank you for coming here so quickly and prioritising these repairs. We appreciate it.”

“That’s nice of you, thanks.” Kyle took the wrapped treats

and smiled, his gaze holding hers. "Right, I'll get back to the work yard and start building your fairy huts."

"Tonight?" Suzanne glanced at her watch and saw it was almost five o'clock already. "Aren't you finished for the day?"

"I promised we'd build these fairy huts as quickly as possible. No time like the present."

"I hope your boss isn't making you work horrible hours just to keep us happy here at the hotel?"

Kyle shook his head. "All part of the job. And the truth is, I'm looking forward to building these little huts. I might even get my nephew to help with some of the easier parts and give him some jobs to do that'll keep him busy and out of trouble."

They left the bar and started walking back towards the lobby. "It sounds like you're close to your nephew?" Suzanne said.

"Jamie's a sweet kid." His voice was soft as he spoke, and Suzanne could see that the man adored his nephew. "He enjoys having manly tasks to do, things involving work tools and muck and messing around outdoors, so I think he'll enjoy lending a hand with these fairy huts."

"That's nice of you to think of him."

"It's hard not to when he's trailing around behind me all evening telling me he's bored."

Suzanne must have looked confused at this because Kyle added, "Jamie and his mother—my sister, Erin—are living with me at the moment. She's just been through a bad break-up from her husband, and she and Jamie are staying with me while they find their feet again."

"I'm sorry, that can't be easy on either of them."

"Erin is a warrior and is battling through it all, although quite how she's managing it is a mystery to me. Jamie acts like everything is fine, but I know he's secretly crushed that his dad…" He broke off and shook his head. "Sorry, you don't want to hear any of this."

"No, it's fine, really."

Although this unexpected sharing of personal details had taken Suzanne by surprise, she found herself wanting to hear more about Kyle and the family he'd welcomed into his home. Her thoughts turned to the photo he'd shown her on his phone, of him play-wrestling with his small nephew. He obviously adored the boy, and if he'd invited his sister and nephew to stay with him following her marriage breakdown, then it sounded like he was a decent and caring man.

Although she'd already sensed that about him when she'd run straight into him on the street corner in town and almost landed on her backside. There'd been deep concern in his expression as he'd asked if she was all right, and she'd felt a bright spark burst inside her as his gaze had travelled across her face, checking for injuries.

But she wasn't about to start daydreaming about the handsome landscaper. It was unprofessional, for one thing. More importantly, she reminded herself yet again, the last thing she was interested in right now was romance. She was much too busy for silly things like that.

They'd reached the lobby doors and they stepped outside into the late afternoon sunshine.

"Well," Suzanne said, offering her hand to Kyle. "Thanks again for helping us to get our woodland play area back into shape."

Kyle shook her hand and smiled. "Thanks for sending your business our way. As soon as we've completed our tree inspection tomorrow, I'll update you on where things stand."

She watched him walk along the wide pathway that led to the visitor parking area, his long muscular legs eating up the distance.

"And now I'm watching the man walking away," Suzanne

muttered to herself as she turned to go back into the hotel. "Idiot."

"What did you say, dear?"

She glanced up and saw Mrs Wishmore walking through the hotel doors towards her, wearing her red jacket and with her blue handbag over her arm. Her first shift at the hotel must be over and she was now heading home.

"Nothing, I was just talking to myself," Suzanne said and gave an easy laugh.

Doris smiled and her gaze shifted over Suzanne's shoulder to where Kyle was getting into his parked van. "He's a handsome young man, isn't he?"

Suzanne gaped. "Uh, well… I'm not sure that's appropriate, Doris."

Now it was Mrs Wishmore who looked astonished. "You don't think he's helpful?"

"Helpful?"

"Yes, he strikes me as an incredibly helpful young man. I thought you'd think so too, dear."

"Oh, I thought you said… never mind."

Humour danced in the older lady's eyes. "Ah, I see. You thought I said he was *handsome*. Well, as it happens, I think he *is* handsome as well as helpful. I might be an old lady, but I'm not blind."

"It was certainly very nice of him to bring the quotation paperwork out here so quickly and to answer my questions," Suzanne said, determined to keep her expression neutral. "I've decided to hire Hill Landscaping to take care of the work."

"That's wonderful news," Mrs Wishmore beamed. "And I'm sure he appreciated the opportunity to talk to you, dear."

The older lady's eyes were twinkling with mischief now, and Suzanne blushed at the obviously intended subtext in Mrs Wishmore's comments.

"So, you're finished for the day, I take it?" Suzanne asked, not wanting to be drawn any further into this odd conversation.

"It was a busy first day on the job but I loved every minute."

"I'm pleased to hear it, Doris. And thanks again for going above and beyond and finding a landscaper who could help us with our woodland emergency. I appreciate it."

"As I said, dear, I'm here to help however I can." Mrs Wishmore smiled and laid a hand on Suzanne's arm, giving her a gentle squeeze. "And if you need a friend to talk to, just let me know."

Suzanne blinked in surprise at this. "What?"

"I said, if you need any other tasks taken care of, just let me know."

"Oh, of course."

Suzanne wondered how she could have misheard the older lady yet again, considering she was standing right in front of her.

And yet, she was sure she hadn't misheard her at all.

"Well, it was lovely getting to know you today, Suzanne," Mrs Wishmore said. "I hope we'll become friends."

There it was again, that word—'friend'. How strange that Doris should say something like this, right after Suzanne had misheard her just a moment before.

"Well, I better get myself home," Mrs Wishmore said cheerfully and adjusted the blue handbag hanging from her arm. "See you tomorrow morning, bright and early."

"Bye, Doris."

Mrs Wishmore started along the pathway. Further over in the car park, Suzanne saw that Kyle Lawson was still sitting in his work van, his mobile phone at his ear. As Mrs Wishmore walked past his van, she gave him a quick wave through the windscreen, which Kyle returned, before she continued towards the exit that led to the main road in the distance.

As Suzanne turned back into the hotel, she wondered how Mrs Wishmore was getting back into town. She'd assumed that the older lady had come here in a car which she'd parked in the staff car park, but she hadn't gone in that direction. She hoped Doris wasn't planning on catching a bus, because at this time of day the service was only hourly, and when Suzanne glanced at her watch, she saw that the next bus wouldn't pass by the hotel entrance for another forty minutes. As the woman was new to the hotel, and no doubt still adjusting to the logistics of her temporary position, it seemed only right to alert her to the bus situation.

Suzanne turned and hurried back out of the hotel. But when she reached the wide pathway that linked the hotel entrance to the road that led out to the main exit, she saw no sign of Mrs Wishmore anywhere.

Peering around, she couldn't help but frown in confusion. There was no way the older lady could have walked out of sight so quickly, because the pathway stretched for some distance before disappearing into the treeline beyond. Perhaps Doris had come here in a car after all and had parked it in the visitor car park by mistake?

To her left, Suzanne heard an engine start, but when she turned she saw it was only Kyle Lawson starting his van. He finished his phone call, before tapping the screen and setting the phone aside. A moment later, he was reversing out of his parking spot and driving away.

Suzanne scanned the pathway and the expanse of front lawns outside the hotel, but still couldn't see Mrs Wishmore anywhere. The older lady had been heading towards the main exit, and Suzanne only hoped she wouldn't be too disappointed to find herself waiting so long for the next bus once she reached the stop out on the main road.

Doris Wishmore was a sweet lady and she'd been a big help to Suzanne today, and she didn't like the idea of her hanging around waiting for a bus when she probably just wanted to get off her feet. Suzanne made a mental note to ask Mrs Wishmore about her travel arrangements the next day. If she was relying on the bus, perhaps they could adjust her shift timings so she could catch the earlier bus back into town rather than waiting for the later one.

Suzanne headed back to her office. It would be nice to do something helpful for the older lady who'd come to work at the hotel and who'd already proven herself to be invaluable.

CHAPTER SEVEN

Kyle steered the work van down the narrow road that wound from the hotel car park towards the main road, pleased with how the meeting had gone with Suzanne Kennedy.

Discussing the work details over coffee had sealed the deal, and Frank Hill would be over the moon. Hill Landscaping might not make a fat profit from the contract, but the fact that they were going all out to repair the woodland play area as quickly as possible might mean that the Star Castle Hotel management would think of them for any future landscaping work. Kyle knew the success of the contract rested with him, because he was the one who'd have to build those little fairy huts in record time, but he could handle that if it kept Frank Hill off his back.

Frank would also be pleased to know that hand-delivering the quotation paperwork had done the trick in securing the work. The nice older lady who worked at the hotel and who'd suggested he and Suzanne look at the paperwork together over coffee had helped, too.

The beautiful woman sitting across the table while he

drank his coffee and secured some business for his boss had been the icing on the cake.

On the road up ahead, Kyle saw someone walking along the narrow path that skirted the road. As he drew closer, he saw it was an older lady with a distinctive cloud of silvery hair and bustling way of walking, and he recognised her as the staff member who'd encouraged Suzanne to have coffee with him. Deciding that a word of thanks was in order, Kyle pulled the van to the side of the road.

"Hello, there," Kyle said after rolling down the window.

The woman peered into the van and smiled. "Well, hello there, Mr Lawson."

"Call me Kyle. I wanted to thank you for the coffee back at the hotel. Getting the chance to sit down and chat with the deputy manager helped me to secure the contract with the hotel."

"So I heard. I'm thrilled that it will all be dealt with so quickly. I know how anxious Suzanne is to get those repairs sorted and I'm sure she appreciates you going the extra mile."

Kyle glanced along the road that stretched for some way before it met the main road. "Are you heading into town? Can I give you a lift?"

"Oh no, dear, I wouldn't want to impose."

"Don't be silly. I'm driving back into town, anyway. I'd be glad to drop you off wherever you're heading."

The older lady's smile widened. "That's a generous offer, Kyle. You really are a lovely young man. Well, in that case, I'd love a run back into town. It will save me waiting for the bus."

"I've just realised I don't know your name," Kyle said once the older lady had shuffled herself into the passenger seat.

"Mrs Wishmore," she replied as she fastened her seat belt. "Doris Wishmore."

"So, where can I drop you, Doris?"

"Anywhere on the main street will be just fine, thank you, dear. I'd like to pick up a few things at the supermarket before I go home."

Kyle pulled back out onto the road. "How long have you worked at the hotel, Doris?"

"I only started today, on a temporary basis. I must say it's been all go since I arrived this morning, but the hotel is a wonderful place to work. And young Suzanne Kennedy is a wonderful manager."

"She seems like someone who knows what she's doing."

"I couldn't agree more. As the hotel is a family affair, she's especially keen to do the best she can to make sure the business is a roaring success. She has big shoes to fill."

"Judging by the smart questions she asked when we were discussing this landscaping contract, I think she's more than up to the challenge," Kyle laughed.

"I think she's up to the challenge, too. In fact, I know she's up to it. But Suzanne is the one who has to believe it."

Kyle turned in astonishment at this comment. It was an odd thing for an employee to say about a boss they'd only just started working for. "It sounds like you know Suzanne Kennedy well. Were you friends before you started working at the hotel?"

"Something like that," the older lady said mysteriously, before turning to Kyle with a smile. "But of course, you know all about the trials and tribulations of running your own business and how challenging it can be."

Kyle frowned. "Do I?"

"But of course. This landscaping business of yours must take a great deal of work."

He realised the woman must have got her wires crossed. "Hill Landscaping isn't my company. I'm just an employee."

"Oh, I see. Gosh, judging by how well you handled your meetings today with Suzanne Kennedy, and the fact that you know so much about landscaping and whatnot, I assumed you were the one in charge."

Kyle laughed. "Don't let my boss hear you say that. He'll get suspicious."

"I would have thought any boss would be delighted to have a smart and competent young man such as yourself helping take his business from strength to strength."

"Actually, I think my boss would say I haven't been pulling my weight lately."

"No, I can't believe that."

Kyle slowed to make the turn onto the main road, just a little mystified about how he'd ended up having this personal conversation with the woman who worked at the hotel.

"Anyway, I'm sure your boss will be thrilled to know that you've secured this important job from the hotel," Doris said. "And I feel sure that when you eventually go into business for yourself, you'll make a tremendous success of it."

"What makes you think I plan to go into business for myself?" Kyle said, looking over at the woman in genuine confusion. How could she know such a thing about him and his plans?

"Well, that's what people do, isn't it?" Doris said, as if it was perfectly obvious. "When someone is good at something, as you are, they want to make a go of things for themselves and take their future into their own hands. That must count for double when someone is working for a boss they don't especially care for, as you are."

"Are you some kind of mind reader?" Kyle joked.

Mrs Wishmore laughed softly. "You just seem like a go-getter to me. I feel sure that when the time comes to go out on your own, it will be a wonderful experience and everything you've always hoped for."

"I appreciate the vote of confidence. But the official line is that my boss is a terrific man to work for and I couldn't be happier there."

The older lady laughed again and mimicked zipping her lips closed. "I won't breathe a word to the contrary."

They drove in silence for a few moments, Kyle watching the road while Mrs Wishmore admired the countryside passing by outside the windows. After a minute or so, Doris pointed to the napkin-wrapped stack of cookies that Kyle had tucked into the coin tray beside the gearstick.

"I noticed as you left that Suzanne insisted you take some goodies with you," Mrs Wishmore said.

"I think she just didn't want me drooling over them anymore," Kyle grinned.

"She has a kind heart." They'd reached the town main street and Mrs Wishmore pointed out the window and said, "Just drop me off here, Kyle."

He pulled to the side of the road and Doris opened the van door and climbed out, clutching her blue handbag to her side. "Thank you so much for the lift, Kyle. I appreciate it."

"Glad to help, Doris."

She closed the van door and threw him a wave through the window before walking off down high street. Kyle pulled back into the traffic, tooting his horn as he passed her and returning her wave.

What a strange lady she was, he thought as he headed towards the Hill Landscaping work yard on the other side of town. Strange… but also nice and comforting, too, although he couldn't exactly say why.

As he drove, his mind turned to the fairy huts he would start building at the yard when he got there. He wanted to do a good job for the hotel—no, he wanted to do a *great* job for the hotel—not just to keep Frank Hill off his back, but because he wanted Suzanne Kennedy to love the play huts he built for her as much as she loved the ones her grandfather had got for her when she was a little girl.

He wanted to make Suzanne smile, he realised, because she had a smile that could outshine the sun. And that was something worth seeing.

After working on the frames for the fairy huts in the Hill Landscaping yard for a few hours, Kyle loaded some lengths of timber into the back of his car and drove home. He planned to do more work in his garden, dealing with the little carved signs and decals that would form part of the fairy hut decoration once the structures were built.

First, though, he wanted dinner. Apart from the cookie he'd wolfed down at the Star Castle Hotel, he hadn't eaten since lunchtime, and his stomach wasn't happy about it.

When he got home, he found his sister, Erin, washing dishes at the sink while Jamie sat at the kitchen table doing his school homework.

"Hey, squirt," Kyle said, ruffling Jamie's hair. "How was school?"

"We played football during gym and I got tackled." Jamie lifted his elbow to show off a bloody scrape he'd sustained, and grinned as he added, "The boy who did it got a yellow card."

"So he should've," Kyle said. "Did you score a goal?"

"I was a defender."

"That's the toughest position." Kyle looked over at his sister. "How was your day?"

"Hectic, as usual," Erin said, finishing the dishes and drying her hands on a tea towel. "We were short-staffed at the hospital and it was all hands on deck, and then we had a surge of new admissions to the ward and no beds to put anyone in. I'm planning on a long bubble bath tonight to recover before I have to do it all again tomorrow."

"I'll keep an eye on this scoundrel while you take a soak."

"I don't need anyone to keep an eye on me," Jamie protested. "I'm all grown up."

"Is that right?" Kyle grinned. "In that case, I've got a woodwork project you can help with tonight. I need a strong lad to lend a hand."

Jamie tossed aside his pencil and shoved his exercise book away. "What is it! Can I use the hammer? Can I pound nails into planks?"

"Maybe, but you don't get to do any of it until you've finished your homework," Kyle said.

"It's finished!"

"Really?"

Jamie frowned. "No."

"Well, the sooner you finish, the sooner I can put you to work." Kyle laughed as Jamie grabbed his pencil again and pored over his exercise book.

"I'll be checking your homework before you help Uncle Kyle, so don't be rushing through it and not paying attention," Erin said.

"I won't!" Jamie said. "Anyway, these sums are easy."

Erin shook her head and shared a smile with Kyle. "You're late tonight. I was about to send a text to see if everything was all right."

"I stayed behind at the yard to get a jump on some work," Kyle said.

"Is Frank Hill still giving you a hard time?"

"He's not happy unless he's harassing someone. It's all just bluster."

Erin didn't look convinced and an unhappy expression crossed her face. "Sorry if you were late again this morning because of the school run."

"It's nothing to do with that," Kyle said. The last thing he wanted was for Erin to worry about him. She had enough on her plate already.

"I saved you some dinner." She took a covered dish from the oven and scooped the contents onto a plate. "Chicken and veggie pasta."

"You're a star." Kyle pulled out a chair and sat at the table beside Jamie. "I'm famished."

As he dug into the meal, he remembered the napkin-wrapped cookies he'd brought home from the Star Castle Hotel for Jamie. Once he'd swallowed his first forkful of food, he pulled over the rucksack he'd dumped on the floor when he'd come into the kitchen, and took out the wrapped treats he'd stuck in the side pocket when he'd got out of the car.

"I brought home some cookies for you, Jamie," Kyle said as he opened the napkin to reveal the treats inside. "Thought you might enjoy one of these for dessert."

"Yum!" Jamie yelled, once more abandoning his homework in order to grab a cookie. "These are awesome!" he announced as he tucked in, spraying crumbs across the table.

"Don't talk with your mouth full," Erin told him as she took a cookie for herself, her eyebrows arching in appreciation as she bit into it. "Wow, these are good. Where'd you get them?"

"The Star Castle Hotel. I was up there discussing a landscaping job, and the woman I spoke to gave me these to bring home. We'd had coffee while we chatted and these biscuits were going spare."

"That was nice of her. What's the job?"

"They need some landscaping and structural repairs done in the hotel's woodland play area. Frank Hill was keen to get the work and get a foot in the door up there. He was pleased tonight when I told him we'd got the contract. First time I've seen him smile in weeks."

Frank Hill hadn't just smiled at Kyle's news when he'd returned to the work yard—he'd slapped him on the back in appreciation and grunted out words that sounded a lot like, "Well done, that's good work". Kyle had been astonished.

"I didn't know they had a woodland play area at the hotel," Erin said. "Although I can't say I spend much time up there."

"I didn't know about it, either. If I had, I would've taken Jamie when he was younger. They have this cute enchanted woodland theme going on, with fairy huts and toadstools and so on." Kyle glanced across at Jamie, who was sneaking a second cookie from the pile on the table. "Think you might like to go up there and check out the play area once we've sorted out the repairs?"

Jamie shook his head. "I'm too grown up for that kid's stuff, Uncle Kyle."

"Thought you might say that." Kyle laughed and turned back to Erin. "Anyway, they're in a rush to get the repairs finished, and as I'm the only one on Frank's staff who knows enough carpentry to build the fairy huts, I'll be busy with it for the next few nights. I wanted to let you know in case you need help with anything related to this nuisance." Kyle poked at Jamie as he said this, making the boy giggle. "Make sure you give me enough warning if he needs dropped off, or picked up, or buried alive in the garden, or anything like that."

"Uncle Kyle!" Jamie shouted. "Don't bury me alive!"

"Don't give me a reason to, squirt."

Jamie collapsed into a fit of giggles and snorts, making Kyle grin.

"I've finished my homework," Jamie announced. "Can I

play on my PlayStation until Uncle Kyle's ready to put me to work in the garden?"

Erin glanced at Jamie's exercise book and then nodded. "All right, go ahead."

Jamie leapt from his chair and stampeded through to the living room, where the sounds of explosions and gunfire were soon booming from the television.

"He made quick work of these homework sums," Erin said, looking more closely at her son's exercise book.

"He's a genius," Kyle said. "He gets it from you."

"I don't know about that. Although I do know he didn't get it from his idiot father." Erin sighed and rubbed at her temple. "Sorry, I don't mean to bitch about him."

"Bitch away. The man's a giant turd."

Erin's lips twitched. "Yeah?"

"Without a doubt. He's a giant, planet-sized, stinking turd." When Erin snorted out a laugh, Kyle added, "I can come up with ruder and more offensive descriptions if you'd like, but I if I start I might not want to stop."

"Tell me about it," Erin said and gave a sad laugh. "Oh, hell. How did I not realise Lee would do this to me one day?"

"We discussed this already. It's not your fault."

"But..."

"It's not your fault, Erin."

She sighed and turned to the sink. "Yeah, I know. But still..."

"You'll get through this. You *are* getting through this."

Kyle rose from the table and carried his empty plate to the sink. Erin took it from him before he had a chance to start washing up.

"What would I do without my smart big brother?" she said with a smile.

"What would I do without my mad little sister?"

"Oh, I don't know. You could enjoy your bachelor pad in

peace, and invite a string of wanton women over to keep you entertained."

"I don't know any wanton women."

"Well, that's a real shame."

They laughed quietly as they finished the last of the dishes at the sink. Much as Kyle hated the pain his sister was going through on account of his no-good soon-to-be-ex brother-in-law, he liked having this time with her and his nephew, and loved these moments they got to share.

"Want me to keep some dinner in the oven for you for the next few days if you're working late?" Erin asked.

"If it's no trouble."

"It's the least I can do." Erin gave him a thoughtful look. "You know I'll never be able to pay you back for everything you've done for me and Jamie these past few weeks?"

"Erin, didn't I say that if you mentioned anything like that again, I'd throw you out onto the street?"

"You'd never do that to Jamie."

"Of course not. Jamie can stay. You're the one I'd toss outside."

She laughed and wiped a cloth across the counter. "I wish you'd hurry up and find a woman to marry and have kids with. You're the best man I know, Kyle, and one day you're going to be an amazing husband and an even more amazing father."

"I appreciate the vote of confidence."

Erin rolled her eyes. "But?"

"But I just haven't found the right woman for me yet."

"You aren't looking hard enough. Why aren't you out there dating and finding the woman of your dreams?"

"Because I'm too busy at work."

"It's because Jamie and I are living here, isn't it?" Erin said, an agonised look crossing her face. "We're cramping your style."

"Don't be daft. And I don't have any style to cramp."

Erin laughed, and he hoped that might be the end of the matter. It was true that while Erin and Jamie were living with him, he didn't want to be dating and bringing women home and risk confusing his poor nephew any more than he already was, but there was also more to it than that. He'd put dating on the back burner while developing plans for his new business, but he hadn't told Erin about his hopes and dreams to start up his own garden design business. If he told her, she'd want to know why he wasn't pushing on with it full-steam, and he wasn't about to lay a guilt-trip on her over a decision that was his and his alone. Erin was already being hard enough on herself following the breakdown of her marriage.

"Look, maybe I'm enjoying hanging out with you and Jamie right now," he said. "Eventually, you'll find a new place to live, one within your price range, and then the both of you will be gone. While you're here, I want to do what I can to help you and spend time with Jamie. If I was seeing some woman, she'd just complicate things."

"Some woman?" Erin said, her eyebrows arching. "You're such an old-fashioned romantic, Kyle."

Kyle shrugged. "The point is, I'm not interested in dating. Not right now. So, let's just leave it at that."

"If that's what you want." Erin put the last of the dried dishes into the cupboard and gave him a look. "I happen to know it's *not* what you want, but if that's what you want to keep telling yourself, that's fine with me."

Kyle flicked the tea towel at his sister, then shouted through to Jamie in the living room. "Ready to come outside and get to work, squirt?"

"Ready!" Jamie yelled. The blasting and explosions from the PlayStation fell silent and Jamie appeared in the hallway two seconds later, his eyes shining with excitement. "Have you decided if I'm allowed to hammer nails into planks, Uncle Kyle?"

"I'm still thinking about it. I'm not sure you've got enough muscles for any hammering work."

"I do have muscles, Uncle Kyle!" Jamie flexed his scrawny, seven-year-old's biceps. "Look! I've got tonnes of muscles!"

"Hmm, that's vaguely impressive," Kyle said. "Maybe you're up to the challenge of some hammering, after all."

"Yay!"

"But you have to listen to your Uncle Kyle and do what he tells you," Erin said. "Understood?"

Jamie nodded and ran to the back door that led to the tiny garden. "Hurry up, Uncle Kyle!" he yelled as he ran outside.

"Enjoy your soak in the bathtub," Kyle told Erin as he followed his nephew to the garden.

"Don't let my boy hammer a nail through his hand."

"Spoil sport."

With a laugh, Erin disappeared upstairs. Kyle stepped outside and called Jamie over.

"We'll unload the wood from the car and get started."

"This will be fun, Uncle Kyle," Jamie announced as they walked around to the side gate and out to Kyle's parked car on the street.

"I think so, too, buddy. Maybe once we've done some work, we can drive into town and get ice cream."

"Yes! I love ice cream, Uncle Kyle."

Jamie grinned up at him as he skipped along, his expression sweet and eager, making Kyle's heart squeeze.

Spending this time with his nephew was worth more to Kyle than anything else right now, and despite what Erin thought, that included dating women.

It wasn't even a close contest.

Yet even as he told himself this, his mind filled with an image of Suzanne Kennedy, smiling at him outside the Star

Castle Hotel as they'd said goodbye earlier that afternoon, the summer sunshine catching her hair and lighting up her emerald eyes.

"Uncle Kyle, what are you grinning about?"

Kyle snapped out of his daydream and looked down at Jamie, who was peering up at him with a curious look on his face as he waited for him to unlock the parked car.

"I was thinking about what ice cream flavour to get later," Kyle said, fishing his keys from the pocket of his jeans as he pushed the image of Suzanne Kennedy from his head.

The woman was beautiful. And as his boss's new client, she was also off-limits. End of story.

If only it were that simple.

CHAPTER EIGHT

Suzanne's work at the office still hadn't finished by the time seven-thirty rolled around. There were emails still waiting to be read, revenue spreadsheets still waiting for analysis, not to mention half a dozen other jobs that had landed on her desk throughout the afternoon. But her rumbling stomach told her it was time to call it a day. After working for almost twelve hours straight, her brain felt like mush. As she closed her laptop and pushed back from her desk, she was already fantasising about gulping down some fresh air outside before heading home and eating dinner.

She was almost at the office door when she turned back and grabbed a folder of paperwork from her desk, sliding it into her bag beside her laptop. She usually ended up working in the evening once she was home, unable to switch off from the hotel and its endless tasks. The paperwork she'd grabbed concerned proposals put together by the events supervisor for the Christmas season, and which needed to be agreed in the next few days. It might only be June, but in the hospitality business, they were already finalising their plans for the festive period. Taking one last look through the proposals before agreeing on the hotel's Christmas and New Year offerings would be a useful way to spend her evening and keep things moving forward.

As Suzanne locked her office door, she glanced along the corridor towards her mother's office. Imogen's door was open and Suzanne saw her sitting at her desk, peering at her computer screen and tapping at the keyboard. She thought about dropping in to say good night, and maybe chatting about what her mother thought about the hospitality proposals for the Christmas season. But she decided against the idea. There were a few details in those Christmas proposals she felt sure her mother would disagree with her about, and the work day had been long enough already without ending it with another tense and frustrating conversation. They'd already butted heads twice today, and when it came to having a difference of opinion with her mother, three times was definitely not a charm.

A glorious summer's evening greeted her when she stepped outside the hotel and headed towards the staff car park at the side of the building. The sun was warm and the sky was a deep blue, and Suzanne smiled to see the bar terrace already buzzing with guests enjoying food and wine in the tranquil setting of the hotel's gardens. The bar and restaurant staff would have a busy evening, and the hotel was lucky to have great staff who always went the extra mile for their guests.

Ten minutes later, Suzanne was driving along Balmarrie high street and wondering what she'd make for dinner when she got back to her flat overlooking the waterfront. She didn't feel like cooking, but wanted something more than the simple sandwich she usually settled for when she'd had a long day and was too lazy to put together something more substantial.

As she slowed for traffic lights, her gaze travelled to the pizza place on the street corner. Through the tall glass front, she saw customers waiting at the counter for takeaway pizzas while diners tucked into their meals at the tables in the small restaurant section. The idea of a hot, cheesy pizza was too much to resist, and once the traffic lights changed, Suzanne pulled into a free parking space further along the road and walked back to the pizza shop.

After placing her order—thin crust with a topping of green peppers, black olives, and extra mushrooms—she stepped out into the street to enjoy the evening sunshine while the staff prepared her food. The pretty high street was busy with holiday-makers coming and going from the ice cream parlours and cafes that stayed open late in the summer to soak up the seasonal trade. As she indulged in a pleasant spot of people-watching, Suzanne saw a familiar face walking in her direction. Shielding her eyes from the low evening sun, she realised it was Mrs Wishmore.

Suzanne was about to call out a hello when the older lady was suddenly clipped on one side by two young boys racing up the street on a pair of motorised scooters, sending the shopping bag Doris was carrying crashing to the ground where the contents tumbled out onto the pavement.

"Sorry!" the boys yelled over their shoulders in unison before continuing on their much too fast journey along the pavement.

"Doris, are you okay?" Suzanne cried and hurried up the street to where Mrs Wishmore was standing with a stunned look on her face.

Mrs Wishmore glanced at Suzanne and then at the shopping now scattered at her feet. "Oh, I'm just fine, dear."

"Are you sure? Are you hurt? Those boys almost knocked you over!"

"The young lad only caught my elbow as he whizzed

past." Doris rubbed at her arm and nodded. "I'm absolutely fine. My elbow is a little tender, but no damage done."

"You're more forgiving than I'd be, Doris," Suzanne said, returning the spilled shopping to the bag.

"They're just young boys and a little too excitable. I don't think they meant any harm."

"Is everything okay over here?"

Suzanne looked up from the shopping she was still gathering on the ground and saw Kyle Lawson striding across the road with a young boy at his side. Seeing the hotel's new landscaping contractor appearing before her sent her stomach into a traitorous somersault.

"I saw what happened from across the street," Kyle said as he stepped off the road. "Are you hurt, Doris?"

"Well, hello Kyle!" Mrs Wishmore smiled. "No, I'm just fine. Thank you for asking. As I was explaining to Suzanne, those young lads only caught my elbow as they sped past. I'm quite all right. Well, apart from my shopping spilling all over the ground."

"Let me help," Kyle said, helping Suzanne gather the remaining shopping. Their hands brushed together as they reached for the same grocery items, and Kyle threw her an apologetic smile.

"Sorry," he said.

"No, it's fine," Suzanne said. "It's nice of you to stop and help."

"Seems like this is the second time today we've done this."

"I guess you're right," she said, feeling heat colour her face at the memory of their collision on the street earlier that morning, and of Kyle's hands touching hers as he'd helped her gather up her scattered paperwork.

Had that really been just this morning? It seemed like ages ago. It had been a long—and strange—day.

When they both straightened up again, Kyle pointed to a

few loose oranges rolling down the incline of the pavement. "Jamie, grab those oranges, will you, pal?"

The young boy darted down the street after the oranges and brought them back. "Here you go," he said to Suzanne and dropped them into the shopping bag she was holding open.

"That's very kind of you," Mrs Wishmore said, smiling at the boy.

"This is my nephew, Jamie," Kyle told them. "Jamie, this is Doris Wishmore and Suzanne Kennedy."

The boy grinned and gave them both an awkward wave. Suzanne liked that Kyle had introduced his nephew properly and she liked seeing the obvious bond that existed between the two of them.

"It's very nice to meet you, Jamie," Mrs Wishmore said, reaching into her jacket pocket and pulling out a bag of wrapped toffees. "Would you like a sweet as a thank you for chasing down those oranges?"

Jamie's eyes widened at the bag of sweets, but he glanced at his uncle before taking one. "If I have a sweet, can we still get ice cream?"

"Of course we can," Kyle laughed. He looked at the two women and added, "Jamie helped me tonight with the prep work for the hotel's fairy huts, and I promised that if he did a decent job, I'd buy him an ice cream cone."

"I worked hard!" Jamie announced as he unwrapped a toffee and popped it in his mouth.

"I'm sure you did," Mrs Wishmore said.

"Doris, are you sure you're okay?" Suzanne asked, turning to the older lady. "It looked like you took quite a knock."

"I assure you I'm fine," Doris said. "I would've even have dropped my shopping bag if it hadn't been for the fact that I got a bit of a fright."

"Can I give you a lift home?" Suzanne said. "My car's parked right over there."

"Thanks for the offer, but I don't have far to go and I want to enjoy the rest of my stroll in this fine sunshine." Mrs Wishmore nodded to Kyle, and added, "Young Kyle here was kind enough to give me a lift into town from the hotel this afternoon after I finished my shift, and I'm keen to get a few more steps in to make sure I've had my exercise."

"I'm sure you did more than enough running around at the hotel today to see to that," Suzanne said. "And that shopping bag looks heavy, Doris. Are you sure I can't drive you home?"

"No, I'm looking forward to the rest of my walk," Doris insisted. She glanced at Kyle and then back at Suzanne, and a thoughtful look crossed her face. "I must say, it's such a lovely surprise bumping into you both here this evening."

"I just stopped off to pick up something for dinner," Suzanne said. "I'm glad I did, too, because it meant I could help you after that nasty bump, Doris."

"Well, now that you can see for yourself that I'm fine and well, you'd better run along and see to your dinner arrangements," Mrs Wishmore said. "You must be hungry if you haven't had your evening meal yet."

"I've ordered a pizza," Suzanne explained, pointing to the pizza place further down the street. "I'm just waiting for them to finish making it."

As if on cue, one of the counter staff popped his head out through the doors of the takeaway and shouted, "Order for Kennedy!" When he saw Suzanne, he gestured with the enormous pizza box he was holding.

"Oh, there must be a mistake!" Suzanne said, hurrying over. "I only ordered a small pizza."

The guy glanced at the ticket taped to the top of the pizza

box and frowned. "Ah, you're right. Our mistake. Never mind, just take it anyway. No extra charge."

"But it's too much for me to eat by myself!" Suzanne said in alarm.

But the guy from the takeaway had already thrust the pizza box into her hands and disappeared back inside, where there was a queue of people waiting to be served and collect their food.

"Gosh, that really is a huge pizza!" Mrs Wishmore chuckled.

"And most of it's about to go to waste," Suzanne said unhappily.

"Perhaps Kyle and young Jamie would like to help you eat some of it," Doris said, turning to them both. "What do you think? Can you fit in a slice of pizza before you treat yourselves to ice cream?"

"Yay!" Jamie shouted.

"Well, hang on a minute, buddy," Kyle said to his nephew. "Suzanne probably doesn't want her dinner plans being crashed by the two of us."

Mrs Wishmore's suggestion that Suzanne share her pizza with Kyle and his nephew caught her off guard. But seeing the excitement on Jamie's sweet face made it impossible for her to do anything other than go along with the idea. She couldn't disappoint the boy now that the idea was out there and he was hopping from side to side next to his uncle and staring at the enormous pizza box with barely concealed glee.

"You're both more than welcome to share this food," Suzanne said. "In fact, you'd be doing me a favour, because there's no way I'll eat even a quarter of this pizza by myself and it would be a shame for it to go to waste."

For a moment, Kyle looked conflicted, but then his gaze

shifted to his nephew and to the pizza box the boy was salivating over.

"Well, if you're sure, we'd love to help you polish off a few slices," he said.

"I'm starving!" Jamie declared.

"He's not starving," Kyle said, rolling his eyes. "His mother fed both of us earlier tonight, but maybe all that fairy hut woodwork has given us an appetite."

"How wonderful that you'll be able to share a quick bite together," Mrs Wishmore said, her smile wide.

"You'll join us too, won't you, Doris?" Suzanne asked.

"I'll have to pass. I ate dinner with an old friend earlier this evening, and must confess I enjoyed rather too much pudding for my own good. I couldn't eat another thing if I tried!"

Suzanne realised that if Doris wasn't joining them, that meant she'd be eating her meal with this man she'd only just met a few hours ago. She wasn't sure how she felt about that.

"You three run along and enjoy your pizza before it gets cold," Mrs Wishmore said and picked up her shopping bag. "I'll see you tomorrow at work, Suzanne. Goodbye, Kyle, and it was very nice meeting you, Jamie."

"Bye, Mrs Wishmore," Jamie said. "Thanks for the toffee."

"You're quite welcome, dear."

The older lady shuffled off down the road. Suzanne watched her walking away, keen to make sure the woman wasn't showing any signs of limping or discomfort following her collision with the careless boys on the scooters, but Doris appeared to be moving with no problems or pains.

"I wish she'd accepted a lift home," Suzanne said.

"Me too." Kyle peered along the street to where Mrs Wishmore was turning the corner. "I think I'll hurry after her and insist she let me drop her off at home, just in case she feels any achiness after that knock she suffered and didn't want to mention it."

Suzanne nodded. "I'll come with you. I don't like her just walking off like this on her own, either."

With Jamie skipping along behind them, Suzanne and Kyle jogged down the pavement to the corner where Mrs Wishmore had turned down another street. But when they got there, there was no sign of the woman.

"Where did she go?" Suzanne said, frowning as she scanned the quiet residential street.

"I don't see her anywhere." Kyle glanced around, as if hoping the woman might emerge from between the cars parked on the side of the road outside the terraced houses that lined the street. But apart from a young couple walking on the other side of the road, and a man exercising his dog further along, there was no one around, and no sign of Doris Wishmore.

"Perhaps she lives in a house further along," Suzanne said, although she didn't think it was likely that the shuffling older lady could have already hurried along the street and up one of the garden paths and inside a house in the short time that had passed.

"Maybe," Kyle said, clearly not convinced either.

"Look, there she is down there!"

Suzanne and Kyle both turned to see Jamie pointing along the main street to a bus stop further along from the pizza place. A bus had pulled into the stop and Mrs Wishmore was boarding it. When she slipped into a window seat as the bus pulled away, she gave the three of them a friendly wave goodbye.

"How did she get to the bus stop?" Kyle wondered. "I saw her turn the corner and walk down this street."

"That's what I thought too." Suzanne scratched her head. "Maybe she changed her mind about the walk home and caught the bus instead, and we just didn't see her turn back to the main street." As the bus disappeared down the road and out of sight, Suzanne shrugged. "I must admit, though, Doris is a little bit mysterious."

"Mysterious?" Kyle said, giving her a quizzical look. "What do you mean?"

"Well, when she left the hotel after work earlier today, something similar happened. I waved her off outside the main doors, then thought of something I wanted to ask her, but when I turned around, she'd already disappeared from sight, even although she couldn't have crossed the front grounds that quickly." Suzanne shook her head and laughed. "Ignore me. I'm being silly on account of hunger." She nodded at the pizza box in her hands. "I hope you both still plan on helping me eat this monster-sized pizza."

"If you're sure you don't mind the company?"

"I'd love it if you both joined me. Shall we grab a picnic bench on the esplanade and enjoy our food in the sunshine?"

"Great idea."

After ducking inside the takeaway and grabbing extra napkins from the dispenser on the counter, they headed for the esplanade that ran along the waterfront on Balmarrie Bay.

"What pizza topping did you get?" Jamie wanted to know as they settled at a free picnic bench.

"Peppers, olives, and mushrooms," Suzanne said, setting the box down on the table and opening the lid.

Jamie scrunched his face up at the pizza. "Why's there no meat? Are you a veggiesaurus?"

Suzanne let out a burst of laughter at the boy's amusing turn of phrase. "No, but I just didn't feel like any pepperoni tonight."

"I don't like olives," Jamie announced, staring at them as if they might leap off the pizza and attack him. "They taste funny."

"You can pick the olives off," Kyle said. "Now, sit down and say thanks to Suzanne for being nice enough to share her dinner with you."

"Thanks Suzanne," Jamie said, sliding onto the bench. "Girls like weird stuff on pizzas. Mum likes ham and pineapple on hers, which is just wrong."

"No argument there," Kyle said.

"I love a ham and pineapple pizza," Suzanne said as they all helped themselves to slices from the box.

"Thank god we caught you on a sane night, in that case," Kyle said and threw her a wry smile.

"Do you want my olives, Suzanne?" Jamie picked an olive from his slice of pizza and dangled it above Suzanne's, before dropping the unwanted veggie on top.

"Uh, thanks," she said, not sure whether to be charmed by his kindness or be a little bit disgusted, considering the kid had had his finger up his nose two seconds before they'd sat down at the table.

"Sorry, Suzanne," Kyle said, seeing her reaction and immediately whipping Jamie's olive off her pizza slice. "We're usually better dinner guests than this."

"It's fine," she laughed.

"Jamie, when you've only just met someone for the first time, they generally don't like it when you scrape food from your plate onto theirs just because you don't want it," Kyle advised the boy.

"I don't have a plate," Jamie said, staring at the pizza slice on his napkin.

Kyle rolled his eyes and laughed. "Just eat your pizza, buddy."

"Okay, Uncle Kyle."

Jamie flicked a few more olives off his pizza and then

tucked into his food. Suzanne bit into her own slice, savouring the crisp crust and the salty olives and the comforting melted cheese. After a few more bites, her rumbling stomach stopped complaining.

"So, you said you already started work on the fairy huts for the woodland play area?" Suzanne asked, keen to make conversation while they ate together.

Kyle nodded. "Most of the time-consuming stuff lies in the underpinning structure and the frame. Once I get to the decorative carving work, I'll check back with you to make sure you're happy with what I'm doing. As time is a factor here, there will be places where I can trim back on the decorative carvings to get it done faster, but without losing the character of the huts. Everything will fit in perfectly with the enchanted woodland theme and I'll make sure you're happy with the decorative decisions."

"I appreciate you keeping me in the loop. So long as the new huts are in keeping with the others, we'll be happy."

"Understood. I think you'll like the finished products. We'll do a good job for you, Suzanne, I promise."

She liked the easy, confident way he said this. It might just have been an extra soothing word to keep a concerned client happy, but she appreciated it anyway. He spoke about his work with obvious passion, and that made her feel happy with the contractor she'd chosen, as well as comfortable with the man who was doing the work.

"Did you have fun working with your uncle on the fairy huts, Jamie?" Suzanne asked, not wanting the little boy to feel left out of the discussion.

Jamie nodded as he licked pizza cheese from his fingers and his expression turned serious. "Uncle Kyle says I might be allowed my own set of tools if I keep helping him."

"That sounds like fun."

"Once I have my own tools, I can build my own stuff."

"What are you going to build?" Suzanne asked, amused by the sweet boy and his plans.

"I want to make an army look-out hut. That way, when my friends come over to play, we can be soldiers and have a war."

"That sounds cool."

Jamie nodded. "Uncle Kyle says we can put the army hut in his back garden and then move it to my new house once we get it." Jamie threw a concerned glance at Kyle. "It won't get broken when we move it, will it Uncle Kyle?"

"Nope," Kyle said. "It'll be just fine, and you don't need to worry about it."

Jamie gave another nod, apparently satisfied, and then his eyes widened as he pointed along the esplanade to the small park where a family of four were playing on the grass. "There's my friend from school, Harry, and his little brother, George. Can I go and play with them, Uncle Kyle?"

"Only if Harry's mum says it's okay," Kyle said. "And if she does, make sure she knows I'm over here keeping an eye on you."

Before Kyle had even finished talking, Jamie was ditching the rest of his pizza slice and leaping up off the bench, before running along the esplanade and through the gates to the park. Suzanne watched as Jamie hurtled towards the group and waved hello to his friend, before saying something to the boy's mother and pointing back up the esplanade to where Kyle and Suzanne were sitting. The woman raised a hand at Kyle in acknowledgement, which he returned, and then Jamie and the two other little boys began kicking a football to each other and running around like wild things.

"Your nephew is a sweet boy," Suzanne said.

"I know it," Kyle grinned. "When his mother finds out I fed him pizza and ice cream tonight after she made us both a wholesome meal, she'll skin me alive."

Suzanne laughed. "Maybe he'll have so much fun running around in the park with his friend, he'll forget he hasn't had ice cream yet."

"I doubt it," he snorted. "The kid's a human vacuum cleaner where food is concerned."

"Says the man biting into a third slice of pizza."

"What can I say? It's a great pizza."

"Agreed, and much better than the sad sandwich I was planning on making when I got home. And I'm sure these green peppers and mushrooms count towards my five-a-day."

Kyle laughed. "I like your thinking."

"I keep telling myself to get to the supermarket and stock up on healthy things for dinner, but I never have time. And then when I do have time, and I buy lots of lovely fruit and veggies for the crisper drawer, I end up hitting an extra-busy patch at work and the whole lot goes off before I even remember it's there. And then I just feel guilty."

"It must take a lot of work and long hours to run a business the size of the Star Castle Hotel," Kyle said.

"It does but I wouldn't swap it for the world. Sorry if it sounds like I'm complaining."

He gave her an odd look. "I didn't think you were. But no matter how much someone loves their work, there are always times when it feels like the balance is off somewhere in life."

"You sound like you're speaking from personal experience."

Kyle set down his slice of pizza and grinned. "I ought to watch what I say, considering you just hired my boss's company. The last thing I want is to make you think he's a dodgy employer who pushes his staff too hard."

"Is he?"

"No. But Frank Hill is old school, and he worked hard to

build his business into what it is today, and he sacrificed a lot, too. He has high standards he expects his staff to meet."

Suzanne was about to say that her mother was the same, but the idea of sharing such a personal detail about her family had her gulping the words back down her throat. Just because she was enjoying this man's company, and enjoying sharing a slice of pizza with him on a warm summer's evening on the waterfront, didn't mean she wanted to divulge every emotion or every thought that wandered through her head.

"What a gorgeous evening," she said instead, looking out across the bay that was sparkling in the late sunshine. "I'm glad I ended up eating dinner out here beside the water instead of back at my flat."

"Me too."

Kyle gave her a look that made her wonder if he meant he was glad he was spending time enjoying the view, or glad she hadn't gone home to eat by herself. Just as a flush of heat crept up her neck at the look in his eyes, it occurred to her that the man probably just felt sorry for her, and the fact that she'd almost spent a summer's evening as nice as this one indoors stuffing takeaway pizza into her face.

"I ought to make more time to get out in the fresh air because I love being out and about," Suzanne said, keen to make sure the man realised she wasn't as sad and pathetic as she seemed at first glance. "But whenever I get lost in my work at the hotel, it's too easy to keep hammering away at the keyboard or dealing with paperwork to make sure things run smoothly. When it's a family business, it's hard to just walk away and leave things to someone else."

"I can imagine." Kyle looked thoughtful for a moment, his gaze sweeping across the bay. "I'm hoping to set up my own business one day. Any words of advice?"

Suzanne wiped her mouth with a napkin and glanced at

Kyle. Given how he'd handled their discussions about the woodland repairs, she could easily imagine him running a successful business of his own.

"So long as you're passionate about the work, you'll be able to overcome any obstacle or problem," she said. "On the other hand, if you aren't interested in the work, then running your own business might feel like more trouble than it's worth after a while."

Kyle nodded. "I guessed as much. I want to go into business for myself because I want to do more of what I like and less of what I don't like. I love gardening and landscaping and design, but there's a lot of work Frank Hill takes on for clients that I wouldn't do if I was working for myself."

"Like building fairy huts for children's play areas and repairing silly little bridges?" Suzanne grinned.

"Actually, I enjoy woodworking, so this job is fun compared to some of the stuff Frank gets me to do."

"Like what?"

He raked a hand through his hair and gave her a nervous look. "Now I'm complaining about the boss, which is never a good idea. Listen, you won't mention anything about me wanting to go out on my own, will you? I haven't told Frank Hill anything about my plans yet."

"Your secret's safe with me," Suzanne said.

"Thanks."

Kyle smiled and the warmth of it flooded over Suzanne like a soft wave. They might only be sharing a simple slice of pizza together while enjoying the view across the bay, but there was something about Kyle that made her relax in a way she hadn't done for too long, and that made her sink deep into the sweet moment she realised they were sharing.

"Suzanne, would you like to go out for a drink with me sometime?" Kyle asked, his blue eyes fixed on her.

Despite the thoughts she'd just had, the question caught

her out. And despite the effect Kyle's gaze was having on her, she felt herself backing away.

"Sorry, but I'm not dating right now," she said.

It was simple and it was true. Although it sounded a little brusque in her own ears, she didn't want to leave this man with any illusions about what might be going on between them. Because nothing was going on between them, it was as simple as that. Even if she had time to date, which she didn't, she would never mix business with pleasure.

"Oh, okay," Kyle said as an embarrassed look crossed his face.

"But I enjoyed sharing my pizza with you, Kyle. I hope we can be friends."

"Absolutely."

Now things just felt awkward, which was a shame, because Suzanne had been enjoying their time on the esplanade, lingering in the evening sunshine at the picnic table and polishing off the pizza.

Maybe agreeing to a drink with Kyle sometime wasn't such a terrible idea?

Except that it *was* a terrible idea. She didn't want the complications of a relationship, no matter how casual. Her work and the hotel were her priorities. She had enough on her plate without adding some frivolous romance into the mix just because this man had made her heart flutter.

It wasn't worth it.

"I should go," Suzanne said, rising from the picnic bench and gathering up the leftover pizza rubbish. "I've got work I need to look over tonight."

"I ought to make a move too," Kyle said, helping to clear the table. "If I leave it any later to buy Jamie that ice cream cone, he'll still be humming with sugar by bedtime."

Suzanne laughed, but it felt forced and she knew it

sounded forced, too. "So, I'll see you tomorrow at the hotel to start the tree inspection?"

"We'll be there bright and early."

"Have a good night, Kyle. Enjoy your ice cream."

"Bye, Suzanne."

After gathering up the pizza box, Suzanne turned for the pavement. When she dumped the box in a rubbish bin further along the esplanade, she couldn't help looking over her shoulder to where Kyle was now walking towards the park to fetch his nephew. The boy spied him, and when Kyle called out that it was time for their ice cream, he waved goodbye to his friend and raced across the grass, barrelling into his uncle's legs, at which point Kyle picked the boy up in one effortless move and spun him around, causing Jamie to shriek with laughter.

The obvious affection Kyle had for his nephew sent a bolt of warmth straight through Suzanne's chest.

"That's enough of that," she told herself, and turned her back on the waterfront and continued on towards her parked car.

She wasn't trying to be hard on herself, or deny herself the romance and fun that most women her age sought and enjoyed as a matter of course. But the hotel and her work came first. She'd never overcome these feelings of doubt about her job and her abilities, and never win her mother's confidence, if she allowed herself to get distracted by some random man who she'd only just met.

And so she simply wouldn't allow herself to get distracted, not even for a split second.

Not even by someone as ridiculously handsome and captivating as Kyle Lawson.

CHAPTER NINE

The early morning sun lit up the hills that rose behind the Star Castle Hotel to the east and scattered diamonds across the waters of the bay to the west. If she lived to be a hundred years old, Suzanne would never tire of this view or fail to be awed by its beauty. As she stood on the side terrace outside the hotel restaurant that overlooked Balmarrie Bay, breathing in the fresh morning air and listening to the birds singing in the trees, her heart filled with love for this place, just like it did every day of her life.

At this hour, the hotel was quiet. Most guests were still asleep in their comfortable beds, with only a few early risers making their way to the restaurant to tuck into the indulgent breakfast on which the hotel prided itself. The scents of salty bacon and herb-infused sausages drifted from the buffet trays that the waiting staff were carrying into the serving area, making Suzanne's mouth water. She'd arrived much earlier than usual at the hotel this morning, just after six-thirty, to deal with paperwork she hadn't got around to last night at home, and hadn't yet eaten breakfast.

After the awkward moment she'd shared with Kyle last night, when she'd turned down his offer to have a drink together, her mind had refused to focus on work tasks when she'd got home to her flat, instead returning to their conversation and whether things would be weird between them when he arrived to start on the job in the woodland play area. Although she wouldn't be looking over his shoulder every moment he spent working at the hotel, they'd naturally have to talk and interact at some point, and Suzanne didn't want there to be any tension with the new hotel contractor.

All she could do was be polite and keep things focused on the work Kyle was there to do. It had been his mistake to invite her out for a drink, after all, and he should be the one feeling awkward about things, not her. She wondered what he'd been thinking, asking out the woman who'd just become his boss's latest business client.

Never in a million years would Suzanne let her personal life seep into her work. She was baffled that Kyle Lawson obviously saw things differently.

That morning, once she'd settled at the desk in her hotel office, she'd buried herself in clearing paperwork and dealing with emails, determined to keep her mind focused on what mattered most, which was the Star Castle Hotel. She'd become so lost in her tasks that she'd forgotten the promise she'd made to herself to fetch breakfast before her day got underway.

Deciding she ought to grab a slice of toast from the restaurant before she left behind the gorgeous view of the bay and returned to her office, Suzanne headed for the doors. She'd only taken a few steps when Mrs Wishmore walked out onto the terrace, carrying a tray in her arms.

"Good morning, Suzanne," Mrs Wishmore smiled. "I heard from one of the other ladies on the reception desk that you've been working in your office since early this morning and I thought you might enjoy some breakfast before things get any busier around here."

Suzanne glanced at the tray bearing a coffee cafetiere and cups, a filled toast rack accompanied with little pots of butter and marmalade, and a bowl of sliced fruit.

"That's very thoughtful, Doris," Suzanne said. "But you didn't have to do that. You aren't here to run around after me."

"It's my pleasure, dear. We can't have the deputy manager of the hotel fainting away from hunger and overwork, can we? Now, shall I pop this tray on that table over there by the edge of the terrace?"

"No, I'll take it to my office and eat there, thanks."

Mrs Wishmore frowned. "And miss out on this beautiful morning?"

"I've been out here for long enough already gazing at the view," Suzanne said with a laugh. "I need to get back to my paperwork."

"Nonsense. I'm sure your paperwork can wait another ten minutes while you eat some breakfast." The older lady carried the tray to the table she'd pointed to at the edge of the terrace and began pouring coffee into two cups. "And if you don't mind, I'll join you for a coffee before my shift begins."

It would be rude to insist on taking the breakfast tray to her office now, Suzanne realised. Pulling out a chair, she joined Mrs Wishmore at the table.

"Aren't you here a bit early for work, Doris?" Suzanne asked as she spread marmalade onto a toast triangle.

"The dayshift supervisor asked me to come in first thing today to cover a member of staff who has a hospital appointment," Mrs Wishmore said, adding milk and sugar to her coffee. "Naturally, I was happy to agree. However, I must say that after such an early start, I'm in urgent need of a caffeine boost."

The older lady chuckled and sipped her coffee. As Suzanne bit into her slice of buttery toast, she wondered just what it was about Mrs Wishmore that made it so easy for her to sit here at this table on the terrace, sharing coffee and eating breakfast. Although she maintained excellent relationships with all the staff at the Star Castle Hotel, she couldn't imagine any of them ambushing her like this and insisting they drink coffee together. It was unthinkable.

And yet here she was, doing exactly that with Mrs Wishmore, a temporary employee who'd only started working at the hotel less than twenty-four hours ago. It was completely baffling.

"Make sure you eat up all that delicious fresh fruit," Doris told her over her coffee cup. "You must get your vitamins and minerals, dear."

Suzanne couldn't help a surprised laugh escaping. "I hope you won't be annoyed if I say that you are a rather odd lady, Doris."

"That's not the first time I've been told that," Mrs Wishmore replied with a grin. "But if you insist on working such long hours, then I see it as my duty to make sure you're paying attention to your nutrition. Talking of which, did you and young Kyle and his sweet little nephew have a nice time together sharing that enormous pizza you bought last night?"

Suzanne kept her gaze on her toast, eager to avoid any conversation about the handsome landscape gardener. "It was lovely. So, I hope you're settling in all right with your job here at the hotel, Doris?"

"Oh, of course. No problems whatsoever." Mrs Wishmore sipped her coffee again, her eyes never leaving Suzanne. "You must have a busy day ahead of you, dear, to have come into your office so early?"

"There's always plenty to do around here."

"I can imagine. You must be looking forward to the weekend. Do you have any nice plans?"

Suzanne let out a laugh. "When you work in hospitality, there's no such thing as a weekend."

"I'm sure that's not true. If you're here working all week, and putting in such long hours each day, surely you take time off on Saturdays or Sundays?"

"Most of our special events and guest functions are booked for weekends. As deputy manager with responsibility for those things, I usually need to be here to make sure everything goes smoothly."

The look of astonishment on Mrs Wishmore's face was unmistakable. "Well, my goodness, how on earth do you make time for yourself if you're working here seven days a week?"

Suzanne shrugged and ate the last bite of her toast. "I love my work, Doris. And I love being here at the hotel. It's no hardship, I assure you."

Mrs Wishmore didn't look convinced. "Well, I only hope you make time to see your friends and spend a little time doing other things that you enjoy, such as your hobbies and so on."

As she lifted a spoonful of fresh fruit to her mouth, Suzanne allowed herself a wry smile. The truth of the matter was that she didn't really have any friends. Acquaintances, yes. Friends, not so much.

Back when she'd been a university student, there'd been people on her business degree who she'd counted as her friends, people she'd enjoyed spending time with after classes and going out with to pubs and clubs every now and again. But throughout her degree she'd worked many weekends and all her holidays at the hotel, not just to earn money but to learn the ropes, and that time spent away from the other students when they were getting together and socialising meant she'd only ever been a casual friend to most of the people she'd known during her university years.

That, too, had been her choice. What mattered was securing a great degree qualification, learning what she had to learn, and leaving university with something solid to show for all that hard work, something that would stand her in good stead for her future at the Star Castle Hotel.

Since graduating, the last few years had zipped by so quickly as she'd immersed herself in the family business. There just wasn't time to make any new friends, and she was too busy to give much thought as to whether that was a bad thing or not.

And as for hobbies, well, the idea of Suzanne having hobbies was ridiculous. There was nothing that interested her enough to take her focus away from work. And even if there was, any hobby would be a disgraceful indulgence when there was always so much endless work to be done at the hotel.

Once she'd found her feet in the new deputy manager role, and had a few wins under her belt in terms of her new responsibilities, and once her mother was no longer scrutinising her every decision and every move… well, maybe then there would be time for friends and for other things, too.

Until then, she had to stay focused on what mattered most.

Perhaps the older lady across the table could see what Suzanne was thinking just by the look on her face, because she said, "Tell me a little about your interests and passions, Suzanne."

"This hotel is my interest and passion, Doris."

"You don't have any hobbies or pastimes, or things you enjoy doing with your free time?"

"I don't have much free time. And when I have a spare

moment, I can usually fill it with some task or other that needs my attention here at the hotel."

Once more, Mrs Wishmore's face was incredulous. "But what do you do for fun?"

Suzanne was getting just a bit tired of this conversation and couldn't help showing it. "Why are you so interested in how I spend my time outside of work, Doris? It's an odd line of questioning, to be honest. And I'm not sure it's any of your business."

She knew she sounded sharp, perhaps even rude, but she couldn't help it. It was one thing to have a friendly chat with an employee. It was another thing altogether to be quizzed and judged by one.

"I apologise," Mrs Wishmore said, before taking a last sip of coffee and rising from the table. "I didn't mean to be nosy and make you uncomfortable. I just thought we were having a pleasant conversation, and I was enjoying learning more about you."

The embarrassed look on Mrs Wishmore's face made Suzanne feel awful. She was never abrupt with people and wondered if she'd misunderstood Doris's chit-chat and read more into it than there was.

Had the older lady's questions about her personal life touched a raw nerve that she hadn't even realised was there? And if so, what did that mean?

"Sorry, Doris, I didn't mean to be rude. There's no need to rush off. Please stay and finish your coffee."

"I already finished it," Mrs Wishmore said cheerfully, and when Suzanne glanced at the older lady's cup she saw it was indeed empty, which was odd because the woman had only taken a couple of sips in the short time they'd sat together. It didn't seem likely that she'd already drained the contents when Suzanne's own cup was still almost full of the still hot coffee.

And yet, Mrs Wishmore had somehow done exactly that.

"Anyway, I ought to get started on the front desk," Mrs Wishmore smiled. "I'm sure there will be plenty to keep me busy. Perhaps I'll see you later, Suzanne."

Suzanne watched the older lady shuffle off back inside the hotel, regretting her sharp tone. Doris's questions about her personal life had put her on edge, and if she'd been rude —which she had—it was because she didn't have any sort of personal life to discuss. The expression on Mrs Wishmore's face when Suzanne said she had no hobbies or particular interests and been one of sadness, and that had embarrassed her.

Did Mrs Wishmore pity her? She didn't want or deserve pity. At twenty-seven years-old, she was the deputy manager of her family's beautiful and prestigious hotel, and she was an essential part of the business. How could anyone possibly pity her? She was hard-working and accomplished, smart and savvy, resilient and tireless.

And an imposter hiding behind a mask of her own creation, terrified that one day she'd be revealed as completely out of her depth.

Where had that thought come from? Suzanne sighed and pushed away the unfinished bowl of fresh fruit, her appetite gone. The morning had started so well, and it had felt good to tackle paperwork in her office before enjoying a few quiet moments by herself and taking in the view from the hotel across the bay. She'd been ready to seize the day… until Mrs Wishmore had turned up and ruined it.

But that wasn't fair. Mrs Wishmore hadn't ruined anything. The older lady had only been making conversation. If Suzanne had taken issue with it, then that was her problem, not Mrs Wishmore's.

She'd chosen this single-minded life. It was what she wanted. The Star Castle Hotel mattered more to her than anything else in the entire world. Friends, hobbies, romances, and anything else that might comprise a personal life were of no interest to her. At least, not right now.

Fine. But if not now, then when? whispered a little voice inside Suzanne's head.

It was a voice that sounded suspiciously like Mrs Wishmore's.

Shaking her head with an irritated sigh, Suzanne left the hotel terrace and went back to work.

That last thing she needed right now were voices inside her head.

CHAPTER TEN

Kyle and his van-load of workmen from Hill Landscaping pulled into a parking space at the Star Castle Hotel just after eight-thirty. The morning was bright and dry which meant they'd make good progress with the repairs in the woodland play area without worrying about rain impeding their work. As they unloaded equipment and tools from the back of the flatbed, Kyle glanced at the hotel entrance, wondering when Suzanne would appear.

When it was the rotund grounds crew supervisor who arrived to greet them, rather than the attractive deputy manager, Kyle couldn't help but feel a little disappointed.

Although it made sense that they'd be met by someone from the grounds crew, rather than the management, he'd been picturing seeing Suzanne's face again during the entire drive from the Hill Landscaping work yard to the hotel. It was stupid, but he couldn't help it. The woman got his heart beating faster and made his head spin like he was a teenage kid again.

Or maybe that was just down to embarrassment after she

turned him down last night when he'd asked her out for a drink.

He could kick himself now for that obvious mistake, but at the time it had felt like the most natural thing in the world to ask her out. Despite what he'd told himself about putting Suzanne Kennedy out of his head because she was his boss's client, it had been easier said than done, especially when he'd seen her on the high street in Balmarrie, helping Mrs Wishmore with her spilled shopping. The sight of her had made his heart beat triple time. And although they'd only spent twenty minutes together at that picnic bench beside the bay, sharing the super-sized pizza the takeaway place had given her by mistake, Kyle felt like they'd made a connection. All he'd wanted was to see if that connection might lead somewhere, and enjoying a relaxed drink somewhere together seemed like a great way to find out.

As Kyle hauled tools from the flatbed, he cringed at the memory of Suzanne's pinched expression as she'd said thanks but no thanks before clearing up the pizza remains and hurrying off.

Yet, even as he cringed, and even as he imagined the awkwardness that surely awaited when he talked to her about the woodland tree inspection once they'd completed it, he still couldn't wait to see her again.

Once the crew carried everything around to the play area, Kyle set one of the younger lads to work completing the measurements for the repairs to the wooden bridge while the rest of them started on the tree inspection. It didn't take long to rig the ropes and send their tree surgeon expert up into the canopy to inspect the trunk and the area where the branch had snapped off.

Fifteen minutes later, Kyle was agreeing a course of action with the tree surgeon when Suzanne appeared in the clearing.

"Good morning," she said to the crew before turning to Kyle. "How are things going here so far?"

Her expression was focused, her tone warm but all business. He knew better than to say anything in front of the crew about the pizza they'd shared last night at the picnic bench overlooking the bay. This was a work environment, and unless Suzanne brought it up first, he had no intention of mentioning it, at least not until they had a private moment together.

If they had a private moment together. Judging by the no-nonsense look on Suzanne's face, that wasn't likely.

Kyle cleared his throat and gestured to the damaged tree with his clipboard. "We've just finished the inspection. As I thought, the tree is healthy. Actually, we're at a bit of a loss to understand why that branch came down in the first place. We can't see anything wrong with it and there are no signs of rot or disease. It's unusual for a big healthy branch to come down from a mature tree like this, especially when there was no wind or bad weather."

"Hmm, how strange," Suzanne said, looking at the tree.

"The good news is that we don't have to do anything to the tree except trim off those ragged parts on the trunk where the branch sheared away to keep the wound clean."

"The wound?" Suzanne glanced back up at the tree with a thoughtful look on her face. "I suppose that's just what it is, a wound, although I've never thought of trees that way before. Will the poor thing be okay?"

He couldn't help stealing a glance at her and smiling at the concerned expression on her face.

"While we've already got our ropes set up, we'll get back up there and trim the splintered edges to stop any disease penetrating. The tree will be just fine, I guarantee it."

Suzanne nodded, apparently satisfied with his assurances. "And once that's done?"

"Then it's just a matter of getting on with the repairs to the bridge and the footpath."

"Right, well, that all sounds wonderful."

They stood for a moment, staring at the tree. When Suzanne looked his way and their eyes met, Kyle felt a zing of electricity ripple straight through his body.

Suzanne's phone pinged, breaking the moment—if it even had been a moment—and pulling her gaze away from his. He watched her tap on the phone screen for a few seconds before looking back up.

"Well, you know how to reach me if there's anything else we need to discuss," she said, already turning towards the path through the woodland clearing. "I'll catch up with you again before the end of the day."

"No problem," he said, returning her wave as she walked off and wishing he'd been able to think of some reason to keep her here a minute or two longer, some unexpected and complicated part of the job they hadn't realised was going to be a problem and that he really needed to chat to her about.

But everything was going smoothly so far. The damaged tree needed only minimal attention. The young apprentice Kyle had tasked with finalising the measurements for the bridge repairs was already waiting for the nod to begin cutting the new wood. The other two workmen were preparing the ground beneath the pathway for the replacement paving stones that Kyle knew would slot into place without any trouble.

Kyle usually prayed for straightforward jobs because straightforward jobs meant there was no need for protracted conversations with clients to get their approval for changes to the agreed work. Clients never liked surprises being sprung on them by the workmen they'd hired. Now, when he wanted some sort of complication to present itself, everything was going perfectly.

And at this rate, they'd have these repairs completed in no time at all.

At least there were still the fairy huts to finish. Until those were done, the Star Castle Hotel job would remain open. And Suzanne had been specific about wanting the decorations and whimsical flourishes on the little huts to be as close as possible to those on the other huts in the play area, and about wanting to see the designs before Kyle finished them.

Cheered by this thought, he got back to work.

Later that morning, Kyle and his men were removing the damaged handrail from the wooden bridge across the stream when he heard movement behind them in the clearing. Hoping it might be Suzanne coming back to check up on them, Kyle turned in expectation, then tried not to let his smile dim when he realised it was one of the hotel employees, Mrs Wishmore.

The older lady bustled into the clearing with a tray in her hands which looked much too heavy for her to have carried all the way out from the hotel.

"Hello there," Mrs Wishmore said, catching her breath as she set the tray down on a child-sized bench by the edge of the clearing. "We thought you men might be in desperate need of a tea break and so I've come with refreshments. The supervisor at the hotel bar insisted I load this plate with plenty of cookies to keep you going."

"That's very kind, Doris," Kyle said. "But we bring our own flasks and snacks to the job. There's no need to feed us."

"But of course there is," Mrs Wishmore smiled. "Workmen deserve a hot brew and a couple of chocolate biscuits from their clients. Just because you're all the way out here in the woodland doesn't mean we've forgotten about you. Now, come and tuck in."

Kyle looked at the tray, which was laden with mugs and a huge teapot, milk and sugar, and a towering plate of biscuits and cookies. He could almost see his work colleagues salivating at the sight of the treats.

"It was nice of you to think of us and come all the way out here," Kyle said. "I hope your arms aren't too sore from carting that heavy tray."

"Not in the least."

When the older lady only stood smiling as the workmen poured tea into mugs and dug into the plate of biscuits, Kyle wondered why.

"I can bring everything back up to the hotel as soon as we're finished," he said. "There's no need to wait for us all to finish our cuppas."

"Oh, it's no trouble to wait," Doris said cheerfully. "In fact, I'm due a mid-morning break myself and thought I'd enjoy it out here in the fresh air, if you don't mind?"

"Of course not." Kyle poured Mrs Wishmore a mug of tea and handed it over. He took a sip of his own tea and found it strong enough to stand a spoon up in, which was just the way he liked it. "I didn't realise I was in serious need of some good, strong tea until just now. Thanks, Doris."

"My pleasure, dear." She drank from her mug and then said, "I happened to deliver a nice tray of breakfast goodies to Suzanne this morning, too. She said you had a lovely time last night sharing pizza."

Kyle glanced over his work colleagues, who had migrated with their tea and biscuits back towards the wooden bridge where they were chatting about the next stage of the repairs. Out of earshot, they looked uninterested in what Kyle might be discussing with the older lady from the hotel. He turned back to Mrs Wishmore and smiled.

"My nephew loved the unexpected treat, and I did too. It was kind of Suzanne to include us."

"And such a stroke of luck that the pizza shop got her order wrong and left her with so much extra pizza going spare," Mrs Wishmore said with a wry smile at her lips. "Isn't it lovely when unexpected circumstances bring people together and help them become friends?"

"I'm not sure I'd go as far as calling us friends."

"Oh?" Surprise creased the older lady's face. "Why ever not?"

Kyle drank more tea and thought about the question. "For one thing, Suzanne is my boss's client. For another, we only spent about twenty minutes together, and she made it clear that..."

When Kyle tailed off, Mrs Wishmore tilted her head, her expression kind. "She made what clear, Kyle?"

"That she's not looking to make any new friends right now, or anything else for that matter," Kyle said and gave an embarrassed smile.

"I see."

For a moment, they stood in companionable silence, drinking their tea. At last, Mrs Wishmore spoke.

"Sometimes what we *think* we want isn't what we actually *need*," she said. "And sometimes what we actually need is just a little frightening for us, and so we pretend not to see it."

Kyle stared at Mrs Wishmore for a long beat, wondering at this wise and yet somehow baffling statement. "I'm not sure what you mean, Doris."

But the older lady only smiled and set her still half-full mug down on the tea tray. "Don't give up on Suzanne just yet. I see something lovely for both of you in the future, if you let her find her way in her own time."

Kyle hadn't the faintest idea what the woman was talking about. "Uh..."

"Well, I ought to get back up to the hotel," Mrs Wishmore said and picked up the tray. "Are you boys finished with your mugs?"

The other men wandered over from the wooden bridge and added their empty tea mugs to the tray and thanked Mrs Wishmore for the biscuits. Kyle gulped down the rest of his own tea and found space on the tray for the mug.

"Good luck with the rest of your work, gentlemen," Mrs Wishmore called out as she turned towards the path through the clearing. In a quiet voice she added, "And Kyle, I hope you'll think about what I said."

As he watched the woman shuffle off, he knew he had no choice but to think about what she'd said.

Don't give up on Suzanne just yet.

He didn't want to give up on her. But it wasn't his choice to make, was it? Much though he might enjoy seeing the beautiful deputy manager of the hotel when she crossed his path, if she didn't want anything more between them than the client-contractor relationship that already existed, then there wasn't much he could do about it.

Mrs Wishmore was wrong. It wasn't about giving up. It was about respecting the wishes that Suzanne Kennedy had made clear last night. He'd asked her out for a drink, and she'd said no. It wasn't the answer he'd wanted, but it was the answer he'd got, and he wasn't about to make a nuisance of himself chasing after a woman who wasn't interested. Nice though it had been to share that pizza last night and watch the sun sinking over the bay, it had never been anything more than a friendly and casual—not to mention accidental—meeting.

And anyway, what on earth did any of this even have to do with Mrs Wishmore?

Kyle had no answer to that question.

But as the older lady disappeared along the path that led

through the wild rose hedge, he knew one thing for sure—Mrs Wishmore was more than a little odd and mysterious.

And yet, despite that, he couldn't get her strange advice out of his mind.

It was almost five o'clock when Suzanne finished her last scheduled meeting for the day and finally had the chance to do something she ought to have done earlier that morning, something that had been troubling her all day. But as ever, the hours had been filled with endless tasks and busy work, and time had run away from her. Between phone calls and staff discussions in her office, and urgent paperwork jobs and administrative decisions that had been popping up and demanding her attention all day, there hadn't been a minute to spare, until now.

Seizing the free time before it was snatched away from her by someone or something else at the hotel, Suzanne hurried from her office and through to the reception lobby, just in time to see a flash of red jacket and cloud of silvery hair as Mrs Wishmore stepped outside through the doors.

"Mrs Wishmore, wait!" Suzanne called out, picking up speed as she dashed outside to catch up with the older lady. At last, Doris turned around on the pathway and smiled.

"Hello, Suzanne," she said. "You look flustered. Is everything all right?"

"Everything's fine," Suzanne replied, catching her breath. "But I wanted to speak to you before you left work for the day, and apologise for being so sharp with you this morning."

For a moment, Mrs Wishmore only stared, her warm smile fixed in place. "My goodness, there's nothing to apologise for."

"But there is. You were kind enough to think of me this

morning and bring me breakfast, and then when we were sharing coffee and you were making casual conversation, I snapped at you and was rude. I apologise."

Suzanne felt shame flood her cheeks at the memory of just how brusque she'd been with the kindly older lady. At the time, Mrs Wishmore's questions had seemed inquisitorial and judgemental, but Suzanne now felt sure that they'd never been intended that way. She might only have known this new employee for a little over a day, but the woman didn't have a nasty bone in her body, of that she was sure. If Suzanne had bristled at Mrs Wishmore's questions, then maybe she ought to think about exactly why that was.

For now, though, what mattered was apologising, and making sure Mrs Wishmore knew it was sincere and heartfelt. Not only did the older lady deserve an apology after all the help and kindness she'd shown Suzanne since arriving, but it was important to make sure that all employees at the Star Castle Hotel knew that the management didn't think they were above the people who worked there and entitled to treat them disrespectfully.

"You weren't rude, my dear," Mrs Wishmore said, her eyes kind. "And anyway, friends sometimes say things to each other that don't quite come across as intended. But that won't stop us being friends, now, will it?"

Suzanne nodded, once more caught off-balance by the older lady's use of that word, 'friend'. How easily Mrs Wishmore applied it to the two of them, even although they were barely more than strangers. And yet how warm that word made Suzanne feel, and how… valued? No, not valued, that wasn't the right word.

Treasured. That was it. Hearing Mrs Wishmore describe Suzanne as her friend made her feel treasured. It was a feeling, she realised with a surprise and regret, that she hadn't felt much lately.

"Oh, but Suzanne," Mrs Wishmore said, her expression soft. "You have *always* been treasured by the people who love you. If only you could see it."

Suzanne could only stare in astonishment, wondering how the woman could have picked the thoughts from her head like that. It was strange and uncanny and more than a little unsettling. But before she could say a single word, Mrs Wishmore reached out and squeezed her arm, sending a warm pulse of comfort straight through her.

"There are many things in this world that are so deeply mysterious and which we can't ever hope to understand," Doris said. "But those mysteries only make life even more wonderful."

"Uh..." Suzanne began, but she had no idea what she wanted to say, and any other words that might have been coming simply evaporated.

"Well," Mrs Wishmore said, releasing Suzanne's arm and smiling. "I ought to make a move or I'll miss my bus."

With a gentle chortle, Mrs Wishmore turned and walked off, bustling along the pathway towards the road that led to the main exit. Suzanne watched her leave, standing transfixed outside the hotel entrance until the woman had disappeared from view. Hotel guests came and went around her, giving her curious looks as they passed by, but Suzanne didn't notice them.

All she could think about was how she'd come out here to apologise to Mrs Wishmore for her churlish behaviour that morning, and had somehow ended up in the middle of yet another strange conversation with the woman that had left her both off-balance and reassured at the same time.

As she walked back to her office, Suzanne turned their exchange over in her head, wondering how Mrs Wishmore could have known what she was thinking about when she'd made that curious comment and told her she had always been treasured.

There was only one explanation—Suzanne must have muttered the private thought out loud and not even realised she'd done it. It was the only thing that made any sense, the only thing that could explain what had happened.

And although a voice inside her head insisted that she hadn't muttered anything out loud at all, Suzanne ignored it. The day had been long and busy, and clearly her mind had become frazzled from the non-stop work and endless activities around the hotel. Her brief conversation with Mrs Wishmore, and whatever had been said or not said during it, had simply been refracted through the prism of a tough day and a tired mind, making Suzanne imagine things.

Considering there was still work to be done before she called it a day, she rerouted to the hotel bar for a large mug of coffee to take back to her office. Clearly, she needed a caffeine boost to get back on track and see her through the rest of today's endless tasks, before her mind played any more silly tricks on her.

CHAPTER ELEVEN

The ballroom at the Star Castle Hotel looked so beautiful it stole Suzanne's breath away.

White twinkle lights danced across the walls, pale pink flowers cascaded from tall glass centrepieces on the tables, and what seemed like a thousand candles waited to be lit and fill the space with romance and magic. No wedding reception taking place anywhere else in the country today could look more wonderful than this one.

It was Saturday afternoon, and in less than two hours a wedding party comprising almost one hundred and forty guests would arrive to celebrate with the bride and groom who were at that very moment exchanging their vows at Balmarrie parish church before detouring to the shores of the bay for photographs. Suzanne had spent the last few hours working with the wedding coordinator hired by the happy couple to oversee their special day and making sure that everything went according to plan. So far, Suzanne had helped source extra flower stocks for the centrepieces to accommodate an extra table of guests added at the last minute by the bridal couple, and had also averted disaster by finding emergency kitchen staff to cover for one of their junior chefs who'd been called away late last night on account of a family emergency. No doubt there was still some other crisis waiting to present itself, and when it did, Suzanne would be ready.

But for now, she took in the beautiful sight of the decorated ballroom, knowing that it met the bride's expectations and that the young woman would love it. The event staff at the hotel had gone the extra mile as usual to make their guests happy. Tomorrow, Suzanne would share photos on the hotel's social media channels of the ballroom dressed up for the wedding, and hopefully they'd go down a storm with their followers and drum up more custom and bookings for the future.

Spurred by the last minute decorative floristry arrangements she'd been immersed in, she made a mental note to ask her staff to check the order numbers for the floral centrepieces for the hotel's summer ball next weekend. If they had to squeeze in an extra table or two to accommodate a late surge in ticket sales, she wanted to make sure they had enough decorative supplies on hand to dress the tables. The last thing she wanted was to skimp on the luxury flourishes, because that would send all the wrong signals to their customers.

"Well, doesn't this place look gorgeous?"

Suzanne turned to see Mrs Wishmore bustling into the grand ballroom, her eyes wide as she took in the beautifully laid tables and the floral arrangements and the stunning lighting.

"What a job you've done," Doris said when she reached Suzanne.

"We take our lead from the wedding planner in terms of the styling," Suzanne said.

"But you and your team put in the hard work to make all

of this happen," Doris said, gesturing around the cavernous space. "The bride will be thrilled."

"I hope so."

"I can't believe the transformation in here, considering this place was hosting a brunch for the Rotary Club just a few hours ago."

Suzanne gave an easy shrug. Although the local delegation from the Rotary Club had been tucking into a special breakfast buffet and throwing back glasses of bucks fizz until almost noon, the hotel staff had transformed the room into its current magnificent state with no trouble under her close supervision.

"We need to make as much money as we can from these spaces inside the hotel," Suzanne explained. "Turnaround is key for the business, and we know how to finish up one event and then quickly set up another, and our staff are trained to follow the procedures we have. It's the only way to survive and stay on top of our running costs in a place like this."

"It's quite astonishing and most impressive."

Mrs Wishmore watched a couple of the hotel staff put the finishing touches to table settings on the far side of the room, while another ran a vacuum cleaner over the floor.

"And now I can imagine just how wonderful this place will look for the summer ball next Saturday," Doris added.

"It won't be exactly like this. I'm changing the styling this year to shake things up a bit and match the new musical entertainment we've hired. We'll use brighter flowers in the table centrepieces, and coloured lights instead of white. The theme will be more hot summer nights rather than wedding romance."

"I can't wait to see it." Doris smiled and looked around the ballroom again. "This is just such a wonderful ballroom. I can almost feel the lingering spirits of all the special memories made here over the years."

As Suzanne glanced around the room, a strange thing happened. The beautifully laid tables and flower-filled centrepieces and clusters of ivory candles all vanished, along with everything else in the space, as if it had all just disappeared into thin air. In their place, there was only the empty expanse of the ballroom, dipped in the sunlight slanting through the tall picture windows and falling in pools on the old burgundy carpet that had once covered the floor so many years ago.

Suzanne gaped at the sight before her, not understanding what she was seeing.

The beautifully dressed and decorated space suddenly looked the way it had decades earlier, right before her grandfather, Robert Kennedy, had launched his master plan to refurbish the ballroom and transform it into a profitable event space for the hotel. Suzanne may have only been a little girl of five or six at the time, but memories of how the enormous and captivating ballroom had looked back then had stayed fixed in her mind. She remembered the old worn burgundy carpet with its timeless pattern of loops and whirls, the undressed windows that had seemed to stretch endlessly up towards the high ceilings, and the way her voice had echoed when she'd danced around the ballroom, pretending to be a fairy princess...

In the centre of the empty room, three figures materialised, like gossamer ghosts. Suzanne's eyes flew wide in stunned recognition.

Her grandfather, Robert Kennedy, looking as smart as ever in his signature three-piece suit and blue pocket square, stood beside Suzanne's mother, Imogen, both of them laughing as they watched a little girl twirling around and around on the ballroom floor, her pink princess dress floating in the air with every turn.

The little girl was Suzanne, her pigtails flying, her cheeks pink from dancing. As she twirled and laughed, she had not a care in the world.

Her grandfather beamed as Suzanne flitted around the ballroom, his eyes bright with joy and fun. Imogen, with the easy grace of the young mother she'd been all those years ago when Suzanne was small, watched her daughter dancing, the smile on her unlined face stretching from ear to ear, before joining her on the ballroom floor, the two of them twirling and spinning and laughing as Suzanne's grandfather clapped his hands in time to their imaginary music.

Suzanne stared at the incomprehensible scene, her utter confusion at what she was seeing—and how she could be seeing it—dwarfed only by the stab of nostalgia and longing she felt for those long-ago days of her childhood, and for the carefree little girl she'd once been.

The little girl twirled, and her mother danced, and her grandfather laughed...

And then they were gone.

The empty ballroom with its sunlit windows and threadbare burgundy carpet dissolved before Suzanne's eyes, taking with it those three happy ghosts, and the reality of the wedding reception ballroom with its floral centrepieces and twinkling lights snapped back into place.

Emotion lodged in Suzanne's throat, the weight of the memory she'd experienced heavy in her chest. For a moment, it had seemed as if she could have reached out and touched that long forgotten memory, stepped into it, and wrapped it around her until she remembered...

"Ms Kennedy, did you hear what I said?"

Suzanne blinked. One of the hotel's young staff members was standing before her and giving her a curious look while gesturing with the nozzle of the vacuum cleaner at her feet. Beside her stood Mrs Wishmore, her thoughtful gaze settled on Suzanne.

"Sorry, what did you say?" Suzanne said, blinking again as the last tendrils of that strange old memory from the ballroom whispered at the edges of her brain.

"I said I've finished vacuuming in here and wondered what you'd like me to do next," the staff member said.

"Oh, right." Suzanne glanced around the ballroom, checking that everything was set up in the beautiful space that was now only waiting for the wedding party to arrive. "If you could make sure the ballroom toilets are ship-shape, that would be great."

The young woman nodded and turned for the toilets along a corridor at the side of the ballroom, leaving Suzanne and Mrs Wishmore alone. The older lady studied Suzanne, looking thoughtful.

"You look like you've seen a ghost," Doris said, her eyebrow arching.

Suzanne let out a strangled laugh at Mrs Wishmore's observation. "I must have got lost in a daydream for a second."

"I hope it was a good one."

She glanced at Mrs Wishmore before looking back towards the spot in the ballroom where that old memory had played out before her eyes. "It was."

"Would you like to tell me about it?"

"Um…" Suzanne was about to shake her head, but instead turned to Mrs Wishmore, her brow creasing even as she spoke. "I was remembering back to when I was a little girl, before my grandfather refurbished this ballroom. I was twirling and dancing with my mother, and my grandfather was laughing, and we were all so happy."

The emotion that had closed Suzanne's throat a moment

earlier now returned, this time threatening tears. An ache settled deep inside her heart alongside the memory she'd watched playing out before her eyes, an ache for all those things that had been lost as the years had passed by. Not just for her grandfather, who she'd adored, but also for that version of her mother who she'd twirled alongside on the ballroom floor, that version of her mother who had known happiness and joy and hadn't been afraid to show it.

And she ached, too, for that carefree little girl she'd once been, and for the memory of how life had felt back then, how full and big and *bright*.

Mrs Wishmore stepped closer and laid her hand on Suzanne's and gave it a gentle squeeze. "That sounds like a wonderful memory, and one worth preserving."

Suzanne nodded, not trusting herself to speak again. *What on earth was wrong with her?*

Pushing back on the emotions swirling inside her head, Suzanne peered at Mrs Wishmore. The older lady's hand was still on hers, bringing comfort and reassurance. Suzanne drew in a deep breath, grateful for the woman's presence and kindness. As Mrs Wishmore's hand squeezed hers once more, she sensed the bright joy of the memory she'd just relived returning, filling her heart with light.

And with it came glimpses of those gossamer ghosts from long ago, twirling and dancing and laughing all around her.

"Doris," Suzanne said, her voice a whisper. "What's happening?"

Mrs Wishmore smiled. "You're remembering, dear. That's what's happening."

"Remembering what?" Suzanne asked, shaking her head in confusion.

Mrs Wishmore's smile softened. "You're remembering what life is supposed to be all about."

Suzanne frowned. "I don't understand."

"You will."

Along with one last glimpse of those dancing ghosts who were once more disappearing around her, Suzanne thought she could almost see what Mrs Wishmore wanted her to see, or understand, or realise. But just before she grasped the knowledge she was sure was there for the taking, it evaporated.

Suzanne stared at the older lady beside her, with her cloud of silvery hair and bright blue eyes, and couldn't help thinking something that seemed crazy…

"Mrs Wishmore," Suzanne whispered. "Who are you? I mean, who are you really?"

The smile on the older lady's face softened. "I'm a friend, Suzanne. No more and no less."

Mrs Wishmore shifted her feet, and the lights from the overhead chandeliers caught the older lady's silvery hair, making it look as if she had a glowing halo above her head.

Suzanne stared at the woman for a long moment and then gaped in astonished understanding.

Was it possible that Mrs Wishmore was...?

"Well, I'd better get back to the reception desk," Mrs Wishmore said, breaking the strange magic of the moment before Suzanne could complete the thought inside her head. "I only came through here to tell you that your mother was on her way to the restaurant and she asked me to remind you to meet her there and not to be late."

With a nod, Mrs Wishmore turned for the ballroom doors. Suzanne watched her leave, her mind flustered and filled with just one thought.

Had she just wondered if it was possible that Mrs Wishmore was… some sort of *angel?*

It was the most ludicrous thought she'd ever had in her life.

Shaking her head, Suzanne adjusted the floral centrepiece

on a nearby table and tried to stop her hands from shaking. The strange memory she'd just remembered and replayed, combined with an admittedly convincing trick of the light caused by the ballroom's crystal chandeliers, had obviously turned her brain stupid.

Stupid enough to conjure dancing ghosts and lost-lost memories and imaginary angels.

Suzanne wondered if she might just be working too hard and going round the bend. She hoped not. Things were much too busy at the hotel for anything ridiculous like that to happen.

WHEN SHE ARRIVED in the hotel restaurant, Suzanne saw her mother seated at a table near the bar and working on her laptop. They met here every few weeks for a quick sandwich lunch and a business catch up. Imogen liked to observe the restaurant in action during one of its busiest times and make sure things were running smoothly, a habit she'd learned from Suzanne's grandfather, who'd valued experiencing the hotel's facilities as a customer as well as an employer and business owner.

Suzanne knew that the efficiency of the multitasking also appealed to her mother—eating lunch while dealing with important business matters pleased Imogen, a woman who liked knowing that every minute was being accounted for and put to good use.

"I already ordered chicken salad sandwiches for us," Imogen said when Suzanne reached the table, her gaze flicking up before returning to the laptop screen. "I thought it would save time while you were making your way over here."

"Good idea," Suzanne said, pulling out a chair. "Everything's all set for the wedding reception in the ballroom. I was just running the final checks before I came over."

Imogen nodded, her eyes still on the screen. After another burst of keyboard tapping, she pushed the laptop aside and turned to Suzanne. "Did you find someone to cover for the staff shortage in the kitchen this evening?"

"One of our other sous chefs has agreed to come in for the overtime."

"And did you liaise with the wedding DJ to answer his questions about loading his audio equipment into the ballroom later today?"

"All done."

"What about the flowers for the centrepieces? I heard you had to source extra supplies because of a late addition of guest numbers?"

Suzanne smiled. "It's all taken care of. You don't have to worry yourself about all these minor details."

"I'm not worrying myself. I just want to be sure that everything's in hand."

"It is."

For a moment, they locked gazes, and when Suzanne saw her mother's steely expression harden, she expected the inquisition to continue. When Imogen only nodded and looked back at her laptop screen, Suzanne was relieved.

"Good. In that case, I'll leave you to it." Imogen peered at her laptop screen before turning back to Suzanne. "Does the kitchen staff know the bride wants champagne and strawberries delivered to the honeymoon suite before she and her new husband arrive?"

"Yes, of course they know." Suzanne tried to hide her exasperation, but it wasn't easy. "Did you hound the last hotel deputy manager the same way you hound me?"

"I *fired* the last deputy manager, in case you'd forgotten," Imogen shot back.

"Yes, but not because he was bad at his job."

Her mother made a face. "I caught him having sex with a co-worker in the second floor linen closet. In my book, that makes him extraordinarily bad at his job. At the very least, it knocked him out of the running for hotel employee of the year."

Suzanne laughed at her mother's quip. Imogen's gaze softened as she, too, let out a soft chuckle.

"I've always been a details person, Suzanne," Imogen continued. "And while you're finding your feet as deputy manager here, you're just going to have to put up with me asking these sorts of questions. But that doesn't mean I'm hounding you, as you put it."

"Fair enough," Suzanne said, keen not to have this same conversation with her mother yet again. "But if you plan on firing me anytime soon, like you did the last guy, I'd appreciate a heads-up."

"Of course I don't plan on firing you," Imogen scowled, then added, "Unless I discover you in a compromising position in the linen closet, in which case all bets are off."

"No danger of that happening." Suzanne heard the wistful tone in her voice, a tone that brought her mother's fierce glare back to drill into her.

"What I mean is, I'd need to have an actual romantic interest happening in my life before there was a chance of a tryst in the linen closet," Suzanne said. "Which I don't, so there isn't."

For a long beat, Imogen scrutinised Suzanne. "Romance is over-rated."

"So you keep telling me."

The response brought deep furrows to Imogen's forehead. "What's that supposed to mean?"

Before she could answer, a young waiter arrived with their sandwiches and drinks. Suzanne took a sip of water and watched her mother prod at the sandwich on her plate, checking the filling and presentation. The woman was never off the clock.

"You think I've steered you away from boyfriends and relationships?" Imogen said after taking a bite of her sandwich. "Well, it's true. I have steered you away from silly nonsense like that, and I make no apologies for it, either. Nor do I make any apologies for encouraging you to focus on your university studies, and now on your career here at the hotel."

"I'm not asking you to apologise for it. I'm where I am right now because of all your good advice. But you can't deny that you have a pretty dim view of things when it comes to matters of the heart."

"Can you blame me?" As soon as she said it, Imogen closed her eyes and sighed. "Sorry, I didn't mean that to sound the way it did."

"You mean bitter and angry?"

"Damn it, Suzanne, are you trying to pick a fight?" Imogen said, anger bubbling in her tone. But as quickly as the fire flared in her eyes, it disappeared, and Suzanne saw sadness in her mother's expression that made her ashamed of her flippant comment.

"Look, Suzanne," Imogen said, "With a solid career beneath you, you can do anything you want in life. You can decide what you want and how you want to go about getting it. With independence comes choice and possibilities. There will always be time for relationships and romance. But first you have to get the foundations right in your life, and that's what you've done. It's what you *are* doing."

Suzanne ate some food and wiped her mouth with a napkin. She knew that what her mother said was true. Their working relationship at the hotel had its frictions, no question, but Suzanne understood how important it was to

Imogen that her daughter make her own way in the world and call her own shots.

She also understood why her mother wanted her attention to remain on her career, and for her not to be distracted by other things. It didn't take a genius to work out what made Imogen Kennedy tick, or why her priorities lay where they did.

Setting aside her sandwich, Suzanne watched her mother for a moment, wondering—not for the first time—at her fierce commitment to her job and to the hotel.

"Can I ask you something?" she said. "Something I've wanted to ask for a long time?"

Imogen glanced up from her plate of food, her expression curious but with that signature wariness lurking beneath the surface. "All right."

"If you hadn't ended up pregnant with me, would you still have stayed here to run the hotel with grandad?" Suzanne asked, the words tumbling out. "Or did you have other hopes and dreams and things you wanted to do with your life, things you would've done if it wasn't for me?"

Imogen's gaze widened, her eyes searching Suzanne's. "You are the best thing that ever happened to me, Suzanne. Being your mother has been—and still is—the most amazing experience of my life. If you doubt that because I have a tendency to drive you crazy as your boss, then I'm sorry, and—"

"I don't doubt that. That's not what I'm asking." Suzanne shifted in her seat, searching for the right words. "All I mean is that you didn't expect to raise me as a single parent. You've never made a secret of that. It wasn't what you planned. So, I'm just wondering what you might have done in life if it hadn't been for that."

Imogen sighed and drank from her water glass before talking again. "I never wanted anything other than to run this hotel with your grandfather. I've always loved this place. It's in my blood. Even if you hadn't come along when you did, and even if your father..." She frowned at the word and cleared her throat. "Look, this is the life I wanted, Suzanne. I got my dream, and then some. I'm in charge of running this business, and I've been lucky enough to run it alongside both my father, who I loved, and now my daughter, who I love beyond measure, even if I don't always do a very good job of showing it."

Imogen reached across the table and squeezed Suzanne's hand, a rare gesture of public affection.

"I have everything I ever hoped for in life, Suzanne," Imogen said, her voice almost a whisper. "And now that's all I want for you, too."

Suzanne smiled, more than a little surprised by her mother's words. She realised it had been a long time since her mother had expressed her emotions like this, and a long time since she'd told Suzanne she loved her.

And Suzanne realised, with a jolt, that it had been a long time, too, since she'd said those same words to her mother.

"I love you, Mum," Suzanne said, her voice a whisper.

Something sparked behind Imogen's eyes, softening her gaze. After squeezing Suzanne's hand one more time, she cleared her throat.

"I love you, too, sweetheart. Now, can we get back to business?"

Her mother tapped at the laptop keyboard, pulling up new paperwork there. Although Suzanne knew this was supposed to be a business meeting, not a mother-daughter heart-to-heart, she wasn't ready to move on yet.

"Mum, can I ask you something else?"

Imogen glanced up from the laptop, and Suzanne took her silence as an invitation to continue.

"Did you love my father?" she asked.

For a long beat, Imogen only stared. Suzanne couldn't tell if the look in her mother's eyes was alarm or irritation. Perhaps it was both.

"Why are you asking about this all of a sudden?" Imogen frowned.

"Because we never talk about him and I can't help but wonder sometimes about what he meant to you."

"There's a good reason we don't talk about him."

Suzanne understood that only too well. Over the years, she'd learned the story about her father, although she'd been a teenager before she'd discovered the full and difficult truth about what had happened between her parents.

Imogen had been twenty-five when she'd met Paul Irvine in a bar in one of the larger towns north of Balmarrie, where his band played regular Friday night gigs. They'd struck up a conversation between sets, and one thing had led to another. For a few weeks, they'd spent every free moment together, enjoying a passionate and out-of-the-blue romance.

Just a couple of months after they started seeing each other, Imogen discovered she was pregnant. When she shared the unexpected news with Paul, any illusions she'd had about what was going on between them and what they might mean to each other had vanished in an instant.

Paul had told her he wasn't interested in having children and wanted nothing to do with an unplanned pregnancy. He was committed to his band and his music, and hoped the new tour they were about to begin would catch the attention of one of the big record labels and propel them to stardom. There was no space in his life for a baby or a family.

If Imogen wanted to have the child, he'd explained, then she'd have to do it alone, because he wouldn't be involved.

Suzanne only knew about this last part of the conversation between her parents all those years ago because she'd once overheard her grandparents discussing it late one night as she'd passed their bedroom. She'd been in her mid-teens by then, and it was the sorrowful tone of her grandfather's voice as he'd said her name that had made her pause at their door and listen, something she would never had dreamt of doing otherwise. Robert had been talking to her grandmother about a recent school project Suzanne had excelled at, and saying how proud he was of her, when he'd added that it was a tragedy that Paul Irvine had refused to have anything to do with his baby daughter, because Suzanne was the light of their lives, and might have been the light of his life, too, if he'd done the right thing and faced up to his responsibilities instead of selfishly telling Imogen he wanted nothing to do with her or the baby.

Until the moment of that overheard conversation, Suzanne only knew that her mother and father had enjoyed a whirlwind romance that had ended with Suzanne's conception. Her mother and grandparents had always made her feel loved, and although she'd become more aware of having no father in her life once she'd started school and heard her new friends talking about their fathers, she had never missed having one around. There was nothing to be done to change his absence anyway, because three months after Suzanne was born, Paul Irvine died in a road accident. While driving between tour stops late one night in a rented minivan with his band, they'd hit a bad corner at speed and skidded off the road. Paul and another bandmate died of their injuries.

Growing up, all Suzanne knew was that her father had died not long after she'd been born. He was just an abstract idea to her when she was a little girl. It was impossible to miss someone she'd never known, although as a young teenager she'd romanticised the idea of the doomed musician who'd died too young and who might have been the best father in the world had he lived. After overhearing her grandfather's words that night, Suzanne had pressed her mother about why there were no photographs of her father in their albums, no pictures of this ill-fated young man holding his newborn baby at the hospital, and Imogen had reluctantly told her the truth about the relationship she'd had with Paul Irvine, or the lack of one. Her father had never been in contact with Imogen again after learning she was pregnant. Although Imogen had reached out once Suzanne was born, giving Paul another opportunity to be involved in his child's life, he'd never responded.

Imogen Kennedy hadn't planned on being a single parent, but that was the hand she was dealt, and she'd played it with courage and commitment. Suzanne never wanted for anything as a child—love, affection, structure, and the encouragement to be whatever she wanted to be in life.

But lately, Suzanne couldn't help but wonder at the young woman her mother had once been. Suzanne was now only a few years older than her mother was when she'd fallen pregnant, and it was hard to imagine the shock she must have experienced. She often wondered what Imogen had felt for the man who'd caught her up in a romantic whirlwind and then turned his back on her.

Yet, although these questions had been swirling around for some time, Suzanne had never asked them. She wasn't sure why she was asking them now, either.

Perhaps it was that strange daydream she'd had a few minutes ago in the ballroom, when she'd remembered being a little girl in a pink princess dress, dancing around the empty ballroom and twirling with her mother while her grandfather clapped and laughed. She couldn't stop thinking about the soft, happy glow on her mother's face in that daydream. It had been so long since she'd seen her mother look that way.

Had Paul Irvine once made her beam with joy, too, back before he broke her heart and changed her life forever?

As Suzanne looked across the restaurant table at her mother, she wondered if she would even get an answer to the question she'd asked. Imogen's scowl had deepened and that tell-tale flash of irritation was burning in her eyes.

But Imogen must have seen something in her daughter's face that made her hold herself in check. Encouraged, Suzanne pressed on.

"I understand why you don't talk about him," she said. "And the truth is, I don't want to talk about him, either. He was never a part of my life, and I made my peace a long time ago with the fact that he never wanted to be a part of it, and that probably wouldn't have changed even if he'd lived. But I can't help wondering what you felt about him before he walked away from you. Did you love him?"

Imogen held Suzanne's gaze for a moment longer before glancing around the restaurant where their guests were enjoying good food and drink while the waiting staff moved between tables and worked hard to keep everyone happy. At last, Imogen looked beyond the bank of windows to the view of the bay in the distance, her expression that of someone who was no longer seeing what was around her, but who was instead falling into the memories inside her own head.

"I didn't love him, no," Imogen said. "I was in lust with him. There's no doubt about that. But love? Maybe in time I would have loved him, but I don't know. The truth is, I'm not sure we would've stayed together just because we were having a child. I hardly knew him when I fell pregnant and had no idea just how important his music career was to him until he told me he wouldn't be staying around to play at happy families."

Imogen gave a sad laugh, then waved a hand at nothing in particular. "Perhaps playing at happy families wouldn't have been right for me, either. I enjoy living life on my own terms, and I always have. I've never yearned for a man or a husband or a partner. It's not who I am. And that has nothing to do with being a single parent, in case you're planning on sending yourself off on some silly guilt trip." She smiled before continuing. "Being your mother never held me back from doing any of the things I wanted to do. But I think that being a wife, being a partner… well, that might just have held me back. I don't do compromise very easily, as you know only too well. Marriage and romantic relationships are all about compromise and making space for another person in your world. I never met a man I wanted to do that for. I like things in my life just as they are. I'm happy."

"Really?" Suzanne fidgeted with her napkin. "Sometimes it seems like you aren't happy at all."

"Oh?" Imogen looked astonished at this.

Not wanting to offend her mother, Suzanne said, "You're always so immersed in work, and you take it so seriously, it just sometimes seems that you don't get the chance to do other things with your time, other things that might bring you joy."

Imogen looked bemused. "I may not go around grinning like an idiot all day long, and it's true that managing this place comes with many challenges and, yes, irritations. But that doesn't mean I'm unhappy. And if I wanted a hobby or extra-curricular activity outside of this place, I'd get one. But I don't." She peered at Suzanne for a second, then said, "Where is all this coming from?"

Suzanne shrugged, once more remembering that strange daydream she'd had in the ballroom while talking to Mrs Wishmore. "An old memory popped into my head earlier. Do you remember back before grandad refurbished the ballroom, and there was that awful threadbare burgundy carpet on the floor?"

Imogen nodded, obviously wondering where Suzanne was going with this.

"I remember I used to love prancing around in there in my silly princess dress, pretending I was at a ball," Suzanne continued. "Grandad would tell me how he was going to decorate the place and make it beautiful and how there would be grand balls and dances every night, with women in dazzling gowns and men in smart tuxedos. It all sound like something from a fairy tale. And I could imagine how it would look. Even back then when the room was just a gloomy shell, I could imagine it all, and I'd dance around in my silly little dress as if the whole place had already been transformed. I was thinking about that today and remembering. In my mind's eye, I could see myself twirling around... and you were twirling with me. And you looked so happy. It seemed like it had been a long time since I last saw you look that way."

Although the restaurant noise and bustle continued around them, a quiet stillness descended as Suzanne and Imogen looked at one another across the table.

"I remember how you used to enjoy twirling when you were little," Imogen said. "But that was a long time ago. We can't just keep twirling through life."

"Why not?"

Imogen sighed and looked away. "You really are in a strange mood today, Suzanne. Asking all these odd questions about the past and talking about these old memories. I'm not sure it does anyone any good."

Was her mother right? Ever since the calamity in the woodland play area when the fallen branch had damaged the fairy huts and footbridge, Suzanne felt like she'd been living halfway in the past. Her regular walks along Star Castle Lane to the enchanted woodland always made her think of her grandfather, but seeing the fairy huts he'd had built for her all those years ago ending up smashed beneath the fallen tree branch had made her think back even more than usual, feeling sad for the little fairy houses and their demise.

And then today, in the ballroom, the strange daydream she'd had, featuring herself as a little girl twirling with her mother and making her grandfather laugh... that memory had filled her with such longing. Not just for the joyful look on her mother's face all those years ago, but for herself, too, and the carefree little girl she'd once been.

Why was she remembering those old memories and pining for days gone by? She wondered what was wrong with her lately. Perhaps the pressures of her new role at the hotel and the responsibilities associated with the upcoming summer ball had turned her brain into mush.

"Now, we need to discuss the plans we drew up for special weekday offers in the spa facilities," Imogen said, pulling her laptop closer. "These lunch meetings of ours are supposed to help us get some work done, so let's get on with it."

Taking a last bite of her sandwich, Suzanne nodded and turned her attention to the task at hand. She had no idea why her mind kept wandering like this, and conjuring old memories of times gone by, but she did know that the work of the hotel ought to be what she was thinking about right now.

Reining in her thoughts, she focused on the projected revenue spreadsheet her mother was scrolling through on the laptop screen, and let the numbers and calculations fill her noisy brain and shut out everything else.

CHAPTER TWELVE

The carved handrail on the little bridge over the stream at the far end of the woodland play area on the hotel grounds looked as good as new.

Well, almost as good as new. Kyle had spied some ragged edges on the handrail, and the little fairy folk faces he'd carved into the side weren't as polished as they could be, but there was time to put those things right.

The team of men Kyle had been supervising on the job had put in a full day yesterday, completing the pathway repairs before removing the damaged footbridge parts and installing the replacement beams and struts. The footbridge work had turned out to be a little trickier than they'd first imagined, with a few miscalculations on their measurements thanks to a slight curve in the old wood of the bridge throwing their lines of out of place.

By the time they'd finished their shift for the day, the carvings and decorative touches weren't yet complete, which was what had brought Kyle back to the hotel grounds late on Saturday afternoon. Hill Landscaping had promised that the woodland area would be reopened to the hotel's guests by the start of the week, and until the handrail was finished and sanded, and Kyle was sure no guests were at risk of sustaining splinters in their hands if they grabbed hold of it, the cordons would remain in place.

With no Saturday plans except working on the replacement fairy hut structures at home, Kyle was happy to press on with the work on site. He'd spent the last half hour sanding down the rough edges on the handrail and now the wood was smooth and pleasing to the touch, with just a few ragged spots remaining to be dealt with where the fittings had been screwed into place. The faces of the fairy folk were coming along nicely, too. Wood carving might not be how Kyle earned his main living, but there was no denying the pleasure he'd found in creating the fairy faces along the edges of the handrail. The work wasn't as intricate or detailed as a skilled craftsman would have achieved, but it did the job and had taken far less time than it would have done if the hotel management had decided to hire a professional woodworker for the task.

As Kyle finished etching a fluttering butterfly beside one of the fairy faces on the bridge handrail, he heard footsteps in the woodland clearing behind him.

"What a wonderful job you and your men have done out here, Kyle!" Mrs Wishmore said as she made her way towards the footbridge. "And you worked so quickly, too."

"It isn't a complicated job and it all looked much worse than it was because of the mess made by the fallen tree branch," Kyle replied.

"And yet here you are, late on a Saturday afternoon, working hard to finish everything off," Mrs Wishmore smiled, drawing closer to inspect the carvings Kyle was dealing with.

"The sooner I can finish and sign off on the work, the sooner the hotel can reopen this area to the guests. There's still some work to complete on these carvings, but by early next week it should all be done."

"I know Suzanne will be thrilled to hear that."

Kyle set down his woodworking tools and drank from his water bottle. "What brings you all the way out here, Mrs Wishmore?"

"My colleague on reception mentioned that you'd dropped by to let them know you'd be working out here for an hour this afternoon, and I thought I'd come over to see for myself how things were going, and to find out if you'd like me to bring you a plate of sandwiches from the kitchen to keep you sustained."

"Thanks, but I'm fine. I'm about to finish for the day anyway. I need a finer woodworking tool to complete the carvings, and I must have left it at home in the shed. I'll come back early next week to complete the job and sign off on the work."

"These carvings are really something," Mrs Wishmore said, peering at the handrail. "You are a talented young man, earning a living as a garden designer and landscaper, and also possessing these woodworking skills, too."

"I enjoy keeping busy. During the winter, the gardening work slows down and it's good to have other ways of making money in the quieter months. It's not a bad idea to develop a side line in something else. I enjoy pottering around with wood design, so this will give me a bit of a safety net for when I set up in business for myself. Plus, people like bespoke touches in their gardens. When I put together garden designs for new clients, I'd like to offer them a signature touch that's unique to them—carved wooden gnomes or wishing wells or seating benches, that sort of thing."

"It sounds to me like you have a brilliant business plan and that it will be a brilliant success when you put it into action." Mrs Wishmore slanted him a look. "But I hope you won't wait too long to make the leap, young man. Waiting gives us too much time to think, and when we think, we all too easily talk ourselves out of the big, brave moves we ought to make in our lives."

Kyle smiled at the woman's easy wisdom. "I'm sure you're right. Well, I'm finished here for now so I'll walk back up to the hotel with you."

After packing his tools away, Kyle accompanied Mrs Wishmore through the woodland clearing and along Star Castle Lane and towards the hotel.

"Do you have any exciting plans for tonight?" Mrs Wishmore asked as they walked.

"It depends what you mean by exciting. I'll be working on the replacement fairy huts for the woodland area for a few hours. We're keen to get this job finished for the hotel as quickly as possible."

"You're a hard-working young man, Kyle, and a credit to Hill Landscaping. I'm sure if those fairy huts you're working on turn out anything like the handrail I just saw, the hotel management here will be thrilled."

"That's the hope. There are some details I need to confirm with Suzanne Kennedy before I complete the fairy hut carvings and decorations, but that can wait until next week."

"Oh, well, Suzanne is working at the hotel this afternoon if you wanted to chat with her," Doris said. "I think she might be leaving shortly, but I'd be happy to find her if that helped speed things along for you?"

"It's nothing I need to trouble her about when she's busy."

"I'm sure Suzanne wouldn't mind."

"What wouldn't I mind?"

Kyle and Mrs Wishmore turned and saw Suzanne Kennedy stepping outside the hotel doors behind them, a leather bag hitched over her shoulders and a stack of paperwork cradled in her arms, her car keys dangling from her finger tips.

"Oh, hello Kyle," she said, offering a smile.

"Kyle was out in the woodland play area working on the footbridge handrail," Mrs Wishmore said. "He was just telling me he plans on doing more work for you tonight on the little fairy huts, but that he has some details he needed to confirm with you on the decorations and whatnot."

"It's nothing that can't wait until next week," Kyle said. It was obvious that Suzanne Kennedy was leaving work for the day and he didn't want to delay her.

"I'm happy to answer questions," Suzanne replied with a smile. "Especially if it helps move things along faster."

"Well, there you go," Mrs Wishmore said to Kyle. "It's perfect timing that you've run into each another again."

Kyle gave Suzanne an uncertain look and glanced at the stack of paperwork in her arms. "If you're sure you're not too busy right now?"

"It's fine," she said. "Anyway, I've been in wedding reception mode all afternoon, and I could use a break before I start on this paperwork."

Seeing Kyle's confused expression, Mrs Wishmore said, "We have the most beautiful wedding reception taking place in the hotel ballroom this evening, and Suzanne has worked non-stop for hours to make sure everything goes as planned for the newly-weds."

"Things are ticking along nicely now that their wedding meal is underway and the champagne is flowing," Suzanne smiled. "The hotel events supervisor will handle the rest of the evening. So, now is the perfect time to ask questions about the fairy huts, because once I get home I'm turning off my phone and collapsing into an exhausted heap."

Suzanne laughed, and Kyle joined her. "I said I'd check with you about the decorative carvings on the fairy huts before I started working on them, to make sure they meet your expectations. You said you had some old photographs I could look at from when the huts were originally installed."

"I forgot I promised to look those out for you." Nodding, Suzanne pulled her phone from her bag and tapped on the screen. "I've made a note now, so I won't forget again. If I get through all this paperwork tonight, then I'll dig out the old photo albums and find a few snaps that might be helpful."

"I appreciate it."

"Although I made time earlier this afternoon to go out to the play area and see how everything was looking," Suzanne said. "I'm impressed with what you've done already. And I was even more impressed by the carvings you'd started on the footbridge handrail."

Before Kyle could answer, Mrs Wishmore jumped in. "Well, you ought to see how it looks now. I've just been over there and the carvings look wonderful."

"In that case, do you need me to find old photographs of the original fairy hut decorations?" Suzanne asked. "It sounds like you already know what you're doing."

"I'm happy to use my initiative, if that's easier," Kyle said. "But I got the impression each of the fairy huts had a unique design above the door, and as the tree branch obliterated the carvings on the damaged huts, I don't have anything to guide me, the same way I did with the handrail carvings which were much easier to deal with because the damage to the original wasn't so bad."

"You're right," Suzanne said. "And after all, I'm the one who said I wanted the fairy huts and their decorations to look as similar as possible to what was there originally. Once I find the old photographs, I'll let you know."

"And perhaps if you can lay your hands on them tonight, you could take some quick pictures with your phone camera and whizz them over to Kyle straight away?" Mrs Wishmore suggested.

"I suppose that would save some time," Suzanne nodded. "Is that all right with you, Kyle?"

"Sounds good to me. Let me give you my number."

Kyle rhymed off his personal mobile number and Suzanne tapped it into her phone.

"If I find what I'm looking for in our old family photo albums, I'll let you know." Suzanne glanced at her watch. "I'd better run. Bye, Kyle. Bye, Mrs Wishmore."

"Goodbye, Suzanne," Mrs Wishmore said as Kyle nodded a quick farewell of his own.

He watched Suzanne hurry around the side of the hotel building to the staff car park at the rear. It was only once she'd disappeared from sight that he realised he'd been unable to take his eyes off her.

When he turned back to Mrs Wishmore, a knowing smile was playing on the older lady's lips.

"Suzanne Kennedy is a special young woman," Doris said.

"I'm sure she is." Kyle adjusted his work bag and cleared his throat. "I ought to get moving myself. It's been a long day."

"Of course. Goodbye, Kyle."

"See you soon, Doris."

"And don't forget what I said."

Kyle turned around and saw that wry smile was back on Mrs Wishmore's face. "What's that?"

"When we wait too long to make the big moves in life, we end up talking ourselves out of doing those things that we really ought to be doing."

With a wink, Mrs Wishmore made her way back inside the hotel. Kyle lingered for a moment on the pathway, wondering at the mysterious woman and her even more mysterious comments.

When it came to offering free life advice, Doris Wishmore didn't hold back… and even although he found the elderly hotel employee more than a little odd, he couldn't help but wonder if he ought to pay more attention to what she had to say.

He also couldn't help but wonder what the older lady had been referring to with her cryptic comment. Was she talking about waiting too long to start his new business? Or was she talking about Suzanne Kennedy?

Kyle suspected that Doris Wishmore might be interested in some meddling matchmaking where Suzanne was concerned. It didn't seem to bother her in the slightest that Kyle had already asked Suzanne out and she'd turned him down.

If Kyle was smart enough to respect that answer, why couldn't Mrs Wishmore do the same?

A crowd of hotel guests came pouring through the main doors just then, laughing and joking with one another as they jostled their way past Kyle on the pathway. Deciding that a tradesman lurking around the place with a grubby toolbox in his hand didn't do the hotel any style favours, he dug out his keys and headed for the car park.

CHAPTER THIRTEEN

Kyle returned home in time to join Erin and Jamie at the kitchen table for dinner. Erin had cooked a casserole with a side dish of roasted vegetables, and while they mopped up chicken gravy with chunks of fresh crusty bread, Jamie chattered on about what he'd got up to that afternoon at the park with his friends, and regaled him with a tale about the contraband chocolate treats he'd snuck into the shopping trolley at the supermarket his mother had 'dragged him to' on the way home. Kyle grinned as Erin rolled her eyes at her son's recounting of the moment she'd reached the check-out and pulled the mega-sized bag of chocolate bars from the trolley before staring at the package in confusion, wondering how it had got there.

Knowing Jamie's love of all things sweet and chocolatey, not to mention his terrible seven-year-old's poker face, he doubted his sister had taken long to solve the puzzle. Inevitably, she'd bought the huge bag of treats. Kyle didn't have to be Sherlock Holmes to work out that, after what Jamie's father had done and the way he'd ignored him since leaving Erin, his sister would indulge her son in some excess chocolate on a Saturday night if it helped chase away the blues the boy must feel.

Once the dishes were washed and the kitchen tidied, Erin and Jamie settled down in the living room to watch a film. When Kyle declined the offer to join them, citing the fairy hut work he wanted to get on with in the back garden, Jamie looked conflicted, torn between a desire to spend time with his uncle, hammering and sawing wood, and excitement about the latest Marvel superhero film he'd been looking forward to watching. After assuring his nephew that there would be plenty of work for him to do some other time, Jamie made himself comfortable on the sofa before turning up the television volume and settling in for the adventure.

At the sight of his sister's pained expression as the Marvel theme tune blasted from the television speakers, Kyle clapped her on the shoulder and asked if *she* wanted to help him in the back garden instead.

"It's a tough choice, but assuming I don't end up deaf on account of the volume, or the speakers don't explode, I'll stick it out in here and see what happens next in the Marvel superhero metaverse."

"It's the Marvel cinematic universe," Jamie groaned. "You never get it right, Mum!"

"Well, since you're the expert on all this stuff, maybe you'll just have to explain to me how this whole cinematic universe thing works."

"Again?" Jamie cried, but he was obviously pleased at the idea of being classed as an expert in all things Marvel. "Okay, but you have to promise to listen this time and pay attention," he said, his tone serious.

As Erin hid a grin while her son began narrating the complicated origin story of the superhero now striding around on screen, Kyle left them to it and made his way outside to the back garden and into the late evening sunshine.

Sticking his ear buds in and turning on some music to enjoy while he worked, he was making progress with the frame of the second fairy hut when his phone pinged with a message. Glancing at the screen, his heart beat out a hard thump when he saw the message was from Suzanne Kennedy:

Hi, Kyle. As promised, here are a couple of old photos of the fairy huts as they looked when my grandfather installed them. You should be able to zoom in on the little carvings and decorative details. Hope this helps! Suzanne.

Kyle set aside the wood drill he'd been using and tapped the phone screen to look at the photographs attached to the message. When he saw the images, he couldn't help but smile.

There were three photographs, snapped from old prints which appeared a little ragged at the corners and faded with age. The photos showed the two fairy huts in the woodland play area which Kyle was replacing, both of them looking bright and brand new, which of course was what they'd been back then, given that the pictures were over twenty years old.

Although the little fairy huts were sweet, they weren't the reason Kyle was smiling.

What made him smile was the little girl grinning out from the photographs as she stood between the cute fairy huts, her hair in bunches and with one small pudgy hand resting on the low roof of the yellow-painted hut closest to her.

The little girl was obviously Suzanne Kennedy. Kyle might only have known the woman for a few days, but he'd recognise that bright smile anywhere.

She looked like she was maybe seven or eight years old in the pictures, and was wearing yellow and blue polka dot leggings and a T-shirt bearing a cartoon image of a cheerful lion with a shaggy mane. The delight on the little girl's face as she posed beside the pristine fairy hut was unmistakable and Kyle could almost hear the laughter from Suzanne's grandfather who stood to the side of the photograph, looking down at his granddaughter with an expression of pure joy on his face.

It was a terrific shot of a treasured family moment shared between grandfather and granddaughter, and Kyle felt somehow privileged to see it.

He wondered who was behind the camera, snapping the shot. Suzanne's mother or grandmother, perhaps? As soon as the question popped into his head, he wondered why he wanted to know. The photograph was only supposed to help him complete a contracted work task, after all. And yet, the intimate image, filled with such love and happiness, had moved him, making him want to know more about the people captured in it and their lovely moment together that had been preserved for all time.

And although he was supposed to be focusing on the decorative carvings above the tiny doors on the fairy huts, Kyle's gaze kept returning to the childhood image of Suzanne and to that smile on her face. Seeing the picture of her as little girl made him feel like he now knew her better than he had just a few seconds ago, even although that made no sense whatsoever.

He zoomed in on the first photograph of the three that she'd sent through, to make sure the detail of the decorative carvings was clear enough to be helpful. After adjusting the image, he picked out a clutch of carved butterflies above the door of the pink fairy hut, and a scattering of stars above the door of the second fairy hut, which was painted a pale yellow colour.

Grabbing his phone, he tapped out a reply to Suzanne's message.

Thanks for these photographs, they'll be a big help. Can see the carved designs just fine, and it's no problem to recreate them. Can also see from these photographs that you were fond of the little yellow fairy hut with the star carvings above the door—will make sure those are extra special for you on the new structures. Cheers, Kyle.

His fingers hovered above the *Send* button. Was that last comment too personal, about noticing how Suzanne, as a child, had favoured the star-decorated yellow fairy hut enough to stand beside it for the photographs, her little hand affectionately touching the roof? Would she think it strange that he'd noticed that detail?

Shaking his head, he pressed *Send*. He was overthinking things, which wasn't usually a problem for Kyle, but had become one ever since he'd met Suzanne Kennedy. Something about the woman made his brain go into overdrive and caused his thought processes to scramble like eggs.

He was about to resume his wood drilling work when his phone pinged with another message.

The yellow hut with the stars was my favourite when I was small! I liked the cheerful colour and my grandfather asked the carpenter for the star carvings because he knew how much I loved them. When you grow up in a family business called the Star Castle Hotel, it's impossible not to love anything with stars on it. My grandfather drew the star design himself for the carpenter, which is why it has sentimental value, and it would be lovely if you can match is as closely as you're able to. Thanks again, Suzanne.

Kyle read the message twice, and then a third time. He liked that she'd shared more of the personal story that lay behind those fairy huts, and liked knowing how her doting grandfather had wanted to make the fairy huts extra special by adding a starry flourish that Suzanne would always cherish. He tapped out a reply.

I'll make sure the star design is the same as the one your grandfather designed for you. It's a shame the original was destroyed, and now I can understand better why you were upset about it and wanted the fairy huts replaced as close to the originals as possible. As the fairy hut with the stars was your favourite as a child, maybe I could add some extra star carvings on to the replacement, maybe some on the roof for extra fun?

A moment later, a reply came through.

That sounds good, I'd like that. But don't take longer on the carvings than you planned to and give yourself more work than you bargained for just to indulge a grown woman's childhood memories!

Grinning, Kyle sent a quick reply.

It will be fun adding some decoration to the roof, I think it will be quirky and the kids will love it. And it's no trouble to do some extra stuff if it's what you'd like.

A reply arrived: *Thanks, Kyle, I appreciate it.*

After reading the message, Kyle saw the three little animated dots in the text box that showed that Suzanne was writing another text. He waited for a message to appear, but then the three dots disappeared with nothing else pinging through. Realising that Suzanne must have said all she wanted to say on the matter, he picked up his wood drill to get back to work. No sooner had he lined up the drill bit with the pencil mark he'd placed on the length of wood than the phone pinged again.

And thanks for the reminder to dig out these photographs. It was fun going through the old photo albums. I haven't done it in ages and I enjoyed the trip down memory lane.

Kyle realised Suzanne had hesitated before sending through the message. Its content had nothing to do with the work he was doing and wasn't necessary. Even so, she'd wanted to share this information with him. He wondered, perhaps too hopefully, if she'd been enjoying their message exchange as much as he had, and—just like him—hadn't wanted it to be over.

It's always fun looking back at old photographs, Kyle typed. *And these are terrific shots of you and your grandfather. You both look as pleased as punch.*

The three animated dots appeared, flashing on the screen for a few seconds before a reply came.

I knew I had these old pics somewhere but had forgotten some of them had both me and my grandfather in them. I felt a bit emotional seeing them again and remembering back all those years ago. It's funny how time flies, isn't it!

Kyle sensed that the exclamation mark at the end of the message was an attempt to smooth over the raw honesty of Suzanne's admission about feeling emotional at the sight of the old photographs. He was curious about why she'd shared this personal detail with him at all. When they'd eaten pizza together overlooking the bay a couple of nights ago, it had been obvious to Kyle that she'd been reluctant to talk much about personal things, and he couldn't forget how easily she'd rebuffed him when he'd asked if they could see each other again for a drink sometime.

And yet here she was, just two nights later, sharing this personal information about how seeing some old family photographs had triggered raw emotions. Kyle wondered if the phone messaging format perhaps made it easier for her to confide in this way, the physical distance making friendly intimacy feel less awkward.

He imagined Suzanne at home, wherever home was and whatever it looked like, kicking back on her sofa with her phone clutched in her hand while surrounded by old family photo albums, spilling memories around her as she sat by herself, alone.

Was she alone? Kyle wondered. He guessed she was, considering she was continuing to exchange these messages with him beyond what was necessary to complete the contracted landscaping job.

And if she was alone, was she also lonely? Was she by herself on a Saturday night, and simply grateful for a response from someone on the other end of her phone, even if that someone was just the hired help who she'd made it clear she wasn't interested in beyond work?

If that was all that was going on here, Kyle could make his peace with that, if it meant they could keep chatting. He began typing again, not wanting their conversation to end.

Time does fly much too quickly. When my sister, Erin, first arrived to stay with me a few weeks ago, she showed me an old photo album she'd found at the bottom of a drawer while packing up her old house. There were pictures in there of me and her when we were kids on holiday at the beach with our parents. When I saw those photos, it felt like that holiday could only have been a couple of years ago. It made me feel old! My nephew, Jamie, had a good laugh at seeing me as a skinny ten-year-old in swimming shorts.

If Suzanne was willing to share memories of childhood, Kyle would do the same. He waited to see how she'd respond, wondering whether she'd want to continue down this road or decide she'd already shared too much with the hired contractor.

Three dots flashed on the phone screen. Kyle watched and waited, his wood working all but forgotten now. At last, Suzanne replied.

Ha-ha, I'm sure your little nephew must have enjoyed seeing his uncle as a boy back in the day. And I'm glad I'm not the only one wandering down memory lane at the moment. I'm not someone who looks back very much, but for some weird reason I've been doing it a lot these past few days, remembering when I was small and, of course, remembering my grandfather and mother when they were younger, too. I don't know what's wrong with me!

Kyle thought about what she'd written before replying.

There's nothing wrong with you. It's good to look back sometimes and remember where we came from and who we used to be.

Those animated dots flashed for what seemed like forever before another message arrived from Suzanne.

Weird you should say that—Mrs Wishmore said something like that today, too. The pair of you aren't in cahoots, are you?!

Kyle frowned, wondering what she meant. *In cahoots about what?* he typed.

Never mind, ignore me. I'm probably just imagining things.

Kyle's frown deepened. *Hey, are you okay?*

I'm fine. Like I said, just imagining things, and it's been crazy busy at the hotel lately, which has probably left me scatty!

Once more, Kyle wondered at that too-bright exclamation mark at the end of Suzanne's message. He couldn't escape the feeling that something was on her mind, or troubling her, and that she wanted to talk about it but couldn't quite work out how.

Deciding to take a risk, Kyle tapped another message on his phone.

Your grandfather looks like he thought the world of you, judging from his expression in these photos you sent through. You must have loved him a lot. And you must miss him now he's gone.

Was he going too far now? He had no idea. All he knew for sure was that Suzanne seemed to have something on her mind, and that he'd like to be here to listen if that's what she wanted.

He was wonderful, a great man and a sweet grandfather. And you're right, I do miss him, even although it's been a few years since he passed away. We always had fun together, as you can see from those photos. When grandad was around, there was always laughter.

Kyle replied: *He sounds like a wonderful man.*

He sent the message, and before he could stop himself, sent another hot on its heels: *And I'm sure you're just like him in every good way.*

Many long seconds passed before Suzanne responded. *Thanks, that's a nice thing to say, even although you hardly know me.*

Kyle had to stop his fingers tapping out an automatic reply that would have read: *I want to know you, Suzanne. I want to know you and learn everything there is about you, and I want to see you smile because it's the most beautiful smile I've ever seen in my life.*

But he didn't write any of that. It would be madness to connect at last with this woman and then risk scaring her away with foolish declarations. They were only exchanging phone messages with one another, after all, and Kyle couldn't escape the idea that Suzanne was only in contact with him right now because he was conveniently available and she was at a loose end.

As this unhappy thought rushed through his head, another message arrived from Suzanne.

Do you ever wish for things in life but have no idea how to get them?

The question was so out of the blue, Kyle could only stare at it on his screen for a long beat, wondering what had prompted Suzanne to ask it and how he ought to respond.

He typed out a reply: *That's a big thought for a Saturday night.*

But as soon as he'd finished typing, he deleted what he'd written. It was too flippant. Suzanne had asked a serious question, and it deserved a serious answer.

After taking a deep breath, he wrote a different reply and pressed Send.

All the time.

Kyle peered at his phone screen. They'd been exchanging these messages for the last fifteen minutes. Texting might have got them this far, but Kyle wanted to hear Suzanne's voice, wanted to talk to her, wanted to find out if talking might keep this conversation moving in the strange yet lovely and intimate direction in which it was already headed.

Taking a risk, he dialled Suzanne's number. The phone rang on the other end—once, twice, three times. He imagined her staring at the screen, seeing his number calling through, imagined her wondering if she should answer it.

When the third ring ended and a fourth began, Kyle assumed she'd let his call go through to voice mail. Resigned to their conversation ending, he sighed.

He'd blown it.

Which was why, when the ringing stopped and he heard Suzanne's voice on the other end of the line, Kyle almost dropped the phone in surprise.

"Hello, Kyle," she said.

"Hi, Suzanne." Now that he had her talking on the phone, he couldn't think of anything sensible to say. So, he decided just to say what he'd been thinking when he dialled her number. "You sounded thoughtful in your messages. I wondered if you might like to talk instead of text."

"Sorry, now I'm embarrassed."

"Don't be."

"You don't want to listen to me wittering on about nothing on a Saturday night."

"Yes, I do. And you're not wittering on. You're just talking. *We're* just talking."

Kyle heard her sigh softly. "I don't know why I started texting you about any of this stuff, Kyle. It seems inappropriate."

"Why? Because you're the client and I'm the hired contractor?"

"I don't know. Maybe you're only listening to me because you feel a professional obligation to be polite and because you don't want to jeopardise getting paid for the work you've done if you give me the brush off."

There was humour in her voice as she said this, but Kyle heard the nervous question that lay beneath it, too.

"That's not why I'm listening. I'm not that shallow, Suzanne."

"I know that. I don't know how I know that, but I do."

The tenderness of her words sent a shiver rippling over Kyle's skin, and the vulnerability in her voice made his heart race.

"So," Kyle said, "what are you wishing for in life that you don't know how to get? It seems to me that if anyone has everything figured out, it must be you."

"If only that was true."

"You're deputy manager of that beautiful hotel that your family owns, and you've got a bright future ahead of you. Surely all your wishes have already come true? If not, I don't think there's much hope for the rest of us."

Suzanne laughed. Kyle was pleased to hear her brighter tone when she spoke again.

"I know how lucky I am, and I don't merit much sympathy at all, when I think about it," she laughed.

"That's not what's going on, and you know it. So, do you want to tell me what's on your mind?"

There was another sigh down the line. "Only if I'm not interrupting your Saturday night."

"I was working on the fairy huts for your woodland play area. If we're not talking, I'll go back to drilling wood. I enjoy drilling wood, but I'd like to listen to you instead."

"Thanks, that's a nice thing to say."

A quiet moment passed. Kyle waited, not wanting to rush her. If she wanted to talk, she'd talk.

"If I tell you something, will you promise you won't think I'm crazy?" Suzanne said at last.

"I promise."

Another sigh. "Something strange happened today. I was working in our hotel ballroom, getting everything ready for the wedding reception we're hosting there while talking to Mrs Wishmore about a few things. Suddenly, right in the middle of our conversation, I remembered back to when I was a little girl, back before my grandfather refurbished the ballroom. I used to dance around in the big open space, pretending I was a fairy princess, and I remembered how much fun it was to twirl and dance."

Suzanne laughed softly at the memory. In his back garden, Kyle leaned against his work bench, listening. He liked the sound of her laugh. It lit him up inside the same way her bright smile did.

"But the thing is, it wasn't like I was remembering that old memory at all," Suzanne continued. "It was more like the memory sort of came alive around me, as if it appeared from out of nowhere. Mrs Wishmore and the other hotel staff and the wedding reception table set-ups all vanished, and instead I saw myself as a little girl in my pink princess dress, twirling with my mother while my grandfather clapped his hands and laughed. It was incredibly strange and yet incredibly lovely too. We all looked so happy, the three of us, immersed in the joy of that single moment. And as I watched this old memory playing out in front of me, I realised how long it had been since I'd felt as happy as I was that day back when I was that little girl, twirling around just for fun, and how long it had been since I'd just lived in the moment and experienced the pure joy that came with it."

She stopped talking and an embarrassed laugh came down the line. "I'm sure that sounds insane. Feel free to hang up."

"I'm not planning on hanging up. And it doesn't sound insane. This memory you remembered must have been very vivid and it must also mean a lot to you, too."

"I don't know why it's been stuck in my head all day. It was all just so… strange. It wasn't like recalling a memory so much as it was like… seeing an old piece of film playing out right in front of my eyes. Has something like that ever happened to you?"

"Maybe not the way you've described it. Although I did have a bad curry once from the Spice Shack on Balmarrie high street that left me with some pretty strange hallucinations."

A burst of laughter rolled down the phone line. "You're saying I ate something that disagreed with me?"

"No. But it's nice to hear you laugh." Kyle was glad he'd injected a blast of humour into their conversation. There was such deep melancholy in Suzanne's voice as she talked about that memory she'd remembered—or relived, or whatever it was that had happened—and it had obviously unsettled her. He didn't want her introspection and thoughtfulness to leave her sad. But he also didn't want her to think he was brushing off the importance of the personal story she'd just confided in him.

"In your text message, you asked if I wished for things in life, but didn't know to get them," Kyle continued. "What are you wishing for, Suzanne, that you don't know how to get?"

A long beat passed before she answered. "It will sound so silly and self-indulgent. And I've got so much to be thankful for in my life."

"But there's something you want, something more. What is it?" He kept his tone gentle. It felt like there was a lot riding on this moment and on her answer.

"I wish I could find more of those fun moments of happiness that I used to have a child," Suzanne said, her voice quiet. "Maybe everyone looks back on their childhoods as some sort of golden era, and it all seems so wonderful in the rear-view mirror, especially once you're an adult with responsibilities. But it would be nice just to do something *fun*, you know?"

"Like what?"

She let out a sad laugh. "That's the problem. I'm so busy with work and with the hotel, and constantly questioning whether I'm doing my job properly and making the right decisions for the business, that I think I've forgotten what it means to have fun."

Kyle thought about what she'd said. An idea began swirling, a crazy idea, one filled with the risk of another rejection to add to the one she'd already dished out when they'd shared pizza together and he'd asked her to have a drink with him. But still, he couldn't get the idea out of his head.

Before he had a chance to speak again, Suzanne was talking in a hurried rush down the phone.

"Listen, I'm sorry, I shouldn't be saying any of this to you. We don't even know each other, and I'm sure this is the last thing you want to hear about on a Saturday night, and if it hadn't been for Mrs Wishmore and the odd things she said this afternoon in the ballroom, then maybe none of this would have happened, and..."

"What are you doing tomorrow?" Kyle interrupted.

There was a long pause. "What do you mean?"

"I mean, do you have plans tomorrow? Do you have work commitments you can't get out of?"

"Um..."

He imagined her on the other end of the line as she thought about her work responsibilities and hotel duties. He imagined her guessing what he might be about to ask next and already thinking of ways to turn him down.

"There's somewhere I'd like to take you," Kyle said, jumping back in before Suzanne had any more time to let her brain get the better of her. "I think you might have fun there."

Silence filled the line for a few seconds. "Where?"

"Let me surprise you. That way, it might be even more fun. You said that's what you wanted to find more of in life, right? So, let me help you do that. Or at least, try to help you do that."

"I don't know, Kyle," she said on a sigh. "Now it feels like you're taking pity on me because I'm sad and pathetic."

"That's not what I'm doing," he laughed. "Actually, this place I have in mind, I have to make a trip there anyway, so you might as well tag along. You'd be doing me a favour and keeping me company on the drive there."

"Well…"

"Come on, it'll only be a couple of hours out of your day. What do you say?"

After another long pause, Suzanne spoke again. "Okay, I'm intrigued. Yes, let's do it, whatever 'it' actually is."

He hadn't expected her to say yes, but he fought to keep the surprise out of his voice. "Great. You'll enjoy it, I promise."

"I have hotel commitments tomorrow until noon, though."

"No problem. How does your afternoon look?"

She paused again. "I don't have anything on the agenda, but…"

"In that case, I'll pick you up at one?" Kyle knew she wanted to back out of this, even although she'd only just agreed to it. He tried not to think about the reasons why that might be. Was it because she really was an incredibly busy person, or because she didn't want to spend time with him after all, but had felt backed into an awkward corner by his invitation?

"Okay. Yes, one o'clock sounds fine."

Kyle blew out a silent breath. "Good, I'll see you tomorrow. You'll have fun, I promise."

"Okay." She didn't sound convinced. But Kyle was sure she'd feel differently once he'd put his idea into practice. At least, he hoped she would.

Just then, Jamie came hurtling through the back door, his face beaming. "Mum says we can have one of the chocolate bars we got at the shops today. Do you want one, Uncle Kyle?"

"Sounds good, squirt."

"Who are you talking to, Uncle Kyle?"

Erin appeared in the door frame. "I'm making coffee, Kyle. Do you want one?" When she saw Kyle had the phone to his ear, she flapped her hands in apology and shooed Jamie back inside the house, mouthing a silent "Sorry" as they disappeared.

"Sorry about that," Kyle said down the phone to Suzanne.

"Don't be silly, I've waylaid your Saturday night plans enough already. I'll let you go. Say hi to your little nephew for me."

"I will. But we can keep talking if you'd like, Suzanne. I was only planning on working on these fairy huts I'm building for this mad and completely unreasonable customer I've got right now."

Suzanne laughed, the sound warm and bright in Kyle's ears. "You'd better not disappoint your mad customer. Get back to work and I'll see you tomorrow afternoon."

"All right. Good night, Suzanne."

"Good night, Kyle."

After he hung up, Kyle stared at the phone in his hand, wondering at the unlikely conversation he'd just had. Following his hastily concluded alfresco pizza with Suzanne on the waterfront two nights ago, she'd kept her distance and maintained nothing more than professional contact with him when he'd been working in the hotel grounds.

Tonight, out of the blue, she'd shared something deeply personal and agreed to see him outside of work. It was a miraculous change of fortunes.

The whole thing may only have come about because Suzanne sent through those old family photographs of the fairy huts in the enchanted woodland, but those photos had been enough to get them talking and for Kyle to get beyond Suzanne Kennedy's tough professional exterior.

He was grateful for it, even if it had pained him to hear the sadness in Suzanne's voice as she'd talked about the happiness she'd once enjoyed as a little girl and which she feared she could no longer find in her life.

Tomorrow, Kyle would show her those fears were unfounded.

Already, his mind was working overtime, thinking about the afternoon he was planning, and that he hoped would give him the chance to see that smile of hers again.

That smile that made his heart do somersaults inside his chest.

"Uncle Kyle, come and choose a chocolate bar!" Jamie yelled from the open back door, his face a picture of undiluted excitement, just like Suzanne's Kennedy's face had been as a little girl in those old photographs she'd shared with him.

"Coming, squirt."

Kyle pocketed his phone and went inside to join his sister and nephew for Saturday night chocolate treats, his mind still whirring with plans for Sunday afternoon.

CHAPTER FOURTEEN

Suzanne figured she must have lost her mind. It was the only explanation that made any sense.

It was almost one o'clock on Sunday afternoon, and she was lingering in the hotel reception lobby, peeking through the doors to where the road swept around the front of the building while she waited for Kyle Lawson to arrive and pick her up.

Pick her up for their date. *Their date.*

Or at least, she thought it was a date. It was just as likely that the poor man had taken pity on her while she'd been mumbling and muttering down the phone to him last night, and had thought it would be a kindness to get her out and about for a while, make sure she got some healthy fresh air and a bit of exercise before she went round the bend altogether.

Even now, as she thought back to their phone conversation last night, she scarcely believed that she'd been the one having it with him.

Had she really told him all about that weird episode she'd experienced in the hotel ballroom when she'd imagined—or remembered, or visualised, or whatever it was—herself as a little girl, twirling around in a pink princess dress?

Yes, she had told him all about that, and in quite a lot of horrifying detail, too.

Worse, she'd told him all those deeply personal things about how she'd pined for that carefree little girl she'd been, that little girl who'd been so happy and joyful as she'd danced around the empty ballroom all those years ago, and how she didn't know how to be happy and joyful anymore, and hadn't the faintest idea what to do about it.

Suzanne cringed as she remembered their conversation, word for excruciating word. *Woe is me, I'm ever so sad and unhappy with my amazing life and fantastic job and beautiful family-run hotel that will be mine one day, because I'm gripped with terrifying self-doubt about myself, and I'm also just so busy all the time and don't give myself a single minute to let my hair down and have a teensy, tiny bit of fun. What a complete tragedy! What an unjust world we live in!*

Embarrassment made her cheeks burn and her stomach tie itself in knots. If she could turn back time and suck every single word she'd said back into her stupid mouth, she'd do it.

And if she could command the earth to open up beneath her feet and swallow her whole before Kyle Lawson's car swung around the road and drove up towards the hotel, she'd do that in a heartbeat, too.

So, why was she still standing here, waiting for him to turn up? She could have cancelled their arrangement. She could have sent a message early this morning, citing some hotel work responsibility that had popped up and made it impossible for her to take time away.

But she hadn't done that, and even now, as she continued peeking through the doors, searching the narrow road for a sign of Kyle's car swinging around the corner, she didn't want to do it, either.

She wanted to know what he'd planned for them both this afternoon, her interest piqued on account of this mystery trip he said she'd enjoy.

But more than that, she just wanted to see Kyle.

The admission made her heart beat much too fast and made her skin prickle with a mixture of nervous excitement and blind terror.

Kyle was handsome, funny, kind, warm-hearted—it was impossible to say otherwise, even if she'd wanted to. And if she was being honest, he'd got under her skin from the moment they'd run into one another on the street in Balmarrie outside the little café. She'd tried to deny it, had pushed back on the flood of attraction she'd felt as soon as their eyes had met. She'd ignored that attraction when Kyle had turned up to inspect the repair job in the enchanted woodland, ignored it when they'd met again that evening and shared pizza at the picnic bench overlooking the bay, because not only did she have no time for romance, but she'd always sworn to herself that she'd never mix business with pleasure.

And yet here she was, waiting for Kyle Lawson—a landscaping contractor who was now working for the Star Castle Hotel—to come and pick her up and whisk her away for a mystery date in a mystery destination.

Meanwhile, back in her office, there were hotel event proposals to work on, revenue estimates to study, supplier contract bids to compare, customer bookings to analyse, plus a thousand other jobs, too.

"I must be insane," Suzanne muttered and turned on her heel away from the doors, pulling her phone from her pocket and searching for Kyle's number so she could call him up and cancel their afternoon together, before he got here and she had to do it face-to-face.

"Well, hello Suzanne! Don't you look lovely?"

Suzanne glanced up in surprise and saw Mrs Wishmore standing right in front of her, so close she almost fell over the woman in her haste to flee the lobby.

"Have you done something new with your hair today, dear?" the older lady asked.

Mrs Wishmore smiled as Suzanne reached up and patted the soft curls she'd worked into her hair when she'd been getting ready that morning, when her thoughts had already been on Kyle and the time they'd be spending together. "I just thought I'd make a bit of an effort with the styling brush today."

"Well, it suits you." Doris's smile widened, and she tilted her head. "So, you're off out this afternoon, are you?"

Suzanne frowned. "What makes you say that?"

"Oh, one of the ladies on the reception desk mentioned you wouldn't be around later today, and because I know how you like to spend so much of your free time here, making sure everything is running smoothly, I assumed you had something nice planned."

When the older lady gave her an expectant look, Suzanne nodded. "I'm seeing Kyle Lawson this afternoon."

"Oh, I see," Mrs Wishmore nodded. "To discuss more matters relating to the repairs in the enchanted woodland?"

"Erm, no. It's not work related. We're… well, we're going out for a nice drive together. Or something like that. I think."

Mrs Wishmore's eyebrows wiggled. "You're going out on a date with Kyle?"

"Possibly. Although it might not be a date. I'm not sure."

Doris gazed at Suzanne for a moment before letting out a low chuckle. "It can be rather exciting when we let go a little and trust the unknown."

"Can it?"

Doris laughed again. "I'm sure you'll have a wonderful afternoon. You deserve a change of scenery, Suzanne, and some well-earned down-time."

"Actually, I was just thinking that I have far too many things to do around here to even think about going gallivanting off for an entire afternoon with someone I hardly even know. I was just about to phone Kyle and cancel."

Mrs Wishmore's expression saddened. "Oh, what a pity. It seems to me that things around the hotel are running nice and smoothly. Are you sure you're needed here today?"

"I have paperwork in my office I should deal with."

"Your paperwork can't wait just a few hours while you have some time for yourself?"

Suzanne frowned at Mrs Wishmore's sensible question. Of course, the paperwork could wait. There was nothing there that had to be dealt with as a matter of urgency. Suzanne knew this, and she also knew that there was always work to be done at the hotel. It was literally never-ending, which was just as it should be. If the work ever ended at the Star Castle Hotel, that would mean they'd gone out of business.

But what if not working as hard as she could meant that things got missed around the hotel, and opportunities overlooked... and they went out of business, anyway? Suzanne wouldn't be able to live with herself if that happened.

It was a worst-case scenario fear but one that always lurked at the back of her mind.

"It feels too indulgent to take time off," Suzanne admitted.

"Well, you know what they say about all work and no play," Mrs Wishmore chuckled. "And who knows? Perhaps a few hours doing something different, something out of your routine, might be just the tonic you need? Perhaps it might even help you be better at what you do here?"

Suzanne knew the woman was making a good point. And yet she still glanced at her phone, wondering if there was time to call Kyle and cancel their meet-up before he arrived.

Before Suzanne could pull up Kyle's number, Mrs Wishmore reached out and laid her hand on Suzanne's arm. As soon as the woman's soft palm rested against her skin, Suzanne felt a calming wave of peacefulness roll through her racing mind.

"Life is always sweeter when we follow our hopes instead of our fears," Mrs Wishmore said. "Do you remember the joy you saw yesterday on the face of that little girl you once were, twirling around in her favourite princess dress just because it made her heart sing to do so? You can still find that joyfulness, Suzanne, if you're willing to allow yourself the space to search for it. But only you can make that choice."

Suzanne let out a low sigh as Mrs Wishmore squeezed her arm. She felt suddenly calm and at peace, in sharp contrast to the agitation that had been surging through her only moments ago.

She'd agreed to Kyle's invitation last night over the phone because she wanted to see him, wanted to spend time with him, wanted to… live a little? Yes, that was it—she wanted to live a little.

And she did want to find joy in her life again. Mrs Wishmore was right about that.

She was also right that only Suzanne had the power to make that happen. No one could *make* her find joy and happiness. She had to *choose* to search for it, and to create it for herself.

The logic of all this was so crystal clear in Suzanne's mind, it made her heart thud hard inside her chest with understanding and desire.

With a final squeeze, Mrs Wishmore released Suzanne's

arm and smiled. "Well, I ought to get back to the reception desk and make myself useful."

Mrs Wishmore crossed the lobby and got busy behind the reception counter, helping a couple who were waiting to be served. Suzanne let out a deep breath she hadn't realised she'd been holding, her gaze on the older woman who'd helped her feel so calm.

How had she done it? Suzanne wondered. How had she helped her push back against those overwhelming waves of doubt that had been racing towards her?

It was a mystery. There was no question about that. But it was also a mystery that Suzanne couldn't seem to focus on too much, because she was staring at the phone in her hand and wondering what she ought to do.

There were still a few minutes left before one o'clock. She could send a message to Kyle if she wanted to and cancel their afternoon plans. She could apologise, make an excuse…

But she didn't want to do that, and she realised she never had wanted to do that, either.

She wanted to see Kyle and spend the afternoon with him. And she wanted to stop making things so hard for herself.

Suzanne had always prided herself on her tough, confident exterior, even when doubt and turmoil raged on the inside. But these past few days, it felt like the strange emotions surging inside her had cracked that brave exterior. Perhaps that wasn't such a bad thing.

Walking back to the hotel entrance, Suzanne glanced through the doors in time to see Kyle's car driving down the road. When he stopped the car and waved at her, his smile warm, her heart beat out a hot tattoo inside her chest.

"Ready to go?" Kyle asked, after opening the passenger door for her, a gesture that made her feel warm and fuzzy all over.

"Ready," she replied with a smile.

"I wasn't sure if you might change your mind," he said, giving her an uncertain look.

"Of course not." She hid her smile as he got back in behind the wheel. "So, where are we going?"

A wide grin lit up Kyle's face. "Let's find out."

THEY DROVE WEST, leaving behind the coastline and following the winding road through the hills where deer roamed and buzzards wheeled on updrafts. The conversation was easy and relaxed, Suzanne pointing out the sights that caught her eye as their journey continued, and Kyle talking about the progress he'd made on the fairy huts last night before his nephew had hauled him indoors to enjoy the epic battle in the superhero film he'd been watching.

When Suzanne asked, for the second time, where they were going, Kyle only grinned.

"You'll find out when we get there. But I promise, you'll love it. Just relax and enjoy the journey."

It wasn't hard to do that, even for Suzanne. The bright blue skies and brooding hills made for spectacular scenery, and the scattering of freshwater lochs they passed caught the sunshine and sparkled so brightly that Suzanne had to put on her sunglasses.

With Kyle behind the wheel, dealing with the twisting roads with ease, she felt herself sink into the journey and the glorious surroundings of the summer-kissed countryside.

At last, Kyle pulled the car off the main road and along a quieter route. Five minutes later, he indicated to turn, and Suzanne read the sign posted beside the T-junction.

"Heatherglen House and Gardens?" she said. "I don't think I've ever heard of this place."

"It only opened earlier this year," Kyle said. "They're just finding their feet. Hill Landscaping did some work for them around the grounds. I brought Jamie along to the grand opening a couple of months ago and he loved it."

"Has he already caught your gardening bug?"

Kyle laughed. "Not particularly. It wasn't the gardens he enjoyed so much as... well, you'll find out soon enough."

Intrigued, Suzanne gazed out the windscreen, wondering what lay ahead. At the end of a twisting narrow road, Kyle steered into a car park bordered by trees and hedges. The place was busy and it took two loops of the car park to find a space. Once they were out of the car, Kyle pointed beyond the lines of parked vehicles to a building a few hundred feet away.

"The house used to belong to some Scottish lord or earl or something like that," Kyle said as the sleek sandstone building came into view. "It lay in disrepair for a long time before being brought back to life."

"Sounds like the story of the Star Castle Hotel. It was a wreck before my grandfather bought it and ploughed everything he had into the rebuild and refurbishment."

"Heatherglen is much smaller than your hotel, as you can see, but the current owners have squeezed in a café and a gift shop, and they're planning to run arts and crafts workshops and a small cookery school. They put a lot of effort into replanting the gardens and making the outdoor areas look good for visitors. They've added a walled kitchen garden, and once it's producing crops, they'll put them to use in the café and cookery school."

As they drew nearer, Suzanne saw the beauty of the place. The sandstone house was perfectly proportioned for the purposes Kyle had described, and she couldn't wait to get inside to see how the rooms looked and how they'd been restored. Beyond the house, gardens spread out on three sides, and even at this distance, she saw how beautiful and lush they looked, with tall pines and firs scenting the air beside broadleaved trees, and sweet pathways winding through flower beds and shrubs.

"Who bought the place? I'm surprised we haven't heard about it over at the hotel. Our guests would love to know all this was here. Holidaymakers often ask for advice about where to visit, and this seems like the perfect place to recommend."

Kyle grinned. "I'm glad you think so. If you haven't heard about any of this yet, then it's because the owners are still finding their way with all of this. It's being run as a social enterprise and many of the people working here are volunteers at the moment."

"Seriously?" Suzanne was astonished. "That's amazing."

"I think so, too. They're a long way from making any profits, but when they do, they'll plough them back into the business and into building it further. I get the impression there had been interest in the house and land from a development company who planned to build new houses here, but locals from the surrounding towns and villages got together and put an alternative offer to the owner. Once they got the backing of the council and some other big voluntary organisations in the area, the previous owner was persuaded to sell to them instead."

"It sounds like you know a lot about the place?"

"Like I said, Hill Landscaping was hired to take care of some of the work around the gardens. The bare bones of the landscaping were solid, but there was a lot of overgrowth, and some pathways needed attention. While I was working here, I got talking with the folks on the community enterprise board and learned a lot about what they're doing and what they're planning for the future. There's more gardening and landscaping to be done beyond this main entrance area that we can see here, but the board had to prioritise how they use their resources. There are volunteers working on other sections we can't see from here, and they're using some of their income to pay apprentice gardeners to learn the ropes as part of their social enterprise commitments. I volunteer my time and know-how for a few hours a month to help with the training."

Suzanne smiled in surprise. "That's a lovely thing to do."

As he blushed and frowned, Kyle shrugged off her compliment. "It's nothing."

"Of course it's not nothing. And this whole place looks wonderful. I can't wait to see inside the house and take a tour of the gardens."

"Actually, it's not the house I've brought you here to see, or the gardens."

Suzanne gave him a quizzical look. "I don't understand."

Kyle grinned. "This place has an amazing secret up its sleeve, which is the real reason I thought you'd like to come here."

Even more intrigued now, Suzanne followed Kyle through a brick arch entrance cut into the low wall that ran around the front of the grounds. They passed through the gardens that were bursting with pink hardy geraniums and nodding foxgloves, and framed by clipped hedges, before taking a winding pathway that led alongside a stretch of wildflower meadow, Kyle pointing out some of the specimens flourishing there and talking about the business's commitment to creating a diverse ecosystem on the site that would benefit the wildlife.

A clutch of mature trees bordered the wildflower meadow on its northern edge. As they neared the silver birches and sycamores, Suzanne realised she could hear tinkling music coming from somewhere.

"Can you hear that music?" she asked Kyle. "Where's it coming from?"

Kyle's expression broke into a grin. "That's the surprise I brought you here to see."

The tinkling music grew louder with every step. When at last they passed beyond the tall trees at the edge of the wildflower meadow and into an open expanse of green field beyond it, Suzanne's eyes flew wide at what she found there.

Spread across the flat, grassy field was an old-fashioned fun fair, the calliope music drifting on the summer breeze from an array of fairground rides. There was a carousel with painted horses, a small Ferris wheel, a teacup ride, Waltzers, and a miniature railway ride with cheerful engines that trundled around the far side of the field.

Suzanne gasped in astonishment.

"This is amazing!" she said, taking it all in. "I can't believe there's a fairground all the way out here in the middle of nowhere!"

"Neither can anyone else," Kyle said, glancing around at the rides with a wry smile on his face. "One of the volunteers on the social enterprise board has a passion for fairgrounds, and he worked hard to make it possible for one to be hosted here during the summer months. These are all old-fashioned rides, many of them in need of a lot of tender loving care, so they're using some of the income generated from the fairground to run volunteer programmes that train young people in the mechanical and engineering skills they need to keep everything working."

"I can't take this in. What an amazing place."

As Suzanne looked at the fairground rides, and the cute candy floss cart and hot dog stand, and the colourful booth selling toffee apples and bags of marshmallows and other sweet treats, she saw the broad smiles on the faces of the people walking around and revelled in the relaxed atmosphere of the place. There were families with young children, older couples meandering around and holding hands, and groups of young teenagers having fun at the hook-the-duck booth and the target range. The people staffing the rides and games and concessions were smiling and joking with one another and with the customers, and although the fairground was tiny compared to most other amusement and theme parks, Suzanne couldn't imagine anyone looking any happier than the folks milling around in this tucked-away little field right now.

"This place has a wonderful feeling," Suzanne said.

"I think so too," Kyle said. He pointed to the carousel ride with its painted horses. "Can I interest you in a turn on the carousel?"

Suzanne glanced at the carousel, where the galloping horses were slowing down as the current ride drew to an end. The coloured lights of the ride danced in the mirrored panels of the carousel and the lovely music played, drawing fun-seekers near.

"Aren't the rides just for the children?" Suzanne asked, taking in the short line of little ones waiting for their turn.

"Of course not. Look, there are plenty of grown-ups waiting to get on. The kids will be lucky they don't get elbowed out of the way, judging by the looks on the faces of some of these adults."

Suzanne laughed as she looked further along the line of people waiting to board the carousel ride. It was true—many of the adults looked more excited than the children they were accompanying.

Kyle gestured towards the end of the carousel queue. "Shall we?"

She didn't have to think about it for long. "Yes, let's do it."

By the time they'd joined the back of the queue, the carousel was already emptying its previous riders from the horses, and the attendant staffing the little metal fence that encircled the ride was ushering new customers up and inviting them to choose their horses for their exciting fairground adventure.

Once they'd climbed onto the platform, Suzanne picked a pale yellow horse with blue flowers painted along its mane and sides. Kyle hopped up on the one beside hers, a bright orange horse with purple polka dots for decoration.

No sooner had Suzanne secured her hold on the gold-painted pole that propelled the horse up and down than the ride began moving around, quickly picking up speed.

Suzanne laughed as her yellow horse galloped and the carousel spun and the fairground music tinkled around them. The little children riding the nearby horses alongside their parents were screeching with delight while their parents held them tight and laughed as they attempted awkward selfie shots with their phones. With the summer breeze in her hair and the sweet smells of the fairground wafting around her with every turn of the carousel, Suzanne let the sheer delight of the moment sink deep inside her.

This is fun! a surprised voice whispered inside her head. *Fun, fun, fun!*

"How did you know I'd love this?" Suzanne shouted across to Kyle as the music around them grew louder.

"Lucky guess," he grinned. "But come on, who doesn't love riding carousel horses?"

His smile was warm, his eyes sparkling with humour as they rode around and around. When the horses slowed and the carousel ride stopped, Suzanne was sorry it was over.

"It's been far too long since I was at the fairground," she said as they exited the carousel and turned to watch the next clutch of children and adults climbing on board with excitement. "I'd forgotten how fast those horses go."

"If you think the horses are fast, you haven't seen

anything yet." Kyle pointed to the Waltzer ride going at full pelt on the other side of the small field, its curved cars dipping and spinning as they hurtled up and down on the undulating platform that spun around and around. "Want to find out if we can survive a turn on the Waltzers without sustaining a broken rib or two?"

"How could I say no to that offer?"

Kyle laughed as they crossed the fairground and waited their turn for the next ride to begin. Looking at the faces of the people disembarking after the last spin had finished, Suzanne thought they all looked rather queasy, and was glad she hadn't offered to buy hot dogs or candy floss before risking the ferocious Waltzers. The last thing she wanted to do was throw up on Kyle on account of a fairground ride.

When it was their turn to board the Waltzers, their first challenge was actually getting into the car. The curved metal car kept swinging up and down on the tilted platform, even although the ride was stationary, and Suzanne more or less fell into the thing in the end, her balance upended. The ride attendant fixed the safety bar into place while Suzanne was still trying to right herself in the seat, and as the platform started moving and the car started tilting and turning, she found herself thrown against Kyle's side, where she remained stuck in a helpless fit of giggles.

"Eek!" she cried as the Waltzer car raced up and down the undulating platform, while spinning around and around at the same time as the music blared and the lights flashed and the world beyond was whipped into a blur. "I think I'm going to die!"

"Me first!" Kyle yelled as he clutched onto the safety barrier. "I think you punctured my lung with your elbow when you slid along the seat and crashed into me!"

The expression on Kyle's face—a hilarious mixture of

mock agony and genuine alarm as the ride got faster—sent Suzanne into another fit of wheezing giggles.

When their car changed direction mid-spin as it plunged down the tilting, racing platform, the force of it sent Suzanne sliding along the slippery plastic seat to the other side of the car, with Kyle in uncontrolled pursuit. Laughing hysterically as she was thrown against the barrier, she let out a grunt of shocked surprise as Kyle fell against her, pinning her to the edge of the car.

"Ouch!" she croaked helplessly between gales of laughter.

"Sorry!" Kyle yelled, his eyes wide as their car spun out of control. "I think they've put a deranged psychopath in charge of operating this thing!"

Hysterical now, Suzanne could barely get air into her lungs because of all the laughing, and when she at last got her voice working all that came out was a strangled grunt that had Kyle peering at her in alarm.

"Are you okay?" he wheezed as the spinning car sent him hurtling back across the plastic seat again.

She managed a nod before the spinning car whipped her back along the seat too, once more sending Suzanne crashing into Kyle's side.

"Ooft!" he grunted.

"Sorry!"

Kyle's laughter mixed with her own, his eyes bright. As the Waltzer car spun and the lights flashed and the music played, Suzanne let the motion and the noise and the fun roll over her.

Her mind filled with that long-forgotten memory she'd conjured the day before, of herself as a little girl, twirling around the old hotel ballroom in her favourite pink princess dress, caught up in the blissful moment and the joy of twirling.

Now, as she sat in the spinning Waltzer car, she realised

she was twirling once more, twirling and twirling around on the fairground ride and simply letting herself fall into the moment... and she was loving every second.

The memory of herself as a little girl dancing in the ballroom mixed with the sensation of the spinning Waltzer car and the colourful fairground lights and the cheerful calliope music and herself in the midst of it all... those two images dissolved together inside her head and Suzanne felt a burst of joy rush through like she hadn't felt for a long time.

I'm happy right now, her mind whispered. *This is what fun feels like. And this is what it means to simply live in the moment.*

She laughed and twirled, the fairground music played and the lights danced, and a weight she'd been carrying inside herself somehow slipped away.

In that moment, Suzanne felt light and alive and completely wonderful.

At last, the Waltzer car slowed and the ride came to a stop. Kyle climbed out and, as the car was still spinning on its axis, he held out his hand to help Suzanne up. She grabbed hold, and his strong fingers closing over hers sent a hot bolt of electricity rippling over her skin, making her blush.

Once they'd stepped off the undulating platform and were back on even ground, Kyle's hand slipped free from hers. They stood for a moment, looking awkward and glancing around them at the fairground.

"What do you feel like trying next?" Kyle asked.

"I like the look of the miniature Ferris wheel," Suzanne said. "After the Waltzers, I think we need a change of pace."

"Sounds good to me."

They crossed to the little Ferris wheel, Suzanne aware of Kyle's arms swinging next to hers as they walked, his hand so tantalisingly close to brushing against her fingers. She cut her gaze towards him, taking in his tall frame and broad shoulders, his muscular arms bronzed from endless days spent working outdoors, and the way his long stride ate up the ground beneath his feet.

When they reached the entrance for the Ferris wheel, Suzanne cleared her throat to bring herself back together again and shake off the flush the man had sent cascading over her skin. "This is my treat," she said, handing money to the young attendant at the admission booth, who gave her change before gesturing towards the steps that led up to the wheel.

They clambered inside the bright red carriage that was empty and waiting for passengers. Once the door clicked shut, they were swung up into the air a few feet to allow the next passengers to board. Moments later, the ride began, sweeping them up into the air, the carriage rocking as the wheel turned.

When they reached the top of the ride, Suzanne looked down to see the pretty wildflower meadow on the far side of the fairground, and the meandering gardens that bordered Heatherglen House. Although the Ferris wheel was small and compact and didn't reach too high into the air, she was still awed by the sight of the brooding hills around them and the rolling landscape dappled with tiny freshwater lochs and woodland and sparkling streams.

"It's so beautiful up here," she said.

"It is."

Kyle's voice was soft and something in his tone made Suzanne turn from the view towards him. His expression made her heart clutch, the way his gaze had darkened as he looked at her, his eyes locked on hers.

He looked at her hand resting in her lap, then reached out and threaded his fingers into hers. Suzanne's breath caught at the warmth of his skin and the way it just felt so *right* to have her hand tucked inside his strong palm, as if it belonged there.

Her gaze fell to his mouth, her heart beating so hard inside her chest that she could hardly breathe. When Kyle shifted closer on the seat, she caught a whiff of the spicy scent on his neck and it sent her mind flying up into the sky.

One exquisite moment passed as they hung suspended at the top of the Ferris wheel, gazing into each other's eyes.

And then Kyle dipped his mouth towards hers and kissed her in a way that made every nerve ending in her body sing with pleasure.

The Ferris wheel turned and the summer breeze whipped her hair and Suzanne sank into the kiss and the lush sensation of Kyle's lips on hers.

When the wheel jolted to a sudden stop at the top of the ride, they pulled apart in surprise and laughed. Kyle ran his fingers over her cheek and along her neck, and Suzanne had to resist the desire to purr in response to his touch.

"I've wanted to kiss you since the moment you hurtled head first into me on the street in Balmarrie," he said.

"Violent collisions are your thing, are they?"

He grinned, wrapping a strand of her hair around his finger. "You made quite an impression."

"So did you."

His gaze turned thoughtful. "Not enough of one to stop you turning me down the first time I asked you out for a drink."

"I thought it was the right thing to do. I thought it was what I wanted. I was wrong."

Their carriage swung forward as the Ferris wheel juddered into motion before stopping again just as quickly as it had started.

"Do you think we're stuck up here?" Suzanne laughed, glancing out of the carriage.

"If we are, I can think of worse places to be stuck."

Kyle squeezed her hand and smiled, his gaze filled with a

heady mixture of romance and intrigue that made Suzanne's head spin. She wondered how she'd ever been able to deny her attraction to this man. That she'd done exactly that for almost four days was nothing short of astonishing, considering the excitement he was now sparking inside her.

Why had she tried to convince herself that she didn't want this in her life, this romance and this fun, and this man who'd given both those things to her? After only a few hours in his company, it already felt as if an empty place inside her was being filled up.

She thought of what Mrs Wishmore had said yesterday in the ballroom, after Suzanne's strange reimagining of herself as a child in that princess dress she'd loved so much.

You are remembering what life is supposed to be all about, Doris had said.

Suddenly, Suzanne thought she might understand what Mrs Wishmore had meant.

With a jolt, the Ferris wheel started moving again. When the ride was over, and they'd left behind the bright red carriage and were making their way across the small fairground, Kyle once more slipped his hand into hers.

"Can I buy you some lunch at the café back at Heatherglen House?" he asked. "They have a little outdoor patio and we could enjoy the sunshine while it lasts."

"I'd like that." She squeezed his hand and smiled. "Thanks for bringing me to the fairground, Kyle. It was a lovely surprise."

"Did you have fun?"

"I had a lot of fun."

He returned her smile as they left the fairground behind. "See? And there you were thinking you'd lost the knack and that you'd never have any fun ever again for as long as you lived."

"I know," she winced, wondering what he must now think

of her and all the insane nonsense she'd spouted last night during their phone call. "Can you chalk it up to over-reaction mixed in with a lot of over-thinking? Or maybe just pretend I never said anything like that in the first place?"

He answered with an easy shrug. "Why would I do that? You meant what you said last night. It was something that worried you. If I helped show that you don't have to worry about it, and that you can kick back and have some fun anytime you want to, then that's all that matters, right?"

Suzanne could only smile in response, breathing in the scent of the wildflowers as they walked through the meadow, her mind filling with thoughts of a lazy lunch enjoyed while basking beneath the sunshine with a man who made her head spin.

ON THEIR WAY to the café, an older man in gardening overalls who was working in one of the herbaceous borders spied Kyle and raised his trowel in the air by way of greeting. Kyle introduced him as Sam, a volunteer with the social enterprise business. After chatting for a few minutes, Kyle excused himself to accompany the man to the greenhouses and sheds at the back of the estate, so he could deal with the errand that had brought him out here and which he'd mentioned to Suzanne on the phone the night before. Happy to tag along rather than wait for him at the café, Suzanne followed the men. When they reached the greenhouses and sheds, she watched Kyle assist Sam with a complicated plant dividing job, amazed by Kyle's patience as he demonstrated the technique and walked his friend through the process.

It was obvious that the older man appreciated the help and the lesson. That task done, Kyle helped Sam with several other jobs where his advice and skills were required, earning himself a clap on the back once they were finished along with a firm hand shake.

"You're a star, Kyle," Sam told him as they made their way back towards the house. "I'll practice these dividing techniques this afternoon on the stock we want to bring on, and hopefully we'll see results once they take and we have lots of plants to plug into our beds."

"The more you can cut and divide from your current stocks, and grow from seeds, the more money you'll save," Kyle said. "And it'll be good for the apprentices to have several folks here they can learn from, and for all you gardeners here to develop a solid pool of knowledge amongst yourselves."

"Coffee and cake is on us, to say thanks for your help," Sam informed Kyle when they reached the café. "It's the least we can do." When they went inside the pretty café nestled inside the house, the man gestured to the woman working behind the counter. "Marjory, complimentary coffee and cake for Kyle and his young lady friend."

"Right you are," Marjory replied, gesturing to the spread of home baking displayed on the counter. "We've got plenty to choose from, Kyle. Just let me know what you'd like."

"That's not necessary," Kyle said, but Sam waved this off.

"You've been generous with your time and help," Sam said. "The least we can do is give you a cuppa and a slice of Marjory's lemon drizzle cake, and that's that." Sam smiled at Suzanne. "It was nice to meet you, love. Hope we'll see you again here soon. Right, I'll get back to my plant dividing, now that I know what I'm supposed to be doing."

Suzanne said goodbye to the cheerful man and grinned at Kyle. "It's nice what you're doing here, helping the staff and volunteers."

He shrugged off her compliment. "It's no trouble. I enjoy passing on what I know. And if any of the young gardeners they're apprenticing here are any good, it might help me find casual staff for when..." He paused and waved a hand in the air. "Well, for when I go into business for myself."

Suzanne saw the blush on his face and the way he cleared his throat. "That's a great idea to keep an eye out for skilled people you can rely on before you've set up for yourself. That way, once you're ready to hire, you'll already know who you want to consider for the jobs you have."

"I won't be able to hire people permanently or full-time, not at first. But if I can find reliable folk who know what they're doing and who are willing to work casual days here and there, it might be good for me and it might be good for them, too."

"It sounds like a win-win situation."

"Maybe." He waved a hand at the café counter. "Anyway, I said we'd get some lunch. Let's see what looks good."

At the counter, they studied the blackboard menu before ordering soup and salad combos, along with slices of Marjory's home-baked lemon drizzle cake to enjoy with coffee afterwards. When Marjory refused to add the cake and coffee to Kyle's bill, despite his insistence, he slid a ten-pound note into the donation tin beside the till, earning himself an exasperated *tsk!* from Marjory.

Suzanne pulled a twenty-pound note from her purse and added it to the donation tin, keen to make a contribution to the wonderful work being done here and to support the local people who were making it happen.

"You didn't have to do that," Kyle said as they stepped outside and found a patio table in the sunshine beside a tub of bright summer flowers.

"This is a terrific place, and I hope it thrives. After the lovely time I've had here already, a few pounds in their donation tin is the least I can do."

While they waited for their lunch order to arrive, they

basked in the warmth of the sunshine and listened to the bees buzzing in the nearby flowers. Suzanne glanced around at the busy café patio and the happy customers tucking into their food, and the folk meandering through the pretty gardens beyond, chatting with the volunteers and staff who were busy working in the borders.

"This place has a wonderful atmosphere," Suzanne said. "I'm glad you brought me here. It was a lovely surprise."

"I'm glad." Kyle grinned and arched an eyebrow. "And if you're interested, I think the team here would love to hear any advice you have to share about running a hospitality business. Maybe you could offer to come and chat with them some day and take a look at their business plans?"

Suzanne was about to say she doubted she had time in her busy hotel schedule for something like that, but snapped her mouth closed before the words got out. When she tamped down on her automatic response, she realised she'd quite enjoy meeting the folk behind this lovely place, hearing more about how they'd done all this and what they planned for the future. There were good people here, working hard to do something worthwhile for their local community, and she'd like to find out if she could help them.

"I'd like that," Suzanne said. "Once the hotel's summer ball is over, and we're clear of the busiest time of the high season, we can set something up. It would be nice to meet the people running this place and see if I can be of any use."

Kyle's gaze softened as she said this. Maybe he'd thought she'd turn down the idea. Seeing the look on his face—surprise, perhaps, mixed with something else she couldn't quite pin down—made her glad she'd said yes.

"They'd love that," Kyle smiled. "Thank you."

Suzanne blushed at his gaze, that deep look in his eyes doing strange things to her. "These are pretty gardens," she said, glancing at their surroundings. "Tell me what you've worked on here. Where are your signature touches around the place?"

"I don't know if you'd call them signature touches, but..." He pointed to where a pathway wound beneath a series of wooden arbours before disappearing into the shrubbery. "Those arbours were my idea. When Hill Landscaping was hired earlier this year, the budget was limited and there was only enough money to deal with the hard landscaping that needed the most attention. Once we'd fulfilled our contract, I talked with the team here and suggested they might want to think about adding some structural features that, with time, would give these gardens character. Arbours and arches are a good way to do that. People like wandering beneath them when they visit ornamental gardens. It turns a walk around some flower borders into a fun adventure, whether the visitors are old or young. It's something memorable. Arbours, arches, bridges... well, you know that thanks to the little bridge over the stream in your hotel's enchanted woodland."

Suzanne grinned. "The children love racing back and forth across that little bridge."

"Exactly. The team had great ideas for plants and flowers they wanted to grow here, but they didn't have the know-how for structural garden design, and they didn't have the budget to hire someone to do it for them, either. So, I suggested they start small and build out around the gardens closest to the house. It made sense to put their resources into structural features that people would see from the café and the patio, because that would create the biggest visitor impact, at least to begin with. I suggested a series of arbours would give the garden some height and variety and interest. It's a fun addition to the pathway, and it's also something the gardeners can train their plants around. I designed the arbours and helped the team here build them, and the volunteer gardeners got to work deciding which roses they wanted to grow on them. There are a few rose experts on their team, so the plants are in good hands. In fact, they're already thriving."

Suzanne glanced over at the three arbours where they arched over the pathway, their thoughtful positioning drawing visitors deeper into the gardens. The wooden arbour structures were solid and attractive, and the roses growing there were already blooming, even although the shrubs were still small and barely reached the halfway point of the arbour's sides. The effect was impossibly lovely and romantic, and Suzanne could see how it would only improve with time—the elaborate lattice work of the arbours, the sweet pink and yellow roses nodding in the breeze, the curve of the pathway as it led further into the garden... it was all incredibly beautiful and charming.

"It looks fantastic," Suzanne said. "You have such an amazing talent, Kyle. How did you get into gardening?"

Before he could answer, a young waitress arrived with their food, setting down bowls of vegetable soup and salad plates before promising to return with their cakes and coffees once they'd finished eating. Suzanne sampled the creamy soup and wasn't in the least surprised by how good it tasted. It was obvious to her now that the people in charge of this place had something special on their hands and that they were dedicated to offering their guests a fantastic experience from start to finish.

"My dad's a keen gardener," Kyle said after sampling his ham salad. "He had an allotment when I was younger, and we'd potter around there tending to the tomatoes and root veg. He preferred his veggie crops to flowers, but once it was clear that I had an interest, he got me started in our tiny back garden with some beginner plants, showing me how to grow from seed, and how to prune and divide plants, and all that stuff. I loved it."

At his fond grin, Suzanne smiled.

"While my friends at school were getting into gaming and music, I was the nerd with the dirty fingernails who enjoyed digging in the dirt and comparing hardy perennials." He laughed and ate more of his food before continuing. "For my twelfth birthday, my parents took me to London to visit Kew Gardens. I loved every second of that trip. I'd never seen anything like it in my entire life. It just blew my mind—the glasshouses and the endless plant specimens, the layout and design, the *feel* of the place as we walked around the grounds. When it was time to leave, my parents had to drag me out through the gates. My sister, Erin, still talks about that trip sometimes, laughing at how she and mum spent most of the time in the café and the gift shop, while I wandered around gawping at the plants and asking my father a thousand questions, most of which he couldn't answer."

He laughed at the memory, the soft sound like music in Suzanne's ears. In his love and passion for gardens, she saw reflected her own love and passion for her family's hotel. Being here with Kyle, and talking this way, was like being with a kindred spirit.

"Anyway," Kyle continued. "From that moment on, I knew I wanted to be a gardener when I grew up. I spent all my spare time gardening and working on plant projects and experiments, and when I left school, I studied horticulture at college. I know how lucky I am to do something I'm passionate about for a living. I love growing plants and turning neglected pieces of land into something beautiful. It makes me feel like I'm doing something worthwhile." He frowned at this and shifted in his seat. "Maybe that sounds a bit dumb."

"It doesn't. You *are* doing something worthwhile, something worthwhile and wonderful, too."

Suzanne watched Kyle give that awkward shrug of his before dipping his spoon into his soup.

"And after hearing you talk like that," Suzanne added, "I don't know why you haven't already started up your own landscaping business. Given how much you love what you do, I'm sure it won't be anything other than a huge success."

Kyle smiled and ate some of his food. A thoughtful look crossed his face. "That's the dream, that it will be a success once I get going with it. I know I'm ready to make the jump. At least I think I am."

"So, you should do it. What's stopping you?"

For a moment, Suzanne wondered if she might have crossed a line, judging by the frown on Kyle's face. Setting up a new business was no small matter, and it wasn't cheap, either. For all she knew, he was still pulling together the money he'd need to get a new business up off the ground, or having trouble getting a loan from the bank. The last thing she wanted was to embarrass him by getting into financial details he might not feel comfortable talking about with her. They might have shared a kiss filled with a lot of heat and promise back on the Ferris wheel in the fairground, but that didn't mean Kyle was ready to share every personal detail with her.

So, when he finally answered her question, his response left her more than a little surprised.

"I was all set to hand in my notice to Hill Landscaping and get going with my own business," Kyle said. "But then my sister's husband walked out on her and their son, and now I have to be there for them. I *want* to be there for them," he corrected himself, emphatically. "Our parents moved away from Balmarrie a few years ago and are now retired near Edinburgh, and when Erin's marriage collapsed and she couldn't afford her house anymore, I know it upset them not to be closer to her to help her through the tough time. So, I told Erin to come and stay with me until she and Jamie get themselves settled in a new place. Until that happens, I'm holding off on making the big move with my business."

Suzanne gazed at him for a long beat. "That's an amazing thing to do for your sister, Kyle—to put your plans on hold to help her out like that."

"An amazing thing to do for my sister would be to drive to her ex-husband's new house, where he lives with his new girlfriend, and punch his face in." He let out an irritated laugh. "But I'm smart enough to know that while doing something like that might make me feel better, it won't help Erin or Jamie, and it would only make things worse. Jamie's gone through enough without seeing his uncle being hauled off by the police and charged with assault."

Suzanne's heart went out to Kyle's little nephew. She thought of the little boy who'd been shovelling pizza into his mouth at the picnic bench on Balmarrie waterfront a few nights ago. He was a sweet kid, and he must be confused and hurt because of his father walking out on their family.

Although it was a different situation, Suzanne remembered her own dawning confusion as a child when she realised that most of her friends at school had two parents, not one, and while she hadn't missed having a father—because you couldn't miss what you'd never had—she'd been aware of feeling different from her friends because of it. Kyle's nephew was probably experiencing all sorts of emotions and doubts about what had happened between his parents, and wondering why his father was no longer living with them.

Kyle was putting his sister and nephew above his own needs and his own ambitions, and all the things he wanted in life. Suzanne was beginning to realise just how much more there was to Kyle Lawson beyond his obvious talents as a gardener and landscaper. He was loyal to his family and generous in helping others. He had a big heart, and Suzanne understood how easy it would be to fall head-over-heels for him.

"Anyway, once things settle down for Erin and Jamie," Kyle said, "and I know they're doing okay and finding their way again, then I'll have all the time in the world to think about my new business and get things moving with it. It won't be easy drumming up custom and finding clients to work with, and that will take a big time commitment I can't make right now."

Suzanne ate some of the salmon salad she'd ordered as an idea rolled through her head. "We've been thinking of redesigning parts of the landscaping around our restaurant terrace at the hotel. Our grounds crew are terrific, but they aren't designers and that sort of work is outside their remit. Once you're up and running with your new business, we should discuss the job and whether you'd be interested in it."

Kyle laid down his napkin, his eyes wide. "I'd love to. There are lots of ideas we could come up with, and it's a terrific terrace already with a lot of potential, but…"

"But what?"

"Ah…" Kyle's expression looked troubled. "The thing is, when you hired Hill Landscaping to come out and take care of the woodland repairs, my boss, Frank, hoped the job might lead to more work from the hotel in the future. In fact, he low-balled the price he gave you because he wanted to make a good impression so that you'd think of his company if you needed work done again. Much as I'd love to jump at the chance of a potential customer for my new business, especially one like the Star Castle Hotel, it wouldn't be fair if I poached the work from Frank."

Suzanne blinked. Kyle Lawson just kept surprising her.

"Your boss is lucky to have a loyal employee like you, Kyle. If you're still working for him when we're ready to explore our terrace plans in more detail, that's fine. But if you've gone out on your own by that point, then we'll be coming to you to discuss the project and get your quote, and your old boss will just have to live with it."

Kyle barked out a laugh, but his expression sobered. "There's another reason I might feel unsure about accepting a job from the hotel."

"What's that?" Suzanne asked, confused.

"I'd like us to spend more time together, Suzanne. I'd like to see if there might be something here between us."

She couldn't help but catch her breath at the intent in his words and the look in his eyes as he said this.

"But I get the impression you don't like mixing your business life with your personal life," he continued. "I respect that and I understand it. But I don't want some potential landscaping job for my new business getting in the way of whatever might happen here with us."

A few days ago, Suzanne wouldn't even have imagined she'd be sitting at this café table in this pretty garden with this lovely man. She'd thought it was the last thing she wanted. Now, though, it felt like the ground had shifted beneath her feet.

"I'd like to see you again too, Kyle, and spend more time with you," she said. "Not just because we had fun today, when I least expected it, but because..." Pausing, she caught her breath as his gaze stayed focused on her. "The way you look at me, it's..."

Wonderful. Heart-stopping. Head-spinning. All those things and so much more.

But the words couldn't capture the way he made her feel. And so, instead of talking any more, Suzanne reached across the table, taking Kyle's strong, rough hand into hers, and then leaned closer and kissed him.

His mouth was soft and waiting for hers. Around them,

the birds sang and the bees buzzed and the sunshine beat down. The kiss only lasted a moment, but for Suzanne it spun out into forever.

When Kyle brushed his lips against her cheek and pulled back, the smile at his mouth lit up his eyes. "So, that's a yes to a second date?"

Suzanne laughed. "Yes."

"Good."

That darkly intense look filled his eyes again, making Suzanne's stomach flip. It had been a long time since a man had surprised her and bowled her over like this. Maybe too long. She couldn't remember when she'd last had so much fun or felt such a deep attraction to a man.

Once they'd finished lunch, they left the café and gardens behind and returned to Kyle's car. As they reached the car park, Suzanne's phone started pinging. Pulling it from her bag, she realised she hadn't even thought of her phone—or work, or anything else for that matter—since the moment Kyle had picked her up back at the hotel. Nor, she realised with a frown, had she heard her phone ping or ring during the whole afternoon, which was more than a little unusual.

Now, as she looked at the phone screen, a string of missed calls and unread messages raced down the display as they arrived, one pinging after the other.

"I forgot to mention that the phone reception here isn't too good," Kyle said as he pulled out his own phone and checked the screen. "I usually get pinged with something I've missed as soon as I hit the car park."

But Suzanne barely heard what he was saying. All she could focus on was the long string of missed calls from her mother.

And the long string of missed text messages, each one more urgent than the last.

Suzanne, why aren't you answering your phone. Call me!

Suzanne, I need you to call me ASAP.

I don't know where you are Suzanne, but this is an emergency. PHONE ME!

"Hey, is everything okay?" Kyle asked, concern flooding his expression as he watched her stabbing at the phone screen with shaking fingers.

But she didn't answer, her mind racing with worry about those missed messages and what they might mean. As she dialled her mother's phone and listened to the ringing on the other end, her heart hammered in her chest as she thought about what might be wrong.

Her mother would never call repeatedly, or send all those urgent text messages, unless there was a serious problem.

At last, her mother's voice came down the line. "Suzanne, I've been trying to reach you for the past hour. Why didn't you answer your phone?"

"I didn't have any phone signal, I'm sorry. What's happened?"

Her mother sounded upset, and Imogen Kennedy never sounded upset. Suzanne braced herself for whatever she was about to hear.

"Suzanne…" There was an anguished sigh on the other end of the line before her mother spoke again. "There's been a fire at the hotel."

CHAPTER FIFTEEN

Suzanne hardly said a word during the drive back to Balmarrie. Her mind was a whir, filled with anxiety and panic. Even if she'd wanted to talk, she doubted she would've been able to string a single coherent sentence together.

The only thing she wanted was to return to the Star Castle Hotel as quickly as possible. Even with Kyle pushing the speed limit along the country roads that led back towards the coast, she still wished he could drive faster. Every time he slowed for traffic, her foot pumped pointlessly at an imaginary accelerator in the passenger footwell, so desperate was she to get home.

During the thirty minute journey, Kyle glanced her way from time to time, and asked if she was okay. Each time, all she could do was nod and offer a polite smile. Her brain was too busy processing what her mother had told her on the phone.

The fire at the Star Castle Hotel had broken out in a ground floor room in the south-eastern guest wing, which Suzanne's grandfather had built onto the main castle fifteen years ago. No one was injured and everyone who'd been inside the building had got out safely; Suzanne had almost collapsed to the ground with relief when her mother had told her this vital information.

However, what she didn't know was how serious the fire was or how badly it had damaged the building. Before Imogen had got into any of those details, she'd had to end the call in order to return to managing the unfolding crisis on their hands, hurriedly telling Suzanne to get back to the hotel as quickly as possible so she could help.

Now, as they sped along the road, the trees and hedgerows just a blur in the side windows, Suzanne's stomach clenched with fear about what awaited her back at the hotel. Had the fire been extinguished or was it still burning? Had the firefighters arrived in time to prevent the guest wing from being reduced to a scene of smouldering devastation? Did the hotel's fire evacuation plan work properly or had there been problems that might have endangered people? Were the hotel staff okay? Were the guests being looked after?

And why, oh why, hadn't she been there at her beloved hotel when she was needed the most?

Suzanne tried to bite back against that bitter thought, but it wasn't easy. While a major incident was unfolding at the hotel, she'd been cavorting around in a fairground with some man she'd just met, and lazing around in the garden café while making bedroom eyes at him.

Shame and regret boiled inside her. She should never have agreed to this silly excursion today with Kyle. She should never have bleated on at him during their phone call last night about how she just wanted to have some fun before she forgot what having fun actually meant. As deputy manager of the hotel, she couldn't afford those kinds of frivolities, and the shocking news her mother had just delivered only proved it. Running a successful family business like the Star Castle Hotel meant she had to make sacrifices, just like her mother and grandfather had done before her.

Why had she thought she should be any different?

At last, Kyle steered the car into Balmarrie and on towards the hotel. When they reached the road that ran to the hotel entrance, Suzanne gasped at the sight of so many fire engines and police cars parked there. Before Kyle had even stopped the car, she was already unclipping her seat belt and opening the passenger door.

"Suzanne, wait!" she heard him call out as she leapt from the vehicle, but she didn't stop.

She *couldn't* stop.

Leaving him behind, she broke into a run. Outside the main entrance to the hotel, there were small crowds of staff and guests lingering on the pathway, and uniformed police officers talking to some of them and writing in notebooks. Acrid smoke hung in the air, the smell dark and foreboding. There was a grim buzz around the place, sparked by the excitement of the day's events.

Because of its position on the far side of the grounds, the guest annex was obscured from the front of the hotel, and every hurried step Suzanne took felt like it lasted a lifetime as she pounded around the main building, wondering what sight awaited her.

When she ran around the side of the hotel and saw the guest annex for the first time, it was like a punch to the gut.

The wall outside the window of one of the ground floor rooms was blackened with soot. The tattered remains of a pair of burned curtains flapped inside the sagging window aperture, and the room beyond looked dark with devastation. The air smelled of danger and disaster, of water and fire.

But as Suzanne barrelled towards her mother, who she'd

spied talking to one of the firefighters, she had the presence of thought to register that there were no flames still licking the building, no sign of flickering heat inside that dark hotel bedroom. In fact, she saw the firefighters were hauling hoses and equipment back towards one of the parked fire engines, their actions calm and measured.

Even as she kept running, she sagged with relief at the realisation that the building was not still on fire. The firefighters had dealt with the emergency, and the emergency was now over.

During the anxious drive back with Kyle, Suzanne had been gripped by the terrible notion that when she'd finally received her mother's messages and spoken to her on the phone, the hotel had still been burning, the fire still raging, and that Imogen hadn't wanted to tell her so, knowing that the news would be too devastating to hear that way, and that the scale of the emergency would have meant that Imogen couldn't talk on the phone to her daughter anyway, bringing her up to speed about what was happening.

Now, though, Suzanne saw that the fire was out. There was damage, a lot of damage, maybe more than she could see as she ran towards the guest annex. But things were in hand.

And there, in the middle of it all, was Imogen, talking calmly to one of the firefighters. The sight of her mother's steady poise and straight shoulders and no-nonsense expression tamped down against the blind panic Suzanne had felt raging inside her for the last thirty minutes.

"Mother!" Suzanne called out as she drew near.

Imogen turned away from the firefighter she'd been talking to. When she saw Suzanne, relief flooded her face.

"Suzanne, you're here at last," Imogen said. "Where on earth have you been?" Before she could answer, her mother frowned and waved the question away. "Never mind, we don't have time for that right now. I need you to get up to reception and help the staff move our guests out of this part of the guest wing and find other bedrooms for them."

Her mother was about to turn back to continue her conversation with the firefighter, but Suzanne wasn't ready to be dismissed.

"Wait, what happened here?" Suzanne said, desperate to know the details. "Do we know how the fire started? How much damage is there?"

The firefighter excused himself to return to the fire engine and the rest of his team. Once he'd gone, Imogen gestured to the damaged hotel room in the annex.

"The two guests in that room were smoking," she sighed. "It doesn't matter that smoking is banned and that there are signs everywhere saying so. There are always people who decide the rules don't apply to them, and that if they just lean out of the window while they puff away, then no one will be any the wiser. Anyway, one of the guests left their stupid cigarette burning in an ashtray near the window while they went into the bathroom, and it set light to the curtains and to a stack of clothes and newspapers they'd piled up on top of the chest of drawers. The other guest had gone out to their car to fetch something and returned to the room just as the sprinkler system kicked in and the alarms went off. We only know any of this because the guests came clean and admitted what they'd done, although the firefighter was just telling me they found the ashtray and cigarette remains easily enough."

"My god," Suzanne said, looking back at the blackened window of the hotel room. "Even with the sprinkler system coming on, that's how much damage there is?"

"There are no perfect systems, Suzanne, and fire is a fierce adversary. Although we have a wrecked hotel room on our hands, what matters is that no one was hurt and the damage was contained."

"The two guests who were inside that room are definitely okay? No smoke inhalation or burns or anything at all?"

Imogen shook her head. "They got out of the room right away and suffered nothing more than a terrible fright and some temporary coughing. There were paramedics here earlier who checked both guests over and declared them to be fine. They didn't even have to go to hospital. In fact, they were both talking to the police the last I heard."

"And all the other guests are okay?"

"They're all fine. The alarm system roused everyone else who was in the guest wing, and the staff did their jobs and put the fire evacuation plan into motion as intended. Although we'll have to go over all that with them later today in our debriefing to make sure our procedures were followed to the letter." Imogen scratched her head, a weary look crossing her face. "We must make sure we organise a meeting for all the staff involved in the evacuation before any of them finish their shifts. It's important that we log statements from all of them and take details of how they executed the evacuation, and note down any problems they encountered. We'll need it for the fire inspectors and for the insurers."

"I'll deal with it," Suzanne said, seeing the fatigue in her mother's face.

Imogen nodded, her expression relieved. "I'm glad you're back, Suzanne. The duty deputy manager is doing a fine job, but in an emergency like this, you're the one I need here to help manage this crisis."

"I'm sorry I wasn't here. But I'm here now. I'm here to work and to do whatever we need to do to deal with this."

"Good, because there's a long list of tasks we have to oversee and assign. Debriefing the evacuation staff, and of course checking that they are all okay and not too shaken up. Helping the reception team move our guests from this part of the annex to other rooms in the hotel. Temporarily reassigning pending room booking allocations while we organise repairs and deal with the fire damage." Imogen blinked and pinched the bridge of her nose. "And the summer ball is next weekend, too, which means we may not have the room capacity we need."

"We can think about any impact on the summer ball tomorrow," Suzanne interrupted. "Right now, we've got enough to keep us busy with the emergency tasks you already mentioned. I'll head back up to the main building and help the reception staff sort out our guests. That's the priority, right?"

Imogen nodded. They were on the same page, as Suzanne knew they would be. After so many years immersed in the business, they both understood their emergency protocols and how to triage urgent tasks during a time of crisis. If Suzanne had been here earlier, many of those tasks would already be underway, and she cringed inside at the knowledge that she hadn't been here to help. Her mother couldn't be in two places at once, after all. At a time like this, both the manager and the deputy manager were required to put their shoulder to the wheel.

But Suzanne hadn't been here to do her part, and she hated herself because of it.

"Ms Kennedy?" called out one of the firefighters as he walked towards them. "We've finished our inspection of the hotel room and are removing our cordons."

"Already?" Imogen said, obviously surprised.

"The room looks much worse than it is," the firefighter replied. "It will be out of use until you repair the fire and water damage, but there are no structural problems, and the fire didn't spread to the rooms on either side or up to the first floor. Your sprinkler system did what it was supposed to do and kept the fire contained and then extinguished it. We didn't even have to use any additional water once we arrived, which is good news because that has helped limit the damage to your building."

The firefighter gestured to the guest annex and looked thoughtful. "You did the right thing installing the sprinkler system. Given the height of this guest annex, I know you weren't required to do it in order to meet building regulations, but it's paid off for you today. Without that sprinkler system, this annex would have been fully alight before we got here."

"My father insisted on installing the best safety systems available," Imogen said. "When he added this guest annex fifteen years ago, a full sprinkler system was non-negotiable, even although it pushed the building budget to the limit."

"Like I said, it's paid off today," the firefighter said. "Without that sprinkler kicking in and suppressing the fire, it would have spread and you would've lost this whole annex. Instead, things look much better than they might have done."

"Can I go inside and look?" Imogen asked.

The firefighter nodded. "I'll come with you, in case you have questions."

"I'll come too," Suzanne said.

"But I need you up at reception, Suzanne," Imogen frowned.

"Once I've seen the fire damage for myself, that's where I'll go. But I need to know what we're dealing with and just how badly things look inside that room."

Imogen nodded, conceding the point, and together they followed the firefighter into the guest annex. The annex connected to the main castle building via a glass walkway, which had the advantage of making it easy to cordon off from public access while they assessed their next steps. There were twenty guest rooms spread over two floors in the annex. The fire had broken out in the last room at the far end of the guest wing.

If it wasn't for the smell of smoke and water, Suzanne wouldn't know from the ground floor corridor that anything had happened at all. As the fire was contained in the guest room, the other sprinklers in the other rooms and in the corridor had not been activated. It was only when the firefighter pushed open the door of the damaged room at the far end that it became obvious what had happened.

Suzanne gasped at the sight inside the room… but in the same breath, realised it didn't look as bad as she'd feared, or as bad as she'd thought it did from outside. The worst damage was confined to the area around the window, where the curtains hung in tatters and the window frame was scorched. A pile of blackened materials sat on top of the chest of drawers—probably the guests' clothes and newspapers which had acted as kindling, according to Imogen—and the television set was damaged, along with the upholstered chairs beside the window. The smell of smoke hung heavy in the air and Suzanne could see where flames had licked the walls before the sprinkler had pushed them back. The carpet underfoot was wet, the bed and furniture soaked from the water from the sprinkler… but the room, while damaged, was intact.

And the damage was confined to one place, just as the firefighter had explained. The fire-damaged room would need work and refurbishment, there was no question about that. But Suzanne saw that the repairs were manageable, and that the business could deal with this setback.

"Like I said," the firefighter said, gesturing around the room, "this damage is all cosmetic. It will take work and money to put things right in here, but it's nothing compared to what you'd be facing if the fire had gutted this entire guest wing." He stepped outside into the corridor and opened the door to the adjoining guest room. "As you can see, this room is fine. No water ingress. No fire spread. No smoke damage."

He closed the door again. "However, I recommend keeping these doors closed and the windows open until the smell of smoke has vented."

Imogen nodded as they returned to the fire-damaged room. "How long will the smell of smoke linger, do you think?"

"Probably at least a couple of days. If it hadn't been for the pile of clothes and newspapers catching fire so easily, it might not have been so bad. As it is, the sooner you clear this room and get rid of all these fire-damaged items, the sooner the smell will clear. However, as things stand, it's only the unpleasant smell of the smoke that's an issue. As far as we're concerned, these other rooms can be used by your guests again."

"We won't allow our guests to return to their rooms while this smell lingers, even if there is no safety issue," Imogen said, her tone firm. "How do things look on the first floor?"

For the next ten minutes, they checked out the first floor rooms with the firefighter and assured themselves that all was fine in that part of the annex. As a precaution, Imogen declared the room above the source of the fire to be out of bounds for the time being. With a clearer sense of the guest room availability now in her mind, Suzanne began shuffling options around in her head for the next steps she'd take in reassigning guest rooms once she went up to the reception lobby in the main building.

Back on the ground floor of the guest annex, Imogen said goodbye to the firefighter who'd helped answer their questions, before turning to Suzanne.

"Okay, this is bad, but not as bad as we thought," Imogen said. "The priority now is moving our guests from the annex and arranging for their belongings to be moved to their new rooms. Once that's done, and we've met with our staff and debriefed them on the situation, we'll look at our bookings for the next few days and make reallocations as necessary until the smoke smell is gone from the guest wing and we can bring some rooms back into use. While the annex is closed off, we'll put together a team to drag everything out of the fire-damaged room, which should help clear away the odours. We ought to book a skip delivery, so we have somewhere to put all the ruined furniture once we've hauled it out, and..."

"Mother," Suzanne interrupted, seeing how Imogen's mind was once more lining up the long list of tasks to be dealt with. "I know what needs to be prioritised, and that's dealing with the guests. I'll go up to reception and start working with the staff there. Once that's done, then we can think about clearing up this mess."

Imogen nodded. "Yes, okay. First things first."

As Imogen looked around at the ruined hotel room again, Suzanne saw the pained look in her mother's eyes. "Are you okay, Mum?"

"I'm all right," Imogen said after a moment. "Just... well, I'm feeling just a little stunned by this."

"Of course you are." Suzanne reached out and laid her hand on her mother's arm. "Were you here when the fire broke out?"

Imogen nodded. "I was in my office. I ran to the guest annex as soon as we knew that's where the fire alarm was going off, but several of our younger staff members were already there, helping evacuate the guests. We have to make sure we thank them for their swift work."

"We will."

Imogen sighed and shook her head. "When I saw the smoke billowing out of the window of this guest room as I ran around from the main building... I felt such *fear*, Suzanne. Such terror."

"I felt the same thing when I got your phone call."

At this, Imogen's expression clouded. "I had enough to deal with here without having to keep dialling your phone all afternoon, trying to get hold of you."

Suzanne blushed at her mother's complaint. "I'm sorry, I didn't realise there was no signal where I was."

Before Suzanne could say anything else, one of the reception staff appeared in the guest wing, peering along the corridor to where Imogen and Suzanne stood staring into the fire-damaged bedroom.

"Ms Kennedy, the duty supervisor sent me to find you," the woman said to Imogen. "She's having trouble with the room reassignments, and the guests who have rooms in this wing are getting agitated about whether their belongings are okay or if they're damaged."

"I'm on my way to deal with all of that," Suzanne smiled. "In the meantime, ask the affected guests make themselves comfortable in the bar, and serve them complimentary tea and coffee until I get there to talk to them."

The woman nodded and left.

"I better get up there," Suzanne said to her mother.

"We both had better get up there. You deal with the guests and the room allocations. I'll put together a team to clear out all this damaged furniture so we can get rid of this awful smell of fire and smoke as quickly as possible."

Leaving behind the guest annex, they walked to the main hotel building. As they neared the entrance, Suzanne saw the last of the fire engines pulling out and heading towards the exit road.

When her gaze fell on Kyle Lawson, standing beside his parked car and watching her drawing near, her eyes widened in surprise.

She'd been so absorbed in the details of the fire and its impact on the hotel that she'd completely forgotten about him. After jumping out of his car and racing to the scene of the incident, she hadn't given him a second thought.

"You're still here?" Suzanne asked when she drew level with Kyle's parked car.

"Of course," he said. "I wanted to wait and find out if everything was okay." He gestured to the fire engine now disappearing along the road. "One of the firefighters said that the damage isn't as bad as it could have been."

"That's right, and no one was hurt, which is the main thing, but…"

"Suzanne, I need you to deal with our guests," Imogen interrupted, her eyes darting between Kyle and Suzanne. "There isn't time for chit-chat."

Suzanne felt her cheeks flush with a mixture of embarrassment and irritation: embarrassment at her mother's tone, which left her feeling like a scolded child; and irritation at being told something she already knew. Of course she had to deal with the hotel guests. Of course there wasn't time for chit-chat. So why was she standing here talking to Kyle instead of assisting her hotel guests?

"Kyle," Suzanne said. "It's hectic here and I need to get to work. I'll talk to you later, okay?"

"Is there anything I can do to help?" Kyle asked.

"We're fine, thank you," Imogen said sharply before Suzanne could answer, her expression cold as she looked at Kyle from the hotel doors. "Suzanne, let's go."

Suzanne threw a quick wave at Kyle as she hurried inside the hotel after her mother. When Imogen gave her a hard stare before leaving her in the reception lobby, Suzanne looked away.

The meaning behind her mother's expression was clear, but Suzanne didn't need to be reminded that her priority right now was the Star Castle Hotel, and not the handsome man who'd waited out in the car park for her in order to make sure she was okay and that her beloved hotel was okay, too.

After the shock and fear caused by what had happened this afternoon, Suzanne would never forget where her priorities lay again.

CHAPTER SIXTEEN

It was after nine o'clock that evening when Suzanne finally paused to draw breath and gather her thoughts. Beyond the main doors of the hotel, the summer sky was washed in pink and peach as the sun dipped to the horizon, but Suzanne had scarcely glanced up from the computer in the reception lobby where she'd been working for the last hour, and the pretty sunset colours had passed her by.

After much room juggling and creative problem solving, she'd assigned the guests staying in the annex to rooms in the main hotel building and organised staff to move their belongings to the new accommodations. To apologise for the inconvenience caused to the guests, she'd also arranged for complimentary drinks and desserts to be served when they next dined at the hotel restaurant, a gesture which had gone down well with everyone. The affected guests turned out to be sensible and reasonable people, who appreciated that the hotel management was working hard to deal with the unexpected calamity, and once they were kept informed of what was happening, they were all understanding and kind.

Suzanne was heartened by the reminder that people were

generous for the most part. Even the guests whose illicit smoking had caused all the turmoil in the first place had opted for apologies rather than belligerence, and when Suzanne had politely but firmly asked them to leave, they had done so without causing any further trouble.

With those urgent tasks sorted, she'd turned to devising a back-up plan for the coming week and into the weekend of the summer ball, in case the acrid smoke smell failed to disappear as quickly as they hoped it would. The last thing they wanted was to welcome guests to the hotel, only for them to complain about a lingering smoke smell ruining their stay. If the smell persisted, she now had a plan to accommodate all guests holding bookings in the main building, and had agreed with Imogen that they wouldn't accept any new room bookings that would require the use of the guest annex until they were satisfied that the smell of smoke was gone.

When Suzanne had checked up on the room reservations for the night of the summer ball, she'd realised that several new bookings had arrived since she'd last checked, and that they'd reached their capacity in the main hotel building. She could tell from the data tracked by their booking software that the new bookings had come through thanks to the social media marketing she'd pushed out after hiring the new band for the summer ball and ordering the new marketing graphics from the printer. Judging by the room sales trends, they might well have booked out all their rooms in time for the summer ball, had the guest annex been available for allocations. Suzanne would have liked that, considering the bookings were only limping along until she'd switched out the musical entertainment. Perhaps the underwhelming summer ball bookings had been a blessing in disguise after all, given what had happened today.

She reminded herself that her emergency room allocation

plan was for a worst-case scenario. If the smell of smoke disappeared from the guest annex, those rooms would be released for sale.

With her work completed on the booking system, Suzanne stepped away from the computer and stretched out the crick in her neck. Beyond the hotel doors, she saw the sweep of colour in the sky and knew the guests who were out on the terrace this evening would be enjoying a spectacular view. Hopefully, the vibrant summer sunset was helping their guests smooth over the upheaval of the afternoon. Their customers were here to relax and unwind, after all.

Imogen walked through the hotel doors just then, a small team of staff following in her wake. After saying a few words to them, the staff dispersed and Imogen walked to where Suzanne stood at the reception counter.

"We've made a good start on clearing out the fire-damaged room," Imogen said. "The staff have done a terrific job, considering what I asked them to do. Dragging fire-ravaged detritus around the place isn't exactly part of their routine activities. I told them all to expect bonuses in their wages this month as a thank you for their efforts."

"I'm sure they'll appreciate that," Suzanne said.

"Until the skip we've booked arrives tomorrow, we stacked the ruined furniture up behind the outbuilding our grounds crew uses. With the window open inside the burned guest room, the smell should now dissipate. First thing tomorrow, we'll start ringing round to find contractors able to come and repair the damage and refurbish the room."

Suzanne nodded. "Sounds good to me. Seems like these last few days we've had too many calamities around this place. Between the damage to the woodland play area and now a burned-out guest room, I'm beginning to think the gods are conspiring against us."

"They say these things happen in threes. Let's hope that won't be the case here."

Suzanne watched her mother rub her forehead and stifle a yawn. "You look exhausted. Why don't you go home and get some rest? We've done everything we can for tonight and dealt with all the priority tasks we had to see to."

"There are still some loose ends I want to tie up with the paperwork we started for the insurers and the reports we took from the staff involved in the evacuation."

"I can take care of that." Suzanne saw her mother wavering, wondering if she ought to leave those remaining tasks to her or deal with them herself. The fatigue in Imogen's expression was obvious. "Mum, you were here during the fire and you were the one who had to deal with the first response in the emergency. That takes its toll. Go home and sleep, and that way you'll be fresh and ready for everything we have to sort out tomorrow."

"Yes, okay," Imogen said. "If I'm being honest, I'm still shaken up from the fire. I think it'll be a long time before I get the image out of my head of all that black smoke billowing from the guest room window. I thought the whole guest wing was about to be destroyed. And I was terrified that people might get hurt… or worse."

Imogen's voice trembled. Suzanne understood in that moment just how frightened her mother must have been to see fire take hold of their hotel.

"I'm so sorry I wasn't here sooner when you needed me," Suzanne said.

A frown etched its way across Imogen's forehead. "You were with the man who's been working on the woodland repairs, the one who was waiting for you in the car park this afternoon?"

"Yes, Kyle Lawson."

"You can't afford to let yourself be distracted by a man,

Suzanne," Imogen said, her tone ice cold. "Even one as handsome as he is."

"He didn't *distract* me. We were just..."

"It doesn't matter. I needed you here this afternoon, Suzanne, and you were nowhere to be found. You're my deputy manager. If I can't rely on you when there's a crisis here at the hotel, then we've got a problem."

"You *can* rely on me," Suzanne said, lifting her chin.

Imogen's gaze raked across her face, hard and piercing, before her features softened and she let out a quiet sigh. "This is a tough business, Suzanne. Running a family business of this size is *hard*. There is no nine-to-five. We don't walk out of here at the end of the day and forget about work until the next morning."

"I know that."

"There will be time for men later, time for romance. I'm not naïve, Suzanne. Just because I didn't want a partner in life doesn't mean I think you won't want one either. But right now, while you're still finding your way in the deputy manager role, this hotel has to be your priority. Is that really what you want?"

"Yes, of course it is."

"In that case, the hotel has to come first in your life, above everything else."

"I know that," Suzanne said again. "I won't be seeing Kyle anymore. It was just a friendly get-together this afternoon, nothing more, nothing less. There's nothing going on between us."

Imogen sighed again. "Suzanne, all I want is for you to be happy. If this job is too much for you, if-"

"It's not too much. It's what I want. This hotel is my life, you know that."

The quiet of the empty reception lobby was broken by a group of guests arriving through the main doors and nodding their hellos as they made their way towards the lifts further along the corridor. Suzanne used the interruption as a good moment to bring the awkward conversation with her mother to an end.

"Look, it's late and we're both tired," Suzanne said. "Go home and get some rest. I'll finish up here and then deal with the paperwork you mentioned before I call it a night, too. Tomorrow, we'll start working on the room refurbishment organisation and everything else that we need to think about because of what happened today. But right now, you need some rest, and as your deputy manager and right-hand woman, I'm insisting that you go home and switch off."

Suzanne gave her mother a smile, keen to end their conversation on a positive note.

"All right," Imogen said, almost returning Suzanne's smile but with no real enthusiasm behind it. "I'll see you tomorrow."

Imogen turned, but then spun around again and pulled Suzanne into a hug. "That fire could have been so much worse, Suzanne," her mother whispered. "We could have been ruined."

Gulping back a hot flash of emotion, Suzanne hugged her mother back. "I know."

Releasing her, Imogen threw a meaningful look at Suzanne before leaving, but she needed no further reminder of just how terribly things might have turned out today. If the fire had wrecked the guest wing, the business would have been in serious trouble. Worse, if the fire had got out of hand and someone had been hurt or killed, the Star Castle Hotel might not have survived the fall-out.

Might not have *deserved* to survive the fall-out.

It didn't bear thinking about. Pushing away the disturbing thoughts, Suzanne rechecked her work on the booking system once more, determined to make sure she'd dealt with everything before turning her attention to the paperwork she'd promised her mother she'd take care of before this long day was over.

TWO HOURS LATER, a knock on Suzanne's office door pulled her out of the paperwork she'd immersed herself in. When she looked up, she was astonished to see Mrs Wishmore pushing open the door.

"You're not still on shift, are you, Doris?" Suzanne asked, glancing at the time on her phone. "It's almost eleven o'clock."

Mrs Wishmore stepped into the office, a warm smile lighting up her face. "After this afternoon's events, I thought I'd stick around once my working day was over, just in case I was needed."

"You didn't have to do that, but I appreciate it anyway."

"I helped the staff keep the guests happy while the room switches were taking place, and because several staff members were redeployed to clear the burned-out guest room, I was happy to step in and pick up their routine work chores." Doris gestured to the empty chair across Suzanne's desk. "Do you mind if I…?"

"Please, sit down."

"Thank you, dear." The older lady settled herself in the chair, her jacket and bag in her lap. "How are you, Suzanne? I imagine you are quite shaken up given all the upset of the fire in the guest annex and the work required to deal with the fall-out."

"I'm fine. What matters is that the guests are okay, the staff are okay, and no one was hurt."

"And thank goodness for it, too. As I understand it, the

sprinkler system prevented the fire from spreading and helped avert disaster."

Suzanne nodded. "My grandfather always said that safety came first at the hotel. He would be pleased to know he made the right call when he incurred the added expense of that sprinkler system during the guest annex construction. It wasn't required to meet the building regulations, but he insisted on it, anyway. Today, it was worth every penny."

"Your grandfather was a wise man," Mrs Wishmore said. "And I'm sure he'd be proud of the way you and your mother dealt with today's emergency."

Suzanne looked away, feeling her cheeks burn. "My mother was the one who dealt with the emergency. I wasn't even here."

"I don't suppose it's possible for you to be here twenty-four hours a day, seven days a week," Mrs Wishmore said, her tone gentle.

"No, that's true. But when I was needed, my mother couldn't reach me because..."

Suzanne stopped talking and cleared her throat. Why was it that every time Doris Wishmore was around, she couldn't help spilling her heart out?

"Your mother couldn't reach you because you were with young Kyle?" Doris said.

"Yes, that's right."

"So, it's young Kyle's fault, is it?"

Suzanne's head snapped up at Mrs Wishmore's humorous tone. "No, but if I hadn't gone out with him this afternoon, then..."

When Suzanne stopped talking again, Mrs Wishmore gave her a puzzled look. "Then what? If you had been here this afternoon, would you have been able to stop the fire from breaking out?"

"No, of course not. But I would've been able to get to work sooner and help deal with everything that happened."

Mrs Wishmore gave an easy shrug. "It seems to me that everything *was* dealt with, and very efficiently, too, I might add. The sprinkler system did its job and prevented a terrible catastrophe from happening, and for that, you can thank your clever grandfather. The guests were safely evacuated, and for that you can thank your brilliant staff. And once you got here, you worked hand-in-glove with your mother to triage the urgent steps that were needed to make sure your guests were looked after." The older lady shook her head. "So, why are you beating yourself up about it?"

"Because I have a responsibility to this hotel and to this business," Suzanne said. "I put my personal life first for a change, and look what happened."

"My goodness, Suzanne!" Mrs Wishmore exclaimed. "Are you saying you aren't entitled to have a personal life because of your job here?"

"It's not about what I'm entitled to. It's about choices and priorities."

"But if you'd made different choices today, and had different priorities, how would events have unfolded any differently from how they did?" Doris asked. "Those silly guests would have smoked in their room whether you were here or not. Those curtains and personal items in their room would have caught fire whether you were here or not. The sprinkler system would have done its duty whether you were here or not."

"I know, but-"

"And don't forget that you were here the other day when that tree branch fell and damaged the woodland play area," Mrs Wishmore continued. "In fact, you were *right there* when it happened! You being there didn't stop it from happening.

But once it had happened, you dealt with it, just as you've dealt with what happened today, too."

Suzanne sighed, the late hour and the day's events suddenly sweeping over her and leaving her weary. "Mrs Wishmore, I appreciate that you're just trying to make me feel better. It's kind of you. But it's been a long day and I don't feel like talking about any of this anymore."

Mrs Wishmore's gaze softened. "You're quite right, it is late." With a nod, she rose from the chair. "I won't keep you any longer. I just wanted to see how you were doing and find out if there's anything I can do to help."

"Thank you, but you've been here all evening already, and it's time for you to go home. We can't have our employees collapsing with exhaustion." Suzanne smiled, not wanting to sound brisk with the older woman who was, after all, only being kind. A thought occurred to her as Doris reached the office door. "Mrs Wishmore, how are you getting home? The last bus was ages ago."

"One of the other ladies who worked late tonight has offered to give me a lift home," she replied. "Don't worry yourself about that."

Suzanne's phone pinged on the desk. When she glanced at the screen, she saw a message from Kyle.

Hope things are going okay at the hotel. How bad is the fire damage? Are your guests doing okay? Are you doing okay? I'm here if you need any help, just say the word. Kyle.

She read the message and tossed the phone aside, frowning at the annoying flutter she felt in her stomach because of the words Kyle had written. When she looked up, Mrs Wishmore had a strange and knowing expression on her face.

"No matter how busy we are, and no matter how big our responsibilities, it's always good to have friends we can count on," Mrs Wishmore said. "Good night, Suzanne."

The older lady smiled and closed the door behind her, leaving Suzanne alone.

For a long moment, she sat in the quiet office, thinking about what Mrs Wishmore had said, her gaze travelling back to the phone on her desk. She picked it up and tapped the button to open the message Kyle had sent.

Are you doing okay? he'd asked. *I'm here if you need any help...*

Her finger hovered as she thought about replying. But in the end, she closed Kyle's message and set the phone aside. There was still paperwork to finish before she left for home. She didn't have time to reply.

And if she did reply, it would only lead to more messages being exchanged, more conversations, more time spent on a man she had no space for in her life.

She knew this. She'd always known it.

Suzanne turned to the paperwork that waited for her and got back to work.

CHAPTER SEVENTEEN

The next two days went by in a blur for Suzanne at the Star Castle Hotel. Between dealing with the consequences of the fire in the guest wing, finalising the arrangements for the summer ball on Saturday night, and tackling all the other routine hotel tasks that filled her time, she scarcely stopped working from dawn until dusk.

When Mrs Wishmore arrived in Suzanne's office late on Tuesday afternoon with the news that Kyle Lawson was waiting for her in the woodland play area, it took a minute for her to sift through the multiple jobs already spinning around in her head and work out what the older lady was talking about. The ongoing repairs to the footbridge and fairy huts had completely slipped Suzanne's mind.

"Kyle says everything is finished and waiting for your approval," Mrs Wishmore said. "When he arrived in reception, I told him I'd come and fetch you while he returned to the play area to gather up his work materials."

"Thank you, Doris," Suzanne said, rising from her desk.

"I suggested to young Kyle that he could just call your

phone and let you know directly he was ready to sign off on the play area repairs, but he seemed reluctant to do that."

Mrs Wishmore's smile was at odds with the question in her eyes. Suzanne looked away as she closed the files she'd been working on at her computer, knowing only too well why Kyle had been reluctant to phone her. She hadn't replied to his text message on Sunday night, and when he'd called her the next day, she'd let it go to voice mail.

"I'll get over there and see how the woodland repairs look and that will be one less thing to deal with around here."

Mrs Wishmore nodded and walked with Suzanne as far as the reception lobby before returning to the counter to help a guest there. Suzanne hurried out to the rear gardens and along Star Castle Lane and into the woodland, part of her excited to see the play area restored and accessible once more to the guests, another part of her nervous about seeing Kyle again.

She hadn't returned his messages and calls because she was too busy with the fall-out from the hotel fire, but also because she'd chosen to ignore them. It wouldn't be easy to keep that deliberate choice out of her eyes when they spoke.

When she reached the woodland play area, Kyle was standing beside two new little fairy huts, taking photos with his phone, while another younger man packed away tools and equipment. Suzanne's heart tumbled inside her chest as she drew nearer to Kyle and saw the look of pride on his face as he photographed the fairy huts.

"Kyle, these look wonderful," she said, gesturing to the wooden structures. Launching into business matters right away was easier than getting bogged down in awkward hellos and how-are-yous.

He glanced up from his phone and smiled. "I'm glad you like them. Come and look at the carvings and tell me what you think."

Stepping closer, Suzanne gazed at the sweet fairy huts, one painted pink, the other painted yellow. They weren't identical to those they replaced, but Suzanne knew that had never been realistic, given how old the other huts were in the play area. Kyle had done a wonderful job on the wooden constructions, and as she looked at the carvings above the doors, she saw how much care he'd taken with these special flourishes. The carved butterflies on the pink hut were adorable, while the scattering of stars on the yellow hut were charming and whimsical. As promised, he'd added additional carved touches to the roofs of both structures, and Suzanne knew children would love seeing the fluttering butterflies and shooting stars there as they played and enjoyed themselves.

As she looked at the pretty fairy huts, with their bright colours and sweet carvings, she couldn't help smiling.

"These carvings are fantastic, Kyle," she said, running a hand over the rooftop stars on the yellow hut. "Better than I could have hoped for. You've gone above and beyond what we asked for, and I'm grateful."

"I know how much these little fairy huts meant to you," he said. "I'm pleased you're happy with what I've put together." He pointed towards the footbridge. "We just finished sanding the last rough spots on the bridge handrail. Come and see what you think."

They stepped over to the footbridge, where Suzanne ran a hand along the smooth wood and across the cute carvings of fairy faces and flowers that decorated the inside edge. "Again, this is perfect. You've done a super job, and so quickly, too. Thank you."

"It was our pleasure."

"And with everything now safe and sound out here again in the woodland, we'll be able to welcome the hospital Kids' Club summer party here tomorrow afternoon, just as we hoped. The kids will have a brilliant time and I'm relieved we won't have to move their party indoors because the play area is out of bounds. I know the little ones will love seeing these new play huts."

"I'm pleased to hear that." Kyle turned to the young man who'd been clearing away the work equipment. "You can take everything back to the van, and I'll meet you there."

With a nod, the young man grabbed a toolbox in each hand and walked off. Kyle pulled a sheet of paperwork from a folder tucked under his arm and handed it to Suzanne.

"If you can just sign this to confirm you're happy with the work, then we're all done here. If there are any problems you haven't noticed, just call the office and we'll sort it out."

Suzanne scribbled a signature on the paperwork and handed it back. This had all gone much easier than she'd thought it would. Perhaps Kyle had taken the hint thanks to her being incommunicado ever since Sunday and had decided to forget about the afternoon they'd spent together and the kisses they'd shared...

Remembering those kisses brought a blush to Suzanne's face. When Kyle's eyes locked on hers, the blush only deepened.

"So, how are things at the hotel after the fire?" Kyle asked, slipping the paperwork she'd signed back into the folder.

"Everything's okay, but we're busy, very busy," she said. "Although the fire didn't spread beyond the guest room where it started, we've got a full refurbishment job on our hands to sort out the damage. The smoke smell is still lingering, too, and until it's gone, we've had to move our guests to other parts of the hotel, and..." She waved a hand, not wanting to bore him with the endless details. "There's a lot going on, put it that way."

"I can imagine." He held her gaze for a long beat before

continuing. "Are you okay, Suzanne? The fire must have left you shaken up."

"I'm fine. Shaken up, yes, but too busy with work to think much about it."

He nodded, then glanced away before once more meeting her gaze. "When you didn't answer my calls or messages, I guessed you must be busy."

Suzanne gave a nervous laugh. "It's been hectic."

"Once things settle down here at the hotel, and you're on top of your fire repairs and so on, maybe we could get together again?"

She drew in a deep breath while finding the right words to answer him. "I don't think that's a good idea, Kyle."

"I thought we had fun together on Sunday?" His eyes darkened as his gaze fell to her mouth for a second. "I know I did."

She looked away, unable to think straight when he was looking at her that way. "It's complicated, Kyle. My work at the hotel has to come first, and I don't have a lot of free time to carve out a personal life. You understand, right?"

"Sure, I understand how important work is, and how important it is to you in particular. But what about everything you said on Saturday night about wanting to have fun? It seemed like you might want more out of life than just work."

"Well, that's what everyone wants, isn't it?" she said with a forced laugh. "But this is a family business, and it takes a lot of hard graft to keep it ticking over and..."

Perhaps it was the stillness of the woodland that made her say what came next, the enchanted peace of the place making her open up in a way she'd never intended.

"The truth is, Kyle, I have a lot of doubt about whether I'm up to the challenge of running this hotel. I second guess my decisions and interrogate every choice I make. I'm terrified of doing something wrong that puts this place in jeopardy. I have so much to learn and so much to understand, and it takes every ounce of energy I have just to stop my fears about whether I'm good enough from running out of control. After the shock of the fire on Sunday and all the decisions we've had to make and are still making in order to put things right, and with the hotel's summer ball coming up in just a few days—an event I'm fully responsible for—I just don't have any space in my life for other things."

"Not even for a cup of coffee with someone who enjoys your company and wants to get to know you?" Kyle said. "I'm not asking for anything more than that."

"Please don't make this anymore awkward than it already is," Suzanne said, wishing this wasn't so hard. "We spent a nice afternoon together, and I enjoyed it. Can we just leave it at that?"

The confused frown that crossed Kyle's face vanished as quickly as it appeared. "Of course," he said at last, giving her an over-bright smile before picking up his work bag. "I ought to get back to the van. We're due at another job this afternoon."

"Thanks again for all this hard work," she said, gesturing to the restored play area. "We appreciate it."

"The boss will be happy to hear that." He smiled again and hoisted the bag over his shoulder. "Bye, Suzanne."

She watched him walk off towards the clearing and turn onto Star Castle Lane. Her stomach churned at the difficult conversation they'd had, and she was glad it was over.

Once he'd disappeared from view, she looked around the play area again, relieved to know the grounds crew could remove the cordons and allow guests to enjoy the woodland once more. Kyle had done a fantastic job with the fairy huts and the restored handrail on the bridge. For someone whose passion was gardening, he had many other amazing talents.

She thought again of how he'd kissed her at the top of the Ferris wheel in the garden fairground, and the way he'd looked at her. Closing her eyes against memories of his tender touch and heart-stopping gaze, she pushed the thoughts away.

Her afternoon with Kyle Lawson at the fairground and roaming around those glorious gardens had been nothing more than an unexpected interlude in her hectic work life. Now it was time to forget about him and focus on what mattered.

And now that Kyle's work at the hotel was completed, forgetting about him would be easy.

Suzanne was sure of it.

CHAPTER EIGHTEEN

Kyle sank his shovel into the soft soil he'd been back-filling and took a look at the work he'd done. The border looked like a picture-perfect scene from a cottage garden, with romantic roses and nodding foxgloves and perfumed lavender, just the way the client had requested. It was another job well done by Hill Landscaping.

It was late on Thursday afternoon, and Kyle had spent the day transforming the back garden that belonged to the retired couple who'd just moved into the cottage attached to it and needed professional help with the garden make-over. After too many long weeks spent focusing on the grunt work of hard landscaping and garden maintenance, Kyle had loved every minute spent lost in the details of the cottage garden design and planting the flowers and shrubs he'd chosen for the clients. As he looked at the roses with their soft pink blooms and watched bees coming and going from the foxgloves and lavender, he felt the satisfaction of the day sink in.

The time spent planting and bringing a garden design to life had left him with a happy buzz. If only there were more days like this. He missed using his creative skills in the garden and knew that the next few weeks of work lined up at Hill Landscaping involved a return to patio laying and hedge trimming.

Still, a job was a job, and he was grateful for it. But he couldn't help but wonder when the time would be right to go into business for himself, and specialise in the design projects that excited him the most, projects like this gorgeous cottage garden he'd just planted and which had transformed a weed-choked border into something wonderful.

Kyle's phone pinged. For a split second, he hoped it might be a message from Suzanne, but he frowned at the stupid thought. Suzanne had made her feelings clear when they'd signed off on the hotel's woodland play area repairs on Tuesday afternoon, and he knew he ought to stop thinking about her.

But that was easier said than done.

When he checked the phone message, it was from his sister Erin.

We're ordering pizza tonight for dinner. Don't be late or Jamie will eat the lot and you'll just have to starve. Also, I've got a big surprise for later... I think you'll like it!

Erin had added a string of question marks and puzzled head emojis at the end of her message, making Kyle wonder what her big surprise might be.

But before he could ponder the mystery, his mind was already hauling out memories of the last time he'd eaten pizza, a week ago, when he'd met Suzanne in town and he and Jamie had shared the pizza she'd ordered for dinner while enjoying the view of the bay from the picnic bench on the promenade.

It seemed impossible that night was only a week ago. It felt like something from ancient history. He might only have spent a few hours with Suzanne after that, when he'd taken her to the garden fairground at Heatherglen House, but their afternoon together still burned brightly in his mind.

It had been special, or at least that's what Kyle had thought.

There was no point hashing over any of that, though, even if only inside his own head. He had no intention of chasing after a woman who'd made it clear, repeatedly, that she didn't want to see him again. If he'd reminded himself of that before he'd called Suzanne on Saturday night and asked her out, despite having been turned down once already, he might not feel like such a clueless idiot right now, and have been spared the brush-off she'd given him.

Kyle tapped out a reply to Erin, confirming he'd be there on time to eat pizza and fight Jamie for the last slice. As he packed up his gardening equipment, he took one last look at the cottage garden he'd planted and smiled.

The new garden looked pretty good. At least he could still do something right.

"So, what's this big surprise you've got?" Kyle asked later that evening, after wolfing down more than his fair share of the pizza Erin had picked up for dinner.

At Kyle's words, Jamie launched himself out of his chair at the table and started prancing around the kitchen. "I know what it is! I know what it is! I know something you don't know! I know something you don't know!"

"Jamie, buddy, you're covering me with pizza crumbs," Kyle said, making a big deal out of wiping his face with a napkin. "Say it, don't spray it."

At this, Jamie started falling around and laughing hysterically.

"What's wrong with your son?" Kyle asked Erin. "Did you feed him too much sugar today or something?"

"Or something." Erin's wide grin got Kyle wondering just what was going on.

"Well, are you going to tell me what this big surprise is, or is Jamie just going to have to pass out on the floor with excitement?"

Erin pushed back from the table and grabbed her car keys from the counter. "Fancy taking a little trip?"

They piled out to Erin's car. As she drove, Kyle watched her from the corner of his eye, intrigued by her expression. It had been a long time since he'd seen her eyes light up that way. After what she'd been through these past months, he was glad to know something other than the son she loved more than life itself could still make her glow with happiness like that. He only wondered what that something was.

Ten minutes after they left Kyle's house, he got his answer.

Erin steered her car down a street of terraced houses on the other side of Balmarrie. She stopped outside a house with a cheerful red front door and an old twisted apple tree growing in the middle of the tiny scrap of lawn in the front garden.

"What do you think of my new house?" Erin asked Kyle with barely concealed glee. "I signed the rental agreement this afternoon."

"Are you serious?" Kyle grinned at the delight on his sister's face, and in the back seat, Jamie was unbuckling his belt and climbing out of the car.

"It's cool, isn't it Uncle Kyle?" Jamie said as Kyle joined him on the pavement. "Wait till you see the back garden! It's huge!"

Jamie barrelled towards the front gate. He was halfway up

the garden path before Erin made it out of the car and caught up with him.

"Hang on, Jamie," she called out. "We don't have the keys yet, and we don't move in until next week, so we can't go roaming around the place just yet."

"But I want to show Uncle Kyle the back garden," he said, hopping around in excitement. "I want to make sure there'll be room for the fort we're going to build together."

"I'm sure there will be plenty of room, squirt," Kyle said. "And we can build the fort to fit the space, anyway. That's the beauty of making stuff for yourself, see? You can have it any way you want it."

Apparently satisfied with this response, Jamie skipped back out to the pavement, yanking the garden gate behind him.

Kyle looked again at the terraced house with its bright red door and solid brickwork. The windows were in good condition, the front lawn was tidy, the adjoining properties well-cared for by their owners. It was a smart little house, and judging by its compact size, most likely a two-bedroom, making it perfect for Erin and Jamie.

"What do you think?" Erin asked.

"I think it looks great, from the outside anyway. You should have let me look inside before you signed the agreement. I would've checked for mould or faulty electrics or dodgy central heating. I don't want you to end up living in some crappy hell-hole."

"If I'd had any doubts about the inside of this place, I would've asked you to look at it with me," Erin said. "But it's fine inside. Actually, it's better than fine and I'm lucky I snapped it up before anyone else did."

"How did you find it? You've been searching for ages and everything inside your price range has been hideous."

"Don't remind me. As it turns out, it was just one of those

moments when I was in the right place at the right time. At work yesterday, I overheard a doctor in the staff room talking on her phone with her mother. I'd never usually eavesdrop, but I couldn't help but tune in when I got the gist of what she was talking about. Basically, she'd just accepted a position with an international medical charity and was about to leave for a year-long stint delivering health care to isolated communities overseas. She was telling her mother about how she didn't know what to do about her house while she was gone. She didn't want to sell it, because she plans on returning to her current job once her leave of absence ends, but she was nervous about renting it out in case the tenants didn't look after the place while she was gone. It's her house, not an investment property, and she was anxious about what might happen to it if renters moved in and didn't love the house the way she did."

Kyle grinned. "I can see where this is going."

"I loitered around until the doctor finished her conversation with her mother and then I jumped right in. We know each other through work, so it wasn't like I was chatting to a complete stranger. I told her I was looking for a place to rent with my son, but couldn't find anything inside my budget, and wondered if we might do each other a favour. She gets a reliable tenant who won't be throwing drunken parties and wrecking the fixtures and fittings. I get a place to live for a little less than market value. It's a win-win."

"It sounds like it. But I hope you're moving into this place because you want to, and not because you think you need to. You and Jamie can stay with me for as long as you want."

"I know. But it's time for us to move into our own place. It's not about needing more space or not wanting to live with you. It's just..." She shrugged, searching for the right words. "It's time for us to get on with our lives, just me and Jamie, and get our little family back on track."

Kyle smiled. He understood what she meant and how big this next move would be for her.

"At the same time, having only a one year tenancy on the place will mean I don't get too comfortable, either," Erin added. "It's time for us to buy a house of our own, so that Jamie and I have some stability in our lives for the next few years. Living here will give me a chance to stash away some savings for a deposit, to add to what I've saved while living with you. Hopefully, this time next year, we'll be moving into our very own place."

"That sounds like a great plan," Kyle said and turned to Jamie. "Do you like your new house, squirt?"

"It's brilliant, Uncle Kyle. Wait till you see my new room. It's got its own cupboards for all my toys and stuff."

"You're all sorted, in that case, buddy." He looked again at Erin and saw the mixture of happiness and relief on her face when as she gazed up at the new house. "When it comes to moving in to this place, or looking for a house to buy further down the line, or anything at all, I'll help any way I can. I hope you know that."

She gave him a thoughtful look. "Actually, there is something you can help me with, now that you mention it."

"Name it."

Erin grinned and jangled her car keys. "Let's go back to your place first."

They got back into the car and drove home. When they arrived, Erin set Jamie up at the kitchen table with his homework and told him she'd be back to help him finish it in a few minutes. Once Jamie was hunched over his exercise book, she turned to Kyle.

"Come with me," she said.

Now more than a little puzzled, Kyle followed his sister into the living room, where she sat down on the sofa before pulling something out of the handbag she'd brought through with her.

"I was tidying away Jamie's clean laundry earlier and trying to make space in the wardrobe to hang up a couple of things," Erin said. "I was shifting stuff around when some folders of yours tumbled down from the shelf. This fell out."

Erin passed him the item she'd been holding. His eyes widened when he realised what it was—one of the business cards he'd designed and printed out months ago when he'd been playing around with the graphics options he might like to use for his new company logo.

On the plain white piece of card, the words *Lawson Landscaping* were printed in smart sans-serif font. Below this, it read *Garden Design Specialist,* with a few simple green leaves framing the text for added effect.

"Why didn't you tell me you were planning on setting up your own business?" Erin asked.

"It's just an idea I was playing around with," Kyle said.

Erin's gaze narrowed. "You put your plans on hold because of me and Jamie, didn't you?"

"No, not at all."

But Erin's gaze only narrowed further at his denial. Kyle sighed. "Okay, it's something I've been planning for a while. But these last few months have been hell for you, Erin, and I wanted to help you and Jamie however I could." He gestured with the business card. "It will take all my time and energy to get a new business up off the ground. If I was running around doing that, I couldn't be here to help with Jamie."

"But"

"You and my nephew come first, Erin," Kyle continued. "It's as simple as that."

He saw tears glisten in her eyes. "You're the best brother anyone could ever hope for, you know that?"

Kyle looked away, the tenderness of the moment making tears threaten at his eyes, too. "Don't be soft."

Erin let out a volley of laughter, before wiping at her eyes and nodding at the business card in Kyle's hand. "You said if there was anything I wanted you to do, I only had to ask." Looking up, her gaze held his. "I want you to set up your business."

"Once I know that you and Jamie are settled in your new place, and you're both doing okay, then I'll look to get the ball rolling."

"That's not good enough," Erin said, her sharp tone taking him by surprise. "You've waited long enough already, and I won't let you wait anymore. I'll never forget how you helped Jamie and me these past few months, but I won't let you use us as a reason not to move on with your own life."

"That's not what this is about. I just want to know you're both okay."

"We *are* okay. We're okay thanks to you." Erin smiled. "And now it's time for you to do this amazing thing and set up your business, Kyle. When I found that business card, and realised what you must be planning, I was so excited for you. I can't wait to see you make a huge success of it. And I don't want you to wait a single minute longer to get started."

Kyle looked at the business card and blew out a breath. "I don't want to let you down if you need help with Jamie, ferrying him to school or picking him up from football practice."

"You won't let me down, Kyle, you never could. And I can't rely on you forever as a taxi service for my son. I'm not the first single parent in the world to have to figure this stuff out for myself, and I won't be the last. You got me through these last few weeks, Kyle. It's time for me to stand on my own two feet again. I'm looking at community nursing roles that would mean more regular hours instead of shifts, and

I've been connecting with other mothers at Jamie's school who help each other juggle childcare around work, and I think that will be a big help too. And now that we're about to move into our own new house, there's no reason you can't get to work on this big dream you have."

A smile spread across Kyle's face. "You've got all this worked out."

"I have. And now you have to do what your little sister is telling you to do."

He laughed, but at the same time felt a sadness fill his heart. "I'll miss you and Jamie living here with me."

"We'll miss being here. But we'll only be ten minutes away and you'll be coming to ours for dinner at least once a week, so I doubt we'll forget each other."

"Fair enough. But the take away is on me the first time I come over to your new place."

"It's a deal." Erin smiled and then reached into her bag again. "I have a present for you, to say thanks for putting up with us these past weeks."

"You didn't have to do that."

"I know, but I did it anyway."

She handed over a small white envelope. Kyle opened it and pulled out the contents. When he saw what Erin had given him, he was a bit stunned.

"I bought us two tickets to the summer ball at the Star Castle Hotel on Saturday night," Erin said. "I know it might be dorky, a brother and sister turning up to something like that together, but I thought it might be fun. Jamie's got a sleep-over at one of his friends' houses, and when I saw there were still tickets available for the ball, it seemed like a nicer way to spend the evening that sat on your sofa watching television. So, what do you think?"

"Uh, it's terrific, thanks."

At his lack of enthusiasm, Erin frowned. "You don't want to go?"

He didn't want to go, actually. Going to the summer ball at the Star Castle Hotel would mean he'd see Suzanne Kennedy there, given that she was the one organising the event. He didn't want to see her again, if he was being honest, because seeing her would only remind him of those kisses they'd shared and how there'd be no more of them ever again.

But Erin's disappointed expression won out in the end. She knew nothing of the romance he'd almost begun with Suzanne Kennedy, because he'd kept things to himself. Not that there had been much to share, anyway. Erin had surprised him with these summer ball tickets, and if anyone deserved a fun night out, it was his sister.

"Of course I want to go," Kyle smiled. "I'm looking forward to it, assuming you do actually want to spend a Saturday night out with your brother."

"We'll have a laugh," she said. "We'll eat a good dinner, drink some good wine, and then I'll insist you dance with me when the band comes on."

"Fine, but don't complain when I stomp all over your toes because of my two left feet and dodgy dance moves."

"You're slicker on the dance floor than you think."

"Clearly you're delusional."

They grinned at one another for a long beat.

"I'll miss you when you move out, Erin," Kyle said.

"I'll miss you too. But it's time for good new things to happen in our lives, agreed?"

"Agreed."

As Kyle glanced once more at the business card in his hand, he hoped she was right.

LATE THE FOLLOWING AFTERNOON, Kyle pulled the Hill Landscaping van to the side of the road outside a corner shop near Balmarrie main street and hopped out. He'd just dropped his work colleagues off at the pub at the end of their shift, having offered to unload the van back at the yard himself so they could get a jump start on their Friday evening plans. The job they'd worked on all day had run late, and Kyle didn't mind taking care of the van chores.

Sending the men off for the day and returning to the yard without them would also give Kyle a chance to talk to Frank Hill alone, without ears wagging. He had no idea how the boss would react to what he was about to tell him, and the fewer people there were around, the better.

First, though, he needed a cold drink to slake his thirst after a long day spent laying driveway bricks. He was nervous enough about the imminent conversation with Frank Hill without having his throat close up on account of dehydration.

Not to mention nerves. For so long, Kyle had anticipated the moment when he'd leave Hill Landscaping behind and set out in business for himself. Now that the moment was here, and he was ready to tell Frank Hill he didn't want to work for him anymore, Kyle felt raw fear surging through his system.

Ever since his conversation last night with Erin, one question kept racing through his mind: was he ready to go into business for himself? Was this the right move?

The certainty he'd once had about the answers to those questions had mysteriously disappeared now that the moment had come to make the big leap.

After buying a cold drink and gulping down half of it while standing outside the corner shop, he thought about what he was about to do—hand in his notice and set up his own business. Where that idea had once left him excited, it now it left him lightheaded and wondering if he was out of his mind.

"Well hello there, Kyle."

Kyle looked around and saw Mrs Wishmore walking along the pavement towards the corner shop, her red jacket slung over her arm on account of the sunny afternoon. The smile on her face was warm as she drew near.

"Hello, Doris," Kyle said. "How are you?"

"I'm just fine, thank you, dear."

"How are things up at the hotel since the fire? Are you all coping?"

"Everyone is doing well, all things considered," she replied, her expression pensive. "The fire was a terrible shock for all the staff and guests, and I know how relieved everyone is that things didn't turn out far worse than they did. But it's been non-stop ever since for the staff, dealing with the consequences."

"I can imagine."

"Suzanne and her mother have worked very hard to organise the repair and refurbishment of the damaged guest room. While some guests are now staying back in that part of the hotel, Suzanne has refused to allow the other rooms on the affected floor to be used to avoid the guests being disturbed by the noisy repair work taking place during the day. I must say Suzanne has handled the whole thing with such skill and professionalism... although I'm not sure she's quite ready to believe that just yet. And so, my work here continues."

Mrs Wishmore chuckled softly, and Kyle wondered at her odd comment. Before he could ask her what she meant, the older lady had turned and was gesturing at the Hill Landscaping van parked at the kerb.

"I hope you're almost finished work for the day," she said.

"It's set to be a beautiful summer's evening and it would be a shame to miss it."

"I'm just about to return to the yard and unload the van and then I'll be done. Well, almost done."

Mrs Wishmore gave him a curious look. "You look like there's something on your mind, young man?"

Kyle laughed. "You're incredibly perceptive, Doris."

"So I've been told," she smiled. "Is there something I can perhaps help you with?"

Her kind words touched him, considering they'd only met a few times. "No, but thanks for the offer. I need to chat to my boss about something and I'm not looking forward to it."

"Ah," Mrs Wishmore said, nodding as if she understood fully. "No one enjoys having difficult conversations. But sometimes we can't avoid them."

Kyle laughed. "I'm wondering if I really ought to avoid this one."

The older lady tilted her head, her expression thoughtful. "In that case, perhaps you *should* avoid it."

Her words caught Kyle by surprise. "Oh?"

"If that's what your gut and your heart are telling you to do, then you should listen to them."

As the older lady smiled at him, Kyle thought about what she'd said. What were his heart and his gut telling him to do?

It didn't take long to find the answer to that question. He wanted to make this big move in his life and start his own business at last, he knew it beyond a doubt. But that didn't mean he wasn't scared half to death about it, too.

"I know I need to talk to my boss, and do what I have to do," Kyle said. "I think I'm just letting nerves get the better of me."

"It's quite all right to be nervous about the big decisions we make in life, Kyle. If you weren't nervous, then it wouldn't be a big decision, would it?" She tilted her head again, as if considering him. "Would I be right in thinking that this big decision you're talking about is connected to what we discussed the other day and your plans to set up in business for yourself?"

Kyle nodded. "You have a good memory, Doris."

She shrugged this off. "Whenever someone crosses my path and trusts me enough to share something personal with me, I make a point of remembering what they've said. In my experience, people only share such personal details with others because they hope, on some level at least, that in doing so they might find the advice and guidance they're searching for." She smiled again, her eyes bright in the warm summer sunshine, and added, "But the answers people are searching for are usually inside them all along."

Kyle gazed at the older lady, wondering at these wise words she said with such ease, and wondering, too, at how easy it was to talk to her, even although she was little more than a stranger to him.

"For the longest time, I've planned to start my own business," he said. "Now that I'm about to do it, I'm terrified."

"Change is always unsettling. There are no guarantees that we'll succeed when we try new things in life. But not trying comes with a cost, too."

Kyle nodded. "If I do this, I might fail," he said quietly.

"And if you don't do it?" Mrs Wishmore asked.

"Then I'll always wonder what might have been."

The weight of what he'd just said hit Kyle square in the chest. Yes, he was scared about what he was about to do. But what scared him more was the idea of one day looking back and regretting the big move he'd never had the courage to make.

Mrs Wishmore smiled, then reached out and squeezed Kyle's arm. He felt a comforting sense of peace roll through him, along with a deep certainty about the choice that lay before him.

"It sounds like you already know what you have to do, young man," Mrs Wishmore said. Giving his arm a final soft pat, she adjusted the blue handbag at her shoulder. "Well, I must be on my way. See you soon, Kyle."

"Bye, Doris."

Kyle watched the older lady shuffle off along the street. As Mrs Wishmore disappeared into the crowds of shoppers and tourists who were enjoying the gift shops and ice cream parlours, the sunlight caught her silvery hair, and for a moment, Kyle couldn't help thinking that it looked like there was a glowing halo above her head.

With a laugh, he finished his cold drink. He'd obviously been standing in the sunshine too long and it had left him addled.

Kyle hopped back into the van and started the engine. It was time to go back to the yard and tell his boss about the decision he'd made.

As he steered into the traffic, the fear Kyle had felt just a few minutes ago suddenly felt a lot like excitement again.

CHAPTER NINETEEN

Suzanne Kennedy stood at the back of the Star Castle Hotel ballroom and let out a quiet sigh of relief. It was Saturday evening, the summer ball was underway, and everything was going to plan.

After the week she'd had, that seemed like a minor miracle, and although Suzanne didn't believe in miracles, she was grateful for this one just the same.

The ballroom, decked out in bright carnival lights and colourful flower arrangements, was buzzing with fun and chattering guests. The staff had just served the starter, and the food appeared to be going down well with everyone. Suzanne had checked up on the kitchen staff a few minutes earlier, where they were already prepping the dessert course, which would be shuttled through to the ballroom just as soon as the guests were ready for it. Both the strawberry cheesecake and chocolate torte options that the chefs had prepared looked almost too good to eat, and Suzanne knew they'd be the perfect way to end the summer ball dining experience.

The delicious desserts would also give the revellers the

sugar boost they'd need to enjoy the musical entertainment that was scheduled to get underway once the coffee and mints had been served and enjoyed.

At that thought, a flicker of unease wriggled into Suzanne's mind. The new band she'd hired, The Soundscapes, still hadn't arrived. Although there was still more than an hour and a half to go until the band was due on stage, she'd hoped they'd already be here by now and getting their musical equipment set up.

Suzanne was about to pull her phone from her pocket and call the band singer to check up on their whereabout when she saw Mrs Wishmore coming through the double doors of the ballroom.

"It looks like everyone is having a wonderful time," the older lady grinned, glancing around at the guests tucking into their food.

"The meal has the thumbs up so far, and once the music starts later, the night should only get better," Suzanne replied. "I didn't know you were working tonight, Doris."

"I swapped with one of the other staff members who needed tonight off for a family matter. I didn't want to miss tonight's festivities. I think this will be an evening to remember."

Suzanne smiled at Mrs Wishmore's generous words.

"And I hope you don't mind me saying this, Suzanne," Mrs Wishmore continued, "but you look just lovely tonight in that beautiful dress."

Usually, Suzanne stuck to her smart suits and capsule combinations when she was working at the hotel. But she'd felt that tonight's summer ball required something a little more special. After supervising the ballroom set up, she'd hurried home to change, and as she'd slipped into the elegant navy silk cocktail dress, she'd felt strangely festive, as if she were a guest getting ready for the ball, rather the manager in charge of organising it.

Now, as she smoothed a hand down the silk dress and nodded at Mrs Wishmore's compliment, she was pleased she'd made the effort and stepped out of her usual work attire. This was the Star Castle Hotel's premier summer event, and as the ranking member of staff in attendance, it was right that she should go the extra mile. Her grandfather, she recalled, had always worn his best suit for the summer ball, and she liked knowing she was now following in his footsteps in this way.

"Thank you Doris," Suzanne said. "You're very kind to notice my dress."

"It certainly is lovely."

Suzanne turned at the voice behind her and was surprised to see her mother standing there, a soft smile on her lips.

"I thought you'd already left?" Suzanne said. "You told me you wanted to work at home on the paperwork and admin for the guest room fire and refurbishment."

Imogen waved a hand. "That's what I planned to do, but once I heard the guests arriving for the ball and saw how good it looked in here, I couldn't resist staying to watch it all get underway." Imogen's gaze swept over Suzanne's dress and she smiled. "And Doris is quite right. You look wonderful. And every inch the confident manager I need in charge of this headline event."

"Thanks, Mum." Imogen's words had left her at a loss for something to say. It was so unlike her mother to offer praise like this.

"Can I steal you away for a quick word?" Imogen asked, gesturing to a quieter corner at the back of the ballroom.

"I'll make myself useful and help these young waiters and

waitresses clear some of these empty glasses from the tables," Mrs Wishmore said with a smile, and bustled off.

Suzanne followed her mother to the other side of the ballroom. When they reached the far wall, Imogen turned and gestured to the guests who were enjoying themselves at the tables, the staff busily serving them, and the bright carnival lights and decorations.

"You've done a superb job with the summer ball, Suzanne," Imogen said. "This place looks fantastic, and the refreshed decorations and lighting have added a real burst of energy to the place."

"Thank you. I'm happy with how it's turned out," Suzanne said. "I overheard several guests commenting on the new look and they all seem to like it. And in the end, we not only sold all the remaining tickets for the ball, but we also sold out of all our available rooms for tonight."

"That's great news." Imogen glanced again at the busy ballroom. "We've had a tough week, Suzanne. Between the fire in the guest room and all the upset and stress it caused, not to mention the woodland repairs you were already handling, you've still pulled everything together for tonight. I know only too well the work involved in making this happen, and the many last minute tasks and processes you've had to manage in order for all this to run smoothly tonight." Imogen turned to Suzanne, her expression soft. "I'm proud of you."

Suzanne blinked as the words sunk in. "Thanks, Mum. That means a lot."

"I don't say it enough. But I am so very, very proud of you, Suzanne."

Imogen's eyes were glistening as she spoke, and Suzanne felt a lump of emotion lodge in her throat.

"I'm not an easy boss to work for, I know that," Imogen said quietly. "But after everything that's happened this past week, I've realised that you are far smarter and far more capable than I've given you credit for, and that…" Imogen sighed as she searched for the words she needed. "I never really doubted you or your abilities, Suzanne. But I did doubt how much you wanted to run this hotel, and whether you only stayed on here after your grandfather died because you didn't want to hurt me by moving on to other jobs and other adventures."

Her mother's strained voice left Suzanne stunned. Although the festivities of the summer ball continued around them, she hardly noticed.

"I love this hotel, Mother," Suzanne said. "There's nothing I want more than to be here. The Star Castle Hotel isn't an inconvenient obligation. It's my passion and it's my entire world."

Imogen let out a muffled gasp, the sound almost a sob, as she took Suzanne's hand into hers. "Is that the truth?"

"Yes, you know it is."

Her mother nodded and squeezed her hand. "I never want you to feel you *have* to stay here. Not for me, not because of family, not because you think you have to."

"I'm here because I want to be here. I only wish you'd known that all along. Maybe then we wouldn't have been at loggerheads quite so much lately."

Imogen laughed and squeezed Suzanne's hand again. "I'll stop trying to micromanage you. From now on, I'll leave you to get on with the job I gave you, and if you need my help or advice, I know you'll come and ask for it."

"Count on it. You've forgotten more about running this place than I'll ever know. If I'm doing something wrong, I need you to tell me."

"Count on it."

They laughed, and Suzanne felt a weight lift from her

shoulders. Perhaps things with her mother might be turning a corner. She hoped so.

"There's something else I need to say," Imogen continued, letting go of Suzanne's hand and fidgeting for a second before speaking again. "I've been horribly unfair to you when it comes to your personal life. I've steered you away from men and from relationships and tried to convince you it was for the best. That was wrong of me."

"You were just looking out for me."

But Imogen shook her head. "Maybe, but I brought my own baggage into this, too. When you asked about your father last week and the choices I made in my life after you were born, I wasn't entirely honest. Yes, my work here at the hotel was important, and raising you was even more important than that. But while it's true that I like living my life on my own terms, and haven't sought relationships with men, I'd also be lying if I said that what happened to me all those years ago with your father didn't hurt me."

There was such naked honesty on her mother's face, Suzanne hardly recognised her.

"It hurt to be cast aside," Imogen said. "And I hated knowing he'd cast you aside, too. For too long, I let those feelings fester. Once you were grown up, I know I became too protective and overbearing when it came to your boyfriends over the years, because I couldn't stand the idea of you going through the hurt I went through on account of some careless man. I took that overprotectiveness much too far."

Imogen held Suzanne's gaze for a long moment before speaking again. "When I saw you talking to that young man, Kyle Lawson, outside the hotel last week after the fire, it seemed obvious to me that you liked him a great deal. The attraction in your eyes was unmistakable."

Suzanne blinked in surprise. "Was it?"

"It was," Imogen said, a sad smile now at her lips. "Seeing that look in your eyes scared me, and my reaction was to insist that this hotel had to be your one and only priority. That was wrong and it was stupid. You are entitled to a full life, Suzanne, just like everyone is. You are my entire world, and I love you. But it took me a while to realise that I was stopping you from making the choices I made freely when I was younger, choices that gave me you, choices that made my life worth living."

Tears glistened in Imogen's eyes. Suzanne gulped to stop her own tears from tumbling down her cheeks.

"From now on, I'll keep my nose out of your personal life," Imogen said, taking in a deep breath and smiling. "And I hope that if you like this Kyle Lawson man, that you'll spend time with him and not let the rantings of an over-protective mother stop you."

Suzanne held her mother's gaze, amazed at this honest and intimate conversation they were having, right here in the crowded ballroom. For the first time in a long time, she felt comfortable enough to share something personal with Imogen, something that wasn't related to the workings of the hotel.

It was just a pity there wasn't anything to share.

"Kyle is a lovely man," Suzanne said. "But I think we got off on the wrong foot and it was a little awkward because of it. Also, there's so much for me to learn here at the hotel, and so much to do. If this week has shown me anything, it's that I need to focus on my work and on mastering this deputy manager role. I have so many doubts about whether I'm up to the challenge of running this place. Until I've got a proper handle on those doubts, I don't think there's room for other distractions."

She thought this response would have pleased her mother, despite what she'd just said about keeping a lid on her overprotectiveness when it came to a life outside of work. After all, the Star Castle Hotel was the number one priority for them both. But Suzanne saw a spark of sadness in Imogen's eyes, even as she nodded.

"Well, you know what's best for you," Imogen said. "But I'm glad we had this little talk."

"Me too."

Suzanne returned her mother's warm smile. Considering the only things they usually ever talked about were work and the hotel, the conversation they'd just had felt like a huge turning point in their relationship. All week, Suzanne thought she'd done nothing but disappoint her mother as she'd battled her way through the various crises at the hotel. She'd felt utterly in over her head. But this long, difficult week had somehow helped convince her mother that Suzanne knew what she was doing after all, and that her commitment to the hotel was genuine. Quite how this had happened, Suzanne had no idea. But she was grateful for it, just the same.

Across the ballroom, Suzanne saw Mrs Wishmore clearing glasses from a table. The older lady smiled and winked. For a fleeting moment, Suzanne had the inescapable feeling that Doris knew what she'd just been discussing with her mother.

Suzanne blinked. The idea was as ludicrous as all the other odd ideas she'd entertained about Mrs Wishmore ever since she'd come to work here.

Still, that strange thought lingered in her mind for a moment longer, that sense that there was something about Mrs Wishmore that Suzanne couldn't quite put her finger on.

Before she could think anything further about the matter, her phone rang. Pulling it from the pocket of her dress, she glanced at the screen, but didn't recognise the number.

"This is Greg Young," said the caller after they'd exchanged hellos. "The lead singer with The Soundscapes. I'm afraid we've got a problem."

The anxious tone of the young man's voice sent a ripple of worry straight to Suzanne's stomach. "What's the matter? I was just about to call and find out where you are. We expected you here a while ago."

Imogen frowned as Suzanne spoke, picking up that something was wrong.

"I know, and I'm sorry," Greg said. "We were on our way to the hotel when our van broke down. We've been trying to organise a lift for the past half hour but can't get hold of anyone who'd be able to come all the way out here to help."

The band was based near Fort William, more than an hour away from the hotel, and so Suzanne understood their dilemma.

"What about a taxi?" she asked.

"We can't find one at late notice that's big enough to transport our equipment," Greg replied. "The drum kit is too big. Listen, I'm sorry, but unless we can solve this problem in the next fifteen minutes, we won't get there on time to set up and play the show."

Suzanne heard the quiver in the singer's voice as he spoke. Glancing up, she looked around the ballroom at the guests tucking into their meals. They were here for a summer ball, and it wouldn't be much of a ball with no music to dance to. If Suzanne had to stand at the front of the ballroom and announce that there'd be no band, just minutes before the band was due to play, it would be a disaster.

She imagined angry guests demanding refunds and venting on social media about the shambles of the summer ball that never was.

She imagined the financial blow they'd sustain. The reputational harm. The sheer toe-curling mortification of the impending fiasco.

"What's wrong?" Imogen said, concern and alarm creasing her brow.

Suzanne took a gulp of air, trying to slow her racing thoughts, and tilted the phone away while she spoke to her mother. "The band I hired for tonight have broken down on the way here. They can't find other transport to accommodate their musical equipment. They might not arrive here on time to play."

A flash of white hot impatience burned in Imogen's eyes at this news. Suzanne braced herself for a barrage of I-told-you-sos. Her mother had been against hiring a new band, especially one they knew so little about, and now she'd been proven right.

But as quickly as that hot impatience had appeared in Imogen's eyes, it was gone. Her mother's expression cleared, as if that flash of angry emotion had never been there.

"You can handle this," Imogen smiled. " I have every faith in you. Just take a second to think it through and you'll find a solution."

Suzanne forced her racing thoughts to slow down. As soon as she stopped thinking about all the terrible things that would happen if the hotel couldn't give the guests the musical entertainment they'd promised for the summer ball, her mind cleared.

And a solution immediately presented itself, a solution so obvious and simple she didn't know why she hadn't thought of it already.

"Greg, how far away are you from the hotel?" Suzanne asked.

"About fifteen or twenty minutes," the singer replied.

"Okay, tell me your exact location," Suzanne said. "I'm coming to get you."

Suzanne listened to Greg describe his location, and when her phone pinged with a map link from the singer, she knew she could just about get there in time to collect the band and ferry them to the hotel in time for them to play as scheduled. It would be tight, very tight, but it was possible that she could save this night from disaster.

Their hasty conversation concluded, Suzanne turned to her mother.

"I'll take one of our hotel vans and drive out to where the band is stranded," she explained and began hurrying towards the ballroom exit. "Hopefully there will be enough room inside to load up their drums and whatever else they have."

"But will there be enough room inside for the actual band?" Imogen asked, keeping up with her pace as they hustled along the corridor towards the lobby.

"I'll find a staff member who isn't busy working at the ball, and ask them to follow me in a second vehicle," Suzanne said, making it up on the spot.

"I could come along and help instead," Imogen said.

"No, we need someone here to supervise the ball, and if I'm gone, you're the one who ought to stay. We're lucky you were still here and you hadn't gone home yet."

As they turned the corner at the end of the corridor where it met the lobby, Suzanne did a double-take when saw Mrs Wishmore standing behind the reception counter helping a guest.

Hadn't she just saw the woman a few moments ago in the ball-room helping to clear empty glasses and plates from the tables?

Yes, she had. There was no doubt about it.

So how on earth had the woman made it out here into the reception lobby ahead of them, and already be working behind the counter?

As the puzzling question spun in her mind, jostling for space with the transport predicaments of the summer ball band that she was now entwined with, Suzanne hurried into the lobby, her gaze still on the startling sight of Mrs Wishmore at the reception desk.

The older lady looked across the lobby at Suzanne and smiled. And then winked.

In that moment, Suzanne's race across the lobby came to an abrupt halt as she crashed into someone walking in the opposite direction and who she hadn't seen because of her confused fascination with the mysterious appearance of Mrs Wishmore at the reception counter. Bouncing back a few steps because of the collision, she let out a muffled *Ooft!* of surprise.

"Suzanne! Are you okay?"

When she saw who it was that she'd hurtled into, she could scarcely believe it. "Kyle? What are you doing here?"

"I'm at the summer ball," he said, gesturing towards the corridor and the ballroom beyond. "My sister left something in the car and asked me to fetch it for her." He frowned, and added, "Are you okay? I didn't see you coming until it was too late."

"I'm fine," she said, rubbing at the spot where her cheek had collided with Kyle's chest. "I'm sorry. I'm in a rush and wasn't looking where I was going."

It occurred to her that this was how she'd first met Kyle, when she'd crashed straight into him on the street while her attention had been elsewhere. The warm zing he'd sent rippling over her skin back then was nothing compared to fierce flush of heat she felt now at the repeat performance.

Things had changed between then and now, after all. The searing kisses they'd shared at the top of the Ferris wheel on that sunny afternoon a week ago made this second collision far more heated than the first.

She couldn't help letting her gaze roam over the man. He looked good in a suit, very good, the charcoal tones highlighting his tall frame and broad shoulders, the open necked white shirt making her suck in a sharp breath as her mind filled with an image of her laying her lips against the smooth exposed skin of his neck and inhaling his spicy scent…

Suzanne cleared her throat and pushed the image away. The soft chuckle drifting across the lobby from Mrs Wishmore's direction didn't escape her notice, and when she caught the older woman's eye, she saw a knowing look there, as if the mysterious lady had once more understood what was going on inside her head.

"Sorry, Kyle, I have to run," Suzanne said, eager to get away from the man and back to dealing with the emergency she had on her hands. But before she could sidestep around him, he was holding up his hands.

"Hang on, wait," Kyle said, his gaze moving between Suzanne and her mother, who was watching the scene unfold with a look of surprised amusement on her face. "What's wrong? Is there something I can do to help?"

Suzanne shook her head and offered him a bright smile. "Nothing you need to worry about. You're a guest at the summer ball, so you ought to get back there and enjoy yourself."

"Suzanne, I'm not going to just walk off and leave you when there's something obviously wrong," he said, his tone laced with a mixture of concern and irritation. "Tell me what happened. I want to help if I can."

She was about to insist again that everything was in hand, but before she could, Imogen spoke.

"The band we hired for tonight have run into a little difficulty getting here," she said. "Suzanne is about to drive out to where they've broken down and collect them, just as soon as we find another staff member to go with her and help."

Kyle looked at Imogen, then at Suzanne. "I'll go with you."

"No, Kyle," Suzanne said. "If you're at the summer ball

then you're a guest at the hotel, and I won't ruin your evening by allowing you to get caught up in any of this."

"You're not allowing it," he said. "I'm insisting on helping."

"But..."

"My car is parked right outside," Kyle said, pulling his car keys from his pocket. "We can be on the road in a matter of seconds. Or, we can debate this and fall out about it, and then you can waste time rustling up some hotel staff member to help you instead, by which point we could already be on the road." He jangled his car keys at her. "Your choice."

She wanted to refuse, not just because Kyle was a hotel guest tonight, but because it would be downright awkward to accept help from the man after giving him the cold shoulder all week.

But her mother made the decision for her.

"Kyle, we'd be very grateful if you could help us with this emergency," Imogen said, giving him a generous smile before turning to her daughter. "Aren't we grateful, Suzanne, that Kyle can lend a hand?" she said, wriggling her eyebrows meaningfully.

Suzanne sighed in defeat. "If you're sure, Kyle?"

"I'm sure." He gestured to the hotel doors. "Lead the way."

"I'll just grab keys for one of the hotel's vans and then we can go."

As Suzanne hurried to the back offices and the key cupboard, she passed Mrs Wishmore at the reception desk.

"Good luck, dear," the older lady smiled.

Thanking her as she picked up speed, Suzanne wondered if Doris was wishing her good luck in her mission to rescue the stranded band she'd hired... or for something else entirely.

CHAPTER TWENTY

During the fifteen minute drive to where the band was waiting to be picked up, Suzanne glanced often in the side mirror of the hotel van she was driving. She told herself it was just to make sure Kyle hadn't lost track of her as they made their way north along the coastal road. But that was only part of the reason. The main reason was that she couldn't take her eyes off the man.

He looked good in that suit. He'd looked good to her in his grubby work clothes, too, and he'd looked good in his casual jeans and T-shirt when she'd shared pizza with him on the waterfront, and when they'd spent the afternoon at the garden fairground last weekend.

But tonight, he was in another league and the sight of him made Suzanne's mouth water.

Worse, it wasn't only that the man looked good enough to eat. The concern in Kyle's eyes when she'd run into him in the hotel lobby, and his insistence that he abandon his evening in order to help with her emergency, reminded her he was a good man.

Not that she'd forgotten. That would be impossible. Kyle

Lawson was a good man with a good heart, a man who made her pulse race and her head spin, and seeing him tonight made her regret how she'd pushed him away.

Had she made a terrible mistake when she'd ignored his calls? Had she made a terrible mistake when she'd decided that the only thing she had space for in her life was the Star Castle Hotel? Might there have been a sweet and wonderful romance with Kyle if she'd chosen differently?

Might there have been even more?

A stab of loss hit her at the idea of what she might have found on the road not taken.

Stop it! she told herself as she steered along the twisting road. There wasn't time to get distracted like this. The only thing that mattered was rescuing the stranded band and driving them back to the hotel as quickly as possible.

When a set of blinking orange hazard lights appeared on the coastal road just at the spot where Greg Young said the band had become stranded, Suzanne heaved a sigh of relief and checked the time.

There was less than an hour left until the band was due on stage. If they moved fast, they could still pull this off.

Pulling to the side of the road, she saw the four figures standing beside the broken-down van raise their hands in a frantic wave in her direction. As Kyle came to a stop behind her, she got out of the van. Already, three of the band members were opening the back doors of their own vehicle and hauling out the musical equipment packed inside.

"Ms Kennedy," said the young singer, Greg Young, as he ran towards Suzanne. "We are so sorry about this, and so grateful you came to pick us up. We know this looks unprofessional."

"Let's not worry about any of that right now," Suzanne said, seeing the embarrassment on Greg's face. "We've got a ballroom filled with guests back at the hotel who are eating their main course as we speak and getting excited about the band we've promised. Let's not disappoint them."

Greg nodded and turned his attention to helping his fellow band members transfer their equipment to the back of the hotel van. With Kyle and Suzanne's help, they did the work in a matter of minutes. Not even Kyle's hand brushing against hers as they stacked equipment bags into the van was enough to slow Suzanne down, even if it did make her heart skip a beat.

Once they'd packed the van, Kyle pointed to his car.

"Okay, guys," he said to the four band members. "Pile in and we'll follow Suzanne back to the hotel."

As the musicians climbed into his car, Kyle nodded to the hotel van. "You're okay driving this heavy load back along these twisty roads?"

"I'll be fine."

He grinned. "Of course you will. See you back there."

They were on the road again just seconds later. Suzanne checked the time. Fifty minutes until the band was due to play. If it took fifteen minutes to return to the hotel, would that leave enough time for them to set up? How long did it take to put together a drum kit and plug in the guitars? Suzanne had no idea.

All she could do was drive as fast and as safely as she could back to the hotel and hope things would work out all right, and that there would be no more disasters to contend with tonight.

Fifteen minutes later, the turn for the Star Castle Hotel swung into view, and Suzanne blew out a long breath of pure relief. Now all they had to do was make sure the band got set up in time to play for the summer ball guests.

Once they'd parked, Suzanne hurried into the hotel to find as many available staff as possible to help the band carry their equipment around to the ballroom's side doors. The musicians got to work, rigging the drum kit and running cables. Turning to the guests seated at the tables, Suzanne saw they were finishing dessert. As she calculated the timings for serving coffee and mints, plus the short break worked into the schedule during which the staff would shift the tables and chairs to the side of the ballroom so there was room for dancing, she thought there might just be enough time for the band to get set up and to avoid any lengthy delays that would leave the guests restless.

It was only as she glanced around that she realised she'd been so busy helping with the logistics of moving the musical equipment around to the ballroom's side doors that she'd forgotten to thank Kyle for his help. Just then, she saw him walk into the ballroom and head towards a table at the other side. When he got there, he pulled out the empty chair and began talking to the woman he was seated beside.

Suzanne recognised her as Erin, Kyle's sister. She'd been in the background of one of the photographs he'd shown her of the little play huts he'd built for his nephew, Jamie. Kyle appeared to be filling her in on the rescue mission he'd volunteered for, gesturing to the band hard at work at the front of the ballroom while catching up on the meal he'd missed.

It was obvious that Kyle and his sister were close, that they were friends as well as siblings. They talked to one another with ease, their conversation punctuated with laughter. Suzanne thought again of how he'd invited his sister and nephew into his home and helped them through a tough time in their lives.

And she thought again of Kyle's good heart. She thought about the kindness he'd shown her last weekend, when he'd helped her remember what it meant to have fun, to let go of her worries, and to live a little more lightly. Kyle's kindness had led so quickly to something else, to that searing kiss at the top of the Ferris wheel in those flower-filled gardens, a kiss Suzanne still felt reverberating through her body whenever she thought about it.

Watching Kyle now across the hotel ballroom, Suzanne remembered how his lips had felt on hers, how her heart had beat wildly at his touch, how he'd made her feel so completely alive, something she hadn't felt in far too long.

The staff supervisor interrupted her thoughts to ask about the coffee arrangements. Suzanne pushed away her romantic daydreams and got back to work.

Between overseeing the final stages of the meal service and lending a hand to manage the guests while the staff reorganised the ballroom to make space for the dance floor, the next part of the evening raced by. Suzanne caught occasional glimpses of her mother helping to serve at the bar and making conversation with the guests. There was a lightness on Imogen's face that Suzanne liked seeing there, and when her mother caught her eye and smiled across the ballroom, she revelled in it, feeling not only the approval of her boss but also the love of her mother.

When the band singer hurried over and told Suzanne that they were all set and ready to play, it was all she could do not to grab the young man into a hug and whoop with joy.

Five minutes later, The Soundscapes kicked off their set with a rousing rendition of a popular chart topper that had the summer ball guests up on their feet and dancing, filling the ballroom with excitement and energy. Suzanne checked her watch and saw the musical entertainment had begun only a few minutes behind schedule.

Not bad, she thought and let out a long breath she hadn't realised she'd been holding. *Not bad at all.*

"It looks like you've saved the day!"

Snapped from her thoughts, Suzanne turned to see Mrs Wishmore at her side. The older lady was looking at the guests twirling and shuffling around on the dance floor, a wide smile on her face.

"It was a close-run thing, but we got there," Suzanne grinned.

"Everyone is having a wonderful time," Doris said. "I hope you're proud of what you've accomplished here."

"Proud might be stretching it a bit far. Right now, I'm just relieved this whole night didn't end in disaster."

"You faced a crisis and found a way to resolve it, and you ought to be proud of what you've done," Doris insisted. "You did the same thing with the unexpected repairs required in the woodland play area, and again when fire broke out in one of the guest rooms. There will always be challenges, Suzanne. What matters is that you trust yourself to face them and don't let self-doubt make you feel less than you are."

Suzanne turned towards the older lady, wondering at her wise words. "You've given me a lot of good advice since you came to work here, Doris. I appreciate it."

"You're quite welcome, dear. Like I said when I first arrived, I'm here to help however I can. That's my job, after all."

Mrs Wishmore gave a warm chuckle, then looked at Suzanne with a soft expression on her face. "And I hope I've helped you to realise that life is best when it's lived fully and with an open heart."

This conversation should have felt downright odd, considering Mrs Wishmore was a hotel employee and Suzanne was her boss. But it didn't feel odd at all. Suzanne wished she knew why that was, and why she could sense that there was something more to Doris Wishmore than met the eye, even if she couldn't pin down what that something actually was.

The band finished playing one song and launched into another with an even faster beat that got yet more guests up onto the dance floor. Mrs Wishmore grinned at Suzanne.

"I hope you'll enjoy yourself and indulge in some dancing tonight," she said.

Suzanne laughed and shook her head. "After everything that's happened this past week and a half, I don't have any energy for dancing. In fact, all I want is to lie down in a darkened room and recover for, oh I don't know, an entire week."

"Well, that's a pity," Mrs Wishmore said. "Because it looks like there's someone here who'd rather like to take you for a spin around the dance floor."

Doris nodded across the ballroom, and when Suzanne followed the older woman's gaze, she saw Kyle walking towards her. As his eyes found hers and held them, she felt her breath catch.

"Kyle, I was so busy once we got back to the hotel earlier with the band, I didn't thank you for all your help tonight," Suzanne said when he reached her, desperate to smooth over the fluster she felt at the sight of him.

"Glad I could help," Kyle said, then smiled at Mrs Wishmore. "Hello, Doris."

"Hello, Kyle. It's wonderful to see you here this evening. I hope you're having fun?"

"I am. In fact, I was thinking it might be even more fun to get up and dance." He held a hand out to Suzanne. "Care to join me?"

She wanted to say yes, but the answer wouldn't come out, trapped inside by her automatic reaction that the hotel had to come first, above all else, always.

"I ought to stay here and make sure everything is running smoothly," she said. "I'm in charge tonight, after all."

A flicker of disappointment flashed on Kyle's face as he dropped his hand away, and Suzanne hated seeing his enthusiasm wilt because of her.

At her side, Mrs Wishmore reached out and touched Suzanne's arm. Instantly, she saw the memory of herself as a little girl, twirling around the empty ballroom in her pink princess dress, while her mother and grandfather laughed with joy. The image played out, superimposed on the reality of the summer ball taking place around her, as if the little girl she'd once been was now spinning around amongst the guests, the two reels of time unfurling together as one.

Suzanne glanced at Mrs Wishmore and saw her warm smile and the kindness in her bright blue eyes. In the older lady's soft expression, she saw encouragement and comfort.

It's time to remember what life is all about, whispered a voice inside Suzanne's head, a voice that sounded just like Mrs Wishmore's.

The older lady had said the same thing a week ago, when that old memory of herself as a little girl prancing around the ballroom had first bloomed inside her head.

Now, Suzanne understood that what she wanted most of all was to do just what Mrs Wishmore said—remember what life was all about before it was too late.

Kyle remained standing before her, the hand he'd offered in an invitation to dance now at his side, his eyes searching hers.

"But on second thoughts," Suzanne said, "dancing sounds like fun."

Suzanne held out her hand, her heart galloping inside her chest. Kyle grinned and took her hand in his. "Then let's get moving, before you discover I've got two left feet."

Laughing, she followed Kyle onto the dance floor. Before they disappeared into the crowd of dancing guests, she looked back over her shoulder at Mrs Wishmore.

"See you later, Doris," she called out.

"Have fun, dear," Mrs Wishmore smiled. "And farewell!"

At the older lady's strange parting comment, Suzanne frowned and once more turned around, wondering what she could have meant. But the crowds of dancers had already closed in around them and Mrs Wishmore disappeared from view.

Before she could give it another thought, Kyle took her in his arms and they began moving to the music. Feeling his hands around her waist sent delicious shivers all over her skin and made her forget those mysterious parting words from the enigmatic Mrs Wishmore.

"I'm glad you agreed to dance with me," Kyle said as they stepped to the beat of the band.

"Me too," Suzanne replied, knowing in her heart that she meant it.

"Maybe once we've had this dance, you'd like to have a glass of champagne with me to celebrate my big news?"

"What big news is that?"

Kyle grinned. "As of today, I'm now the boss of my very own garden design company."

"You are? That's fantastic." Suzanne beamed, thrilled to hear that Kyle had taken such a big leap, and so quickly, too. Perhaps the big leap he'd taken with his business plans wasn't so different from the big leap she'd just taken when she'd stepped into his arms and begun dancing. "I'm so happy for you, Kyle. I hope it will all be a terrific success."

"Me too." He gave her a sheepish smile. "Frank Hill wasn't happy to find out I was handing in my notice, but once he stopped yelling and blustering, he was pretty decent about it. Despite how much he's been on my case about turning up late because I've been helping with Jamie's school run in the mornings, I got the impression he might actually miss me after all."

"Of course he'll miss you. He'd be mad not to. And if you need business advice or someone to chat to about things, I'm happy to share what I've learned here at the hotel."

"Thank you."

"And I've been thinking about the people I met at Heatherglen House last weekend, too, and all the wonderful work they're doing. Now that the summer ball is almost off my desk, I'd like to take you up on your suggestion to meet with the team there and find out what I can do to help." Smiling, she felt a weight lift off her chest. "I want to feel like I'm contributing and get out there into the world."

"Then we'll make sure that's what you do." A smile curved at his lips and his gaze softened. "But maybe for the next five minutes we ought to forget about work, and instead just dance and have fun?"

Around them, the ballroom hummed with energy, the music played, and the magic of the summer ball glittered in the air. As Suzanne looked into Kyle's eyes, her heart soared.

"Yes," she smiled. "Let's dance and have fun."

Tilting her mouth up to his, she kissed him, and her heart soared higher still as it opened to the rich fullness of life that she was ready, at last, to welcome.

EPILOGUE

Mrs Wishmore stepped out through the doors of the Star Castle Hotel and breathed in the cool evening air. Her work here was done and it was time to move on.

As she walked along the road that led away from the hotel, she took one last look behind her. The Star Castle Hotel looked achingly beautiful tonight, its façade illuminated against the soft summer sky. From the open windows of the ballroom on the far side of the building, Mrs Wishmore could hear the music and fun of the summer ball, and she thought of Suzanne dancing there in Kyle's arms, and thought too of the bright smile she'd seen on the young woman's face just before the crowds had closed in around them.

There had been a world of promise and happiness caught up in that smile, and Mrs Wishmore knew Suzanne would now find her way to the full and rich life she deserved. The young woman had a good heart and she was glad to have helped her learn how to trust herself and her abilities. She was glad, too, that she'd helped Suzanne uncover the deeper issues that lay beneath her self-doubts. Suzanne had denied herself a life beyond work, and eventually her work would have suffered because of that false choice.

Now, though, Suzanne Kennedy was beginning to see just how wonderful life could be when she allowed herself to live it fully. That Suzanne and her mother, Imogen, had now found new respect and understanding for each other, and begun to recast their relationship on a surer footing, was the icing on the cake.

And as for Kyle, well, Mrs Wishmore was only too happy to have been there to help nudge the ambitious young man in the direction he already wanted to go. People always knew in their hearts what they wanted and what was best for them, but all too often, courage was in short supply. If Mrs Wishmore had helped Kyle summon the courage he needed right at the moment he needed it in order to make some big moves in his life, then that only made this adventure at the Star Castle Hotel all the sweeter.

As she left the hotel behind, Mrs Wishmore wondered what might lie ahead for the young couple. She saw great things in the future for their respective businesses, which was just as it should be. She saw, too, how Suzanne and Kyle would champion one another through these next big steps in life, cheering one another on to ever greater accomplishments.

And as for romance, she saw something rather lovely blossoming for the young couple. She saw moonlit walks beside the waters of the bay, and more kisses stolen at the top of the Ferris wheel in those garden fairgrounds they'd claimed as their own special place, and she saw a great passion that would sweep them both off their feet.

Would their romance be forever? Sometimes the future didn't always reveal every detail in advance, not even to Mrs Wishmore. But as she let her mind open to what might come next for Suzanne and Kyle, she caught a wisp of ivory lace on the edge of a wedding dress, and a bouquet of pink roses grown by a besotted groom for his bride, and a sprinkling of confetti on the lawns of the Star Castle Hotel... and she knew that forever was what Suzanne and Kyle had already found in each other.

Mrs Wishmore took one final glance back over her shoulder and wished the young couple every happiness in the years to come. Soon, they'd both forget all about the mysterious older lady who'd come into their lives for a few days during one glorious summer and helped them through a few tough spots. That was how it worked. Wishes were made, and Mrs Wishmore appeared in order to lend a helping hand where she could, but once she was gone, no one ever remembered her.

Which was just as it should be.

But Mrs Wishmore remembered those she'd helped, and there would always be a special place in her heart for Suzanne and Kyle and the Star Castle Hotel.

The road led further into the summer twilight of the tall trees. When Mrs Wishmore reached the main road, she walked to the bus stop in the layby and waited. The last bus was due any minute. When it swung into view and pulled over to let her climb aboard, Mrs Wishmore said a silent goodbye to the friends she'd made here during her all-too-brief stay.

Once she'd taken a seat by the window, the bus pulled back onto the road. Mrs Wishmore watched the sun sinking towards the horizon and into the waters of the bay, leaving behind a tapestry of dazzling colours and fond memories.

With a smile, Mrs Wishmore settled in for the journey and wondered about the next adventure that might be waiting at the other end of it.

A MESSAGE FROM ALIX

Dear Reader

After writing the last words of *A Wish On Star Castle Lane*, I was rather sad when Mrs Wishmore boarded the bus and left behind the beautiful hotel where she'd come to lend a hand. I loved daydreaming about this location, both the wonderful hotel-castle and the Scottish coastal setting, which became a real home-from-home while I was writing. I like the idea that we spent a pleasant trip there, you and I, as we accompanied Mrs Wishmore on her journey.

This story was especially close to my heart for another reason, too. Despite putting on a brave face for the world, Suzanne Kennedy had many doubts about herself and her abilities, and had put her life on hold to focus on work. I know only too well how easy it is to get lost in busyness and forget to actually live. If I had a guardian angel who appeared at my side from time to time to remind me not to worry so much and to enjoy life a little more, I'd be very grateful!

If you'd like to keep up to date with news about future Mrs Wishmore books, pop over to my website and join my Reader's Club to receive my newsletter, along with a lovely heartwarming book to enjoy as a gift to say thank you for signing up. You can find me at www.alixkelso.com

Thank you for reading *A Wish On Star Castle Lane* and I hope you'll join Mrs Wishmore again soon. Until next time...

With all good wishes,
Alix Kelso

What to read next

Mrs Wishmore returns for a new adventure in ***A Wish At The Christmas Village***, filled with plenty of festive wonder and romance.

You might also enjoy my Mrs Wishmore short stories, which you can find in my Story Collection volumes. I recommend starting with her lovely tale in ***A Dog's Heart And Other Stories***.

Stay in touch

If you'd like to hear about new book news, then join my Reader's Club and I'll also send you an exclusive and heartwarming story to enjoy. Pop over to my website at www.alixkelso.com to sign up.

Please consider leaving a review

If you enjoyed this book, I'd be so grateful if you'd leave a review at the store where you bought it. Reviews are very helpful for readers searching for new books and for authors hoping for new readers. Thank you!

Acknowledgements

Special thanks to David Swan for his help with my questions about how long it takes for a live band to set up on stage - I took liberties with these details in the service of the story, and any errors in the book are the author's.

ABOUT THE AUTHOR

Alix Kelso writes warm-hearted stories about romance, friendship and family. She's happiest with her nose in a book and loves being whisked off to imaginary story worlds. Alix lives in Glasgow with her husband, where she enjoys pottering in the kitchen, exploring the great outdoors, and buying far too many Christmas decorations.

Alix loves to hear from her readers - find her online on Facebook, Instagram and Twitter at @AlixKelsoAuthor

Visit her website at www.alixkelso.com

ALSO BY ALIX KELSO

Mrs Wishmore Series

A Wish At The Daffodil Cafe

A Wish On Star Castle Lane

A Wish At The Christmas Village

Foxglove Street Series

Neighbours On Foxglove Street

Friends On Foxglove Street

Sisters On Foxglove Street

Autumn Leaves On Foxglove Street

The Fairhill Series

The Perfect Moment (Book 1)

The Next Forever (Book 2)

The Magic Hour (Book 3)

A Little Romance (Novella)

The Story Collections

A Dog's Heart and Other Stories

The Food Of Love and Other Stories

A Dream Of Christmas and Other Stories

The Magic of Christmas and Other Stories

Home Sweet Home and Other Stories

Printed in Great Britain
by Amazon

48484214R00179